Take It All

Sawyer's Cove: The Reboot

Libby Waterford

This is a work of fiction. Names, places, organizations, and events are either products of the author's imagination or are used entirely fictitiously.

Also by Libby Waterford

Sawyer's Cove: The Reboot

Take Two

Take a Bow

Take it All

Take a Chance

Take Me Over

Hot Take in Steamy Shorts: A Kissed by Romance Anthology

Take Another Look in A Kiss at Midnight: A Kissed by Romance Collaboration

Never a Bride

Can't Help Falling in Love

Can't Make You Love Me

Can't Fight This Feeling

Can't Hurry Love

Weston Reunion

Flirting with Her Professor

Her Reunion Fling

Falling for Her Ex

For Sara, Tara, and Annette

"Sometimes I wonder if men and women really suit each other. Perhaps they should live next door and just visit now and then."

— Katharine Hepburn

Prologue

JULES: So my clever little data reports show me we have a bunch of new listeners since we found out *Sawyer's Cove* is getting another season.

ERIKA: Another season? You make it sound like we time traveled to twelve years ago and the powers that be decided to renew the show, instead of canceling the best show on TV after three measly seasons.

JULES: Wow, you're still bitter, aren't you?

ERIKA: My 16-year-old self will never get over it. But my 28-year-old-self is delighted. Sometimes good things do happen to good people.

JULES: So if you just started listening to us, hello and welcome and let me tell you a little about us. We started as a fan rewatch podcast of the iconic, as previously mentioned, short-lived teen primetime drama *Sawyer's Cove*. We never thought we'd be getting new *Cove* content in this lifetime, but news about a revival with the entire original cast broke in May. Our little podcast now covers all the reboot news, in addition to spending plenty of time waxing eloquent about everything we love about the original.

Erika: Do we wax eloquent?

Jules: I don't know about you, but I wax fucking eloquent.

Erika: Damn straight.

Jules: Now it's August and reportedly production is getting underway in Misty Harbor, Connecticut, which is where they shot the original show. All the actors are on hand, they're building sets, they're doing all that TV magic. I don't know that much about it, but I'm sure it's a lot of work.

Erika: Should we remind folks at home who-all is going to be in these shiny new ten episodes of streaming television?

Jules: Let's do it.

Erika: First up, there's America's sweetheart Camille Corsair, playing the quintessential girl next door, Amy Green. Her real-life paramour, Jay Orlando, plays Amy's true love, Parker Wild. If you don't think they're soul mates, I invite you to watch my PowerPoint on this topic.

Jules: Wait, isn't that this entire podcast?

Erika: Yeah, what are you even doing here if you don't love Parker and Amy together? Anyway, I digress. We also have Nash Speedwell as Will O'Connell. No word on if Will's first love, Noah, played by Darren Silverstein, is returning to the show. We can only hope. Next is Ariel Tulip as the original feminist icon Lily Fine. Last, we've got the incomparable Spencer Crosby playing the titular character Sawyer North.

JULES: Don't forget that behind the camera we've got Camille Corsair doing double duty as a producer, which is badass. And running the whole shebang is Selena Echeveria, who was a staff writer on the original *Cove* and has since done a bunch of awesome shows and projects.

ERIKA: I have to say I'm relieved they have an OG writer to guide the show, even if it's not Ryan Saylor, who created the show.

JULES: Getting Ryan back would have been incredible, but I'm down to see what Selena does with the characters.

ERIKA: I believe in this reboot, revival, redo, whatever you want to call it. We're here for it.

JULES: Now all we have to do is stay alive until the show airs.

FROM THE SAWYER'S COVE REWATCH PROJECT PODCAST: SUMMER MAILBAG

Chapter One

Jake inventoried the woman occupying his usual booth. Red hair that sometimes went by the name "strawberry blonde" and was really more of a copper. Simple clothes, but expensive. The suggestion of freckles under her makeup. His gut told him she would be trouble, one way or the other. His bank account told him to sit down and hear what the possible client had to say.

— *Gunsmoke,* by Warner Mathis

Selena needed stimulants. She dragged herself to the electric kettle in what passed for a kitchen in her temporary home and flicked it on. She didn't need a fancy range, but it would have been nice to be able to prepare something besides black tea and instant oatmeal before she went to work.

Still, she was grateful for the roof over her head. She'd left finding a place to stay during the production of the *Sawyer's Cove* reboot to the last minute, and Cami, brilliant producer she was, had found this spot. For the next three months, her home was the pool house of a mid-century modern mansion.

The wood-and-glass two-story structure was easily five thousand square feet, not counting the garage or her pool house. The property was meticulously landscaped with prolific roses, glossy rhododendrons, and opulent hydrangeas, plants that would never work in her arid, Los Angeles, desert-inspired front yard.

Between her tiny abode and the massive main house was the centerpiece of the place—a 25-meter lap pool lined in cobalt blue tile, surrounded by an attractive beige flagstone patio, complete with fire pit. She'd seen nicer pools in Beverly Hills, but not many.

Selena unwrapped a tea bag and set it into a mug while she waited for the morning's entertainment. Only a few moments later, the back door of the house opened, and her landlord emerged in swim shorts and a wrinkled T-shirt, a thin towel slung over his shoulder.

The view of the pool was turning out to be the best feature of her living situation.

Her landlord stripped off his tee and let it drop to one of the lounge chairs on the edge of the pool deck. This time of morning, the pool was in full sun, so she had an unimpeded view of him as he dove into the water without so much as dipping his toe in first.

He stayed under a long time, so long she almost grew alarmed, groping around the back of her mind for some long ago learned, long ago forgotten lifesaving knowledge. But CPR would not be needed, because he burst out of the water at the far end from where he'd started, on the side nearest Selena. She took an involuntary step back from the window, though he couldn't have seen her with the reflection on the glass even if he'd been looking, which he wasn't. He executed a flip turn and started freestyling in the other direction, his tanned arms coming out of the water with impressive regularity. A white, frothy wake trailed him to the other end of the pool.

Her landlord, Warner Mathis, was just doing laps. But Warner wasn't some rich hedge fund manager with a conveniently empty pool house. He was the author of one of the bestselling mystery novels of the last decade. She glanced at the paperback edition of *Gunsmoke* she'd coincidentally brought from her personal library. It was sitting next to a pile of scripts. The guy who seemed to spend his days digging in the dirt of the flowerbeds outside or coming and going from his gorgeous house in a rusty minivan was also the author of her favorite detective novel. Unless there was another Warner Mathis with intense blue eyes, a serious mouth, and perpetually stubbly cheeks.

Truth was so much stranger than fiction sometimes.

The kettle clicked off, and she filled her mug with steaming water, allowing herself to keep watching while her tea steeped, not sure why she was compelled to. There was something about Warner that aroused her curiosity.

He was a strange duck, that's for sure. To call him taciturn was generous—they'd exchanged less than fifty words since she'd arrived nearly a week ago. But he wasn't mean; just gruff. He touched the flowers with gentleness, and he always left room for her rental sedan in the driveway.

Selena finally turned away from the window and woke up her trusty laptop. Shooting on the first hour-length episode started Monday, and there was so much to do before then. She took a deep breath. It would all get done. She had an amazing team. Everything was on schedule, or as on schedule as something with as many complex moving parts as a television show could be.

She'd been up late working on rewrites for the first episode that had been inspired by yesterday's full cast table read. There was nothing like hearing actors speaking lines out loud to give her a new perspective on the story.

Writing for television was like being part of a relay race. She and the other writers put the story into words, and the actors picked those lines up, breathed life and physicality into them. Then all the layers of art and craft came into play, costumes and lighting and editing and music, transforming the initial idea into more than the sum of its parts. The show crossed the finish line when it played on a fan's screen, where they took the next step, sharing their opinions with friends, making gifs of their favorite scenes, writing fanfiction, speculating about the next episode.

Selena couldn't do her job of delivering a spectacular hour of entertainment without countless other people doing theirs, and she liked it that way.

After dealing with a few emails, she took a super-fast shower, lamenting the lack of a tub and that while she was in Connecticut, she wouldn't be able to indulge in a bath. She had a big clawfoot tub in her 1930s house in Los Angeles, and she loved to soak in it, book in one hand, glass of wine in the other.

She dried off and put on a simple wrap dress that had been her uniform lately. This one was red, to match her glasses and tinted lip gloss. She slid her feet into practical black sandals, loaded her bag with her computer and the latest copy of the script, and grabbed her car keys.

She swore she hadn't timed it, but somehow Warner was hauling himself out of the pool when she passed by on her way to her car.

"Morning," she called.

The sun glinted off the water streaming from his lean, six-foot frame. He had a serious farmer's tan, arms bronzed up to his biceps, pale and dotted with the occasional mole everywhere else, light-colored chest hair between flat pecs. His sandy blond hair was graying a little at the temples, but it looked good on him.

He was probably around forty, but his face was far

more weathered than Selena's own. She was thirty-seven but routinely mistaken for someone ten years younger. Not that she was complaining. It had bothered her to look young in her twenties; now she thanked her good genes and round face and body for keeping her youthful in an industry that prized elastic skin.

"Morning," he returned, squinting against the sun.

"Nice morning for a swim." Just because she never had engaged him in successful conversation didn't mean she was going to stop trying.

"Going to be hotter later," he said.

She already felt the heat of the day seeping into the stone patio beneath her sandaled feet. Thank God the pool house had central air—so far, late August in Connecticut had proven to be hot and humid. When was fall supposed to start around here?

"I'll keep that in mind."

He leaned over to grab his towel, and his wet shorts tightened snugly over his well-shaped ass. He wasn't beefy or unnaturally muscular; he was just a guy with no extra body fat who seemed to have gotten that way through physical labor. He must have to work hard to stay warm in the winter.

"Well, I better get to work. See you...around," Selena said after a beat when he didn't say anything back.

"Goodbye," he said, nodding at her. Dismissing her.

She turned her back on him to walk to her car but couldn't suppress her smile. She'd gotten him to say three sentences to her. Granted, two of them had been one-word sentences, but she still felt like progress had been made. By the time she left Misty Harbor to return to Los Angeles, they might have advanced to saying two sentences in a row to each other.

A woman had to have goals.

Chapter Two

Warner surreptitiously watched Selena trace the flagstone path to the side gate at the end of the driveway, a flash of red as she slipped through to her car. She liked red, he'd noticed. It was practically the only color he'd seen her wear. And why shouldn't she? She looked magnificent in the color. It made her light brown skin glow, and paired with her curly black hair, it drew eyes to her the way a cardinal stood out against the bare trees of winter. Her glasses were red, too, round and oversized, like the young people were wearing them these days. *Golden Girls* chic.

He wondered how old she was, exactly. She couldn't be that young to be in charge of a television show, but she barely looked thirty. Or maybe he just didn't know how to judge anymore. It had been quite a while since he'd looked at a woman and done more than a cursory once-over. It was disconcerting to realize the first woman in years he wanted to take a second look at was also living a hundred feet from him.

And that was his own damn fault. He should have said no when Cami had called him, desperate and pleading, two weeks ago, asking if he had any rental properties available for her friend Selena. He owned three rental houses in Misty Harbor, but they were all booked. The only thing he had to offer was the pool house, a one-bedroom shoebox with a mini fridge and microwave. But he found it exceedingly difficult to say no to Camille Corsair. Not because she was a famous actress. Not even because she was Jay Orlando's girlfriend, though given that Jay owned the bar where Warner spent a few nights a week, it wouldn't do to get on his bad side. No, he'd offered because she was a nice person whose big doe eyes could implore the pope to condone murder. He was certainly powerless to deny her request.

He'd imagined a middle-aged suit-clad ballbuster when she'd explained his new tenant was the *Sawyer's Cove* showrunner and head writer. Then Selena had turned up a week ago in jeans and a T-shirt, all ass and tits, her pretty round face nearly hidden by big hair and glasses, her Lauren Bacall-low voice friendly. She looked like a college student, not the most powerful person on the set. Not that he knew much about set hierarchies. But Cami seemed even younger, and she was a producer, too; he had no idea how Hollywood worked, outside of how it was depicted in the movies themselves.

He finished toweling off, jogged to the house. It was going to be a scorcher. The summer humidity hadn't quit, but fall would be there before they knew it. He needed to stop by the Edwards Avenue house and look at a leak in one of the bathrooms, then he wanted to go by the nursery and see if they had any one-gallon asters. He showered off the pool water in the downstairs bathroom, dressed in his usual work clothes, and switched on the TV in the kitchen to the classic movie channel. He kept it on for company more often than not.

Speaking of Bacall, *The Big Sleep* was halfway through. He let the noise run in the background as he made himself an omelet. He ate standing up and watched Humphrey Bogart flirt with an improbably attractive bookshop clerk. Flirting while on a stakeout was always fun. Flirting and drinking on a stakeout for double points. They drank from Marlowe's stash of rye, and he vaguely wanted a slug himself, notwithstanding the fact that it was ten in the morning. That was why he didn't keep alcohol in the house. He'd been there once, and it wasn't a good scene.

His desire for a swallow of something brown and 40 proof intensified when he opened his laptop, meaning to order bulbs for fall planting, and his eyes fell on his inbox instead. Nestled between the nursery newsletters and seed store sales notices was an email from someone whose name meant trouble.

He stared at the subject line for a minute. *Just checking in.*

The most banal three words in the English language. And the biggest crock of shit he'd ever heard. Joanna Munroe was never "just checking in." He stared for another minute, as if he could delete the email with the power of his mind.

When that didn't work, he clicked on the damn thing. No use letting it linger and ruin his entire day.

Hey Warner,

How's summer been treating you? We just got back from Montana. Big Sky Country sure is beautiful! The kids had the best time. We took them dinosaur bone hunting, and we even found a few fossils! Hope everything in Connecticut is going well!

So Daphne and I were thinking we'd like to do something for the anniversary this fall. We're

thinking dinner at that brasserie we used to go to all
the time when we were all living in the city. Just a
small group. But we'd really love it if you could
come down. Think about it.

Love you,
Jo

Warner's eyes burned. He wanted to blame it on the
chlorine from the pool. But it was Joanna, with her egre-
gious use of exclamation points and relentless positivity.
Her inability to let him fade out of her life. She was cruel
like that.

He shut his laptop without bothering about the
bulbs, washed his plate and fork, and left the omelet pan
to soak. He picked up his keys from the narrow table by
the front door and stopped to stare at the silver-framed
wedding photo he kept there. The couple in the photo
was so young, so bright and shiny, like a couple of
pennies fresh from the mint. They were smiling hugely,
as if they were happy.

Poor stupid kids.

He grabbed his keys and left.

Chapter Three

Erika: Lacey, aka, ParkerWildsWife19, wants to know what we think of the casting of Henry Yu, a complete unknown, Glen Michaelson, a guy with a few credits, and Stephanie Mae, the only household name in the bunch.

Jules: Yeah, I mean, I'm excited about it. It's just so hard to know, since we know literally nothing about the plot or what characters they're going to be playing. Since the news came out about Stephanie, I went back and watched some of the episodes of her cable show, and I loved her in it. She's got that same girl-next-door quality that Camille Corsair has, but she obviously brings her own twist. It's fucking cool she has a prosthetic leg, I mean, the way they accessorized it on her show was genius.

Erika: Yeah, she's kind of a fashion icon for the generation behind us, I think.

JULES: Ugh, is there already a generation behind us? How did we get so old?

ERIKA: We're not old. We're not even thirty yet. But Stephanie Mae is, what, nineteen?

JULES: Henry Yu and Glen Michaelson are in their early twenties, I think. Clearly, they decided not to cast sixteen-year-olds to play the new kids, which is probably smart. Anyway, as far as the casting goes, I say bring it on.

FROM *THE SAWYER'S COVE REWATCH PROJECT PODCAST: SUMMER MAILBAG*

"So this is The Cove."

Selena stopped inside the entrance and took in the gleaming copper-top bar, the small stage on one side that overlooked an open space for dancing, surrounded by a scattering of tables. Cozy lighting offset the dark brick walls. Nothing about the place screamed its association with *Sawyer's Cove*, beyond its name. The casual visitor would have no idea the owner was Jay Orlando, hometown boy-turned-heartthrob who'd found his second act as a Misty Harbor small business owner and productive member of society.

"Selena, over here."

She followed Cami's voice to one of the booths on the opposite side of the bar from the stage and spotted her co-producer, as well as two other members of the production. She walked over and slid in next to Becca Melis, her trusty assistant and the person who knew the most about the production outside of herself and Cami, who was not only producing but also playing the part of Amy Green. Producer was no vanity title—Cami was boots on the ground, seven days a week, dealing with everything from hiring to budget decisions right alongside Selena. Together, they had assembled a rock-solid team. Some folks from the old show they'd been able to hire back, but they had added plenty of fresh faces.

One of the new additions was writer Bo Christopher. He was young and goofy and had been a huge help in writing for the new generation of Cove kids, especially the character of Kai. Bo had drawn on his experience as a pop culture-loving Chinese American midwestern kid to inform Kai's character. He said hello and then blew his straw wrapper at Becca, who tried very hard not to look charmed. Selena grinned. Becca could use something of a social life. Goodness knows she had her working long enough hours. It would do her good to have a reason to go home at night.

"Welcome to The Cove." A woman with wavy brown hair pulled back into a ponytail and wearing a shirt with The Cove's logo appeared at their booth.

"Hey, Danica," Cami said. "Meet Selena, Becca, and Bo. Everyone, you need to know this woman. She's the manager, and the one who calls the shots around here."

"Don't tell Jay." Danica laughed. "He thinks he reigns supreme. And it's very nice to meet you."

She smiled at Selena. "It's super to meet you in person, I've heard so much about you from Cami."

"So you've heard what a bitch I am?" Selena said.

Danica's gray eyes went wide. "No! Only good things."

Selena waved her hand airily. "Sorry, I'm kidding. I forget that line only works in L.A."

"Selena's really a pussycat, she just pretends to be tough so people don't mess with her," Cami said.

Becca let out a snort, while Bo looked between Cami and Selena, as if not sure what part was true and which was the joke. He wisely kept his mouth shut.

Danica smiled uncertainly. "Well, when you're here, you eat and drink gratis. Boss's orders. So, let me know what you want."

Selena looked at Cami. "Jay knows we have a budget, right? He doesn't have to feed us for free."

Cami shrugged. "He wants to. It's his version of New England hospitality."

"Well, what's yummy here?" Selena asked.

Cami wrinkled her nose. "Honestly? The food's kind of mediocre. No offense, Danica."

"None taken. I finally got Jay to agree to hire a company to develop a new menu for us. Just don't say the word 'gastropub' around him, or it'll erase all the progress I've made."

"Noted." Selena glanced at the menu in the stand-up plastic display on the table. "I guess I'll get a bacon cheeseburger."

"The sweet potato fries are decent," Cami said.

"And sweet potato fries."

"I'll have the same," Becca said.

Cami ordered a grilled cheese, and Bo asked for a

burger and fries and potato skins. He looked about sixteen, and he apparently had the metabolism of a teenager, too.

Despite having spent most of the day together, their conversation immediately turned to work. There always seemed to be something to do, someone to cajole into doing something the way they wanted it done, something to make, something to decide. Selena sometimes felt like her job was an endless cascade of decisions. Should Lily Fine wear a leather skirt in the first episode in a callback to the pilot from fifteen years ago? Do they need a stunt double for Henry Yu for the fight scene outside of Cloudy Cove High? If they cut the scene at the pizza parlor, can they use the money to pay for more extras for the carnival scene? And the most difficult decision she was currently apparently unable to make—how should they end the new series? She had to make it satisfying for the audience, wrap up the season-long story arcs, but needed to keep it open-ended in case they were going to have a second season.

Getting the second season order would be the validation that Selena had made the right decisions, which meant every single decision felt like it could be the one that tipped them toward success or the one that held the show back from greatness. Sometimes she felt paralyzed; endless decisions, and no way to know if she was making the correct ones.

Cami would tell her to trust her gut, which right now was trampolining up and down as she recognized the man taking over a stool at the bar.

Warner was wearing more clothing than the last time she'd seen him, but she still recognized him easily in the un-cool work jeans he seemed to favor, clean at least, and wrinkled button-down shirt. She'd never seen him in anything that wasn't wrinkled, come to think of it.

She watched from the corner of her eye as Danica waited on him with a friendly smile and poured him a short glass of something brown. They chatted for a minute, which interested her. Warner *could* hold a conversation, it seemed. Just not with her.

"—meeting with the other writers tomorrow afternoon? Will that work for you?" Becca's voice filtered in.

Selena redirected her focus to her assistant. She must be tired if she was letting her attention wander when there was still so much work to do.

"Uh, yeah, put it on my calendar, please," she said.

Becca tapped her trusty tablet. Sometimes it seemed like it was embedded in her arm. "Okay, I'll send the rest of the writers the invite."

"What time?" Bo asked, getting out his phone.

How did anyone remember anything before they all had computers in their pockets?

"Three," Becca said. "That way, Selena can make her meeting with Brad at five."

"Ugh. What's my meeting with Brad about?" Selena asked.

"He wants to loop in the marketing team on some of the online response to the reboot."

"What about it?" Cami asked, instantly concerned. "I thought everyone was in raptures about the reboot."

"The initial response was unbelievably awesome," Becca said reassuringly. "But I guess lately there have been some snarky things written about the casting."

Cami frowned. "But we haven't even announced the full cast yet."

"Facts never stopped the Internet, you know that," Bo said. "Let me guess—some creeps are arguing you're ruining the show by casting, gasp, a non-white person."

"Or more than one, in this case," Cami said calmly. Two of the three new cast members were Asian American, and the third was a white gay man. "People are so disappointing sometimes."

Selena patted Cami's arm. "It's okay, sweetie, they'll still love you."

"I don't care about me," Cami said, suddenly fierce. "But I care about the show. Is this going to cause problems?"

"You know there's never unreservedly good press," Selena said, willing herself to believe her own spin. "Besides, a little controversy raises our profile, gets people talking about the show. It'll be fine." She couldn't waste time thinking about stuff she couldn't control.

"Well, I think the casting is perfect," Becca said loyally. "And as soon as people see the show, they'll think so, too. Steph and Henry and Glen are perfect. They embody the spirit of the show. They're the spiritual heirs."

"The spiritual hairs? They do have great hair," Bo

joked, while Becca rolled her eyes. "And I hope you're right. People kind of suck, but the show will speak for itself."

Conversation died down once the food arrived. Her burger was hot and filling. Selena had no complaints. On the other side of the bar, an acoustic guitarist began a solo set, and the melody of her songs wafted over to them.

The noise level rose as more folks filtered in to take up seats on the stage side of the bar. Bo and Becca were laughing, heads together, and Cami was watching them, amused.

Selena caught her eye. "This place is awesome."

Cami's smile grew. She looked pleased and proud, and Selena wondered if maybe Cami had been nervous she wasn't going to like it.

"Jay's done a good job with it," Cami said.

"And you're doing a brilliant job, too," Selena said, holding her friend's gaze.

Her big blue eyes went even wider. "Really?"

"Really," Selena said firmly. "I couldn't do this without you, Cami."

Her pale cheeks went rosy. "It's going to be good, isn't it." She wasn't asking. She sounded certain. And Selena wanted to believe her, just like the characters on the show were always saying.

It was too soon to tell if the chemistry they were building behind the camera would translate to magic in front of it, or if all this time and money would simply result in an embarrassing footnote on the *Sawyer's Cove* IMDb page.

But Selena was going to do everything in her power to make the magic happen. She needed this to be a success, because everyone who'd worked so hard on this deserved it. And because Ryan Saylor, the original creator of *Sawyer's Cove*, had trusted her with his show, and she'd be damned if she was going to mess it up. She owed him a worthy follow-up, and she was going to deliver.

She shoved the specter of the final episode to the back of her mind. The staff writers would be turning in their scripts for episodes eight and nine in the next couple of weeks, and only after that would it be crunch time for the finale. She'd figure something out before then, because she had to.

"Who's thirsty? Should I get another round?" She couldn't have another beer without getting too sleepy to drive home, but water sounded appealing after the salty meal.

"I'm going to go back to the inn," Becca said.

"I'll walk you," Bo offered quickly.

Selena hid a smile. He wasn't subtle, but she didn't think Becca minded. "Don't forget to stop working," she reminded her assistant. "It's a marathon, not a sprint."

"Pot." Becca pointed to Selena, then at herself. "Kettle. Why don't you come back with us, and we can watch some reality TV and veg out?"

Bo, to his credit, didn't look disappointed at the

suggestion. "I think *Single and Stranded* has new episodes out," he said enthusiastically.

"Is that the one where they drop all those twenty-two-year-olds on a desert island, armed with nothing but liquor and sunscreen?" Cami said skeptically.

Bo and Becca said, "It's amazing," simultaneously.

"I think I'll pass," Selena said, laughing. "You enjoy. And I'll take it easy tonight, I promise."

Cami left first, to go back to the house she shared with Jay Orlando, bar owner, co-star, and the love of her life.

"Drive safe," Selena ordered. Her friend had only recently gotten her license at the ripe old age of thirty.

"I will," Cami said, hugging them all goodbye.

Bo and Becca took off, after Becca left a big tip for Danica with petty cash from the production budget. Selena pretended to check her phone, waiting until they were out the door before she slid out of the booth and made her way to the bar.

Chapter Four

Hers wasn't the first dead body Jake had ever seen, but no matter how many corpses he'd stumbled upon in his rotten life, the experience always made him thirsty. He took the bottle of 12-year off the shelf with shaking fingers but didn't spill any pouring it into the glass. Each drop was too precious to waste. More precious than his client's life, apparently.

— *Gunsmoke,* by Warner Mathis

Selena took the stool next to Warner, who was bent over a thick paperback, a half-eaten plate of fries at his elbow. His glass was nearly empty. She angled her head to try to see the cover of the book.

She couldn't make it out in the dim light, and the

way he held his body kept the cover in shadow, but her nosiness caught his attention, and he straightened slowly. He looked at her, his mouth an unchanging flat line. Did the man ever smile?

"Hey," she said brightly. "Fancy meeting you here."

"I'm here a lot," he said gruffly.

"My first time," she said. "But I like it."

He didn't say anything back. She stifled a sigh.

"What are you reading?"

In answer, he held up the book. It was a recent thriller. She hadn't read it, but she had read an earlier book by the same author. "I liked the one about the first lady assassination attempt," she said. "Is this one good?"

If he was surprised she knew the author, he didn't show it. "It's not as tight as *High Crimes*, but it's managed to surprise me a couple of times."

Selena got the feeling Warner wasn't frequently surprised. She'd been waiting for a chance to bring up the elephant in the room. Since they were talking books, she decided to go for it.

"I'll never forget the first major twist in *Gunsmoke*, when Jake thinks he's discovered the body of Margot, but it turns out to be Maggie. Chills every time."

As if she was Medusa and he was a hapless Greek warrior, Warner seemed to turn to stone before her eyes. He didn't even seem to be breathing.

She waved a hand in front of his face.

"Warner? Are you okay?"

He didn't so much as flutter an eyelash, but he seemed to unthaw slightly.

"Is it okay to talk about *Gunsmoke* with you?"

He shifted on the stool, opened his mouth. So, not petrified. She was relieved she hadn't accidentally been channeling a basilisk.

"You recognized me. The first day you moved in."

"You're pretty sharp." She hadn't been certain if he'd noted her reaction to his name.

"So are you," he said. "No one in Misty Harbor has ever asked me about *Gunsmoke*."

"Seriously? Did I just blow your super-secret cover?"

His lips twitched. Had she almost gotten a smile out of him?

"I'm not undercover. They know me as Warner, the curmudgeon with his own stool at The Cove."

"To be fair, that seems pretty accurate."

"Oh, it is," he said dryly.

"But you are also the author of one of the biggest books of the last ten years. No one here knows you're an author?" Selena found that hard to believe. She wasn't the only reader in this town. Jay's sister Mimi, Misty Harbor's head librarian, had to know his identity.

"If they do, they do me the very great favor of keeping it to themselves," Warner said.

Selena shifted on her seat, his attitude making her prickly. "I'm sorry if I brought up a sore subject. I thought you should know your tenant knows your big secret."

He looked at her then, really looked at her, his piercing blue gaze pinning her to the stool. She felt immobilized in her own way, but the longer she stared back into his eyes, the more she realized he wasn't angry or irritated with her. He looked…sad.

Warner was an enigma—he wasn't old, but his body carried the weight of more than his years. He obviously didn't care how he came off to the rest of the world, but he couldn't hide his intelligence, his quick wit. He had to be smart to write the deviously twisty thriller that was so beautifully done, it invited reread after reread. *Gunsmoke* was no one-trick pony; the expertly crafted puzzle was only part of its appeal. The main characters, layered and complex, were what kept Selena coming back to read it at least once a year.

But he had only written the single book. It had sold well, won a bunch of awards. He'd launched a hero who easily could have starred in his own series, à la Dan Brown's Robert Langdon or Lee Child's Jack Reacher. Or to be more accurate, Philip Marlowe, the scathingly intelligent, world-weary gumshoe invented by Raymond Chandler. Jake Wilton was the contemporary heir to Marlowe. But there had never been a follow-up. Warner Mathis had never cashed in on his successful debut.

What had stopped him? Did it have something to do with the sad eyes and hard liquor? Had Warner confused himself with the noir anti-hero he evoked so perfectly in *Gunsmoke*?

"Well, thanks for coming clean," Warner said eventually.

"I'm very brash," Selena said, "as you might have noticed. But…" She thought about how alone Warner seemed. She'd never seen anyone else stop by his house, except for the occasional delivery driver. No one except Danica had so much as looked his way since he got to The Cove. Except her. "I won't go blabbing it around, if there's some reason you want to stay on the down-low."

He looked surprised. Perhaps the concept of her talking about him with other people hadn't occurred to him. "I'd appreciate if you kept it on the QT."

"Oh yes, I'll keep it hush-hush," she said, not bothering to hide her amusement at his old-fashioned slang.

His lips did that almost-smile again. "Cheers," he said, raising his glass.

She didn't have one to raise with him, but she nodded. "You need a ride home?"

He blinked, set the glass down without taking a sip. He didn't answer.

"I'm heading back, and I had one beer, like, an hour ago, so I'm good to drive."

He looked uncomfortable. Selena tried not to take it personally. There could be any number of reasons why he didn't want to leave with her. The most obvious being he simply wasn't ready to leave. Perhaps she'd interrupted his drinking as well as his reading.

"It's okay," she said, getting off the stool. "I'll see you around, Warner."

"See you around, Selena," he said gravely. The way he said her name made her sound like a femme fatale he was expecting to be the death of him, literally or figuratively. "Drive safe."

She left without looking back.

Chapter Five

It was raining the day of the funeral, slate gray drizzle. The freeway was backed up. Jake's necktie felt too tight, probably because he hadn't worn one since the last time he'd been to Hollywood Forever Cemetery. Maybe he should get into a line of work where his clients didn't die with above-average regularity. If he was a mortician, for example, he could count on them already being dead.

— *Gunsmoke,* by Warner Mathis

Warner's schedule didn't change much from weekends to weekdays. He often lost track of exactly which day it was. So, when he looked out of his kitchen window and glimpsed a flash of red on the pool deck, at first he didn't understand what he was seeing.

Then Selena dove into the pool with a cheerful splash and he realized it was his tenant, using the pool to swim laps at...he glanced at the wall clock. Ten A.M. It must be the weekend, then.

As far as he knew, this was the first time she'd made use of the pool. He watched her for a few moments, to make sure she was an adequate swimmer. She was doing the breaststroke, slow but steady, her voluminous hair somehow stuffed into a sleek bathing cap, wearing tinted goggles. Okay, so likely she was an experienced swimmer. She was from California, wasn't she? Perhaps she had a pool wherever it was she lived out there.

When he realized there was very little danger of her needing his impromptu lifeguard services, he turned away from the window abruptly. He had no business watching her like a common voyeur.

He busied himself putting away his breakfast dishes and draining the last of his morning joe. He was getting low on coffee, which meant a stop by the Bakeshop. Zelda stocked a roast he'd gotten hooked on. He could pick up a few sticky buns at the same time. Did Selena like sticky buns? He snorted at himself. Who didn't like sticky buns? Someone with a pecan allergy, perhaps.

He slid his gaze back to the pool. Damn the perfect sight lines of the house. He could easily see the entire pool, the deck surrounding it, even the pool house, though the pool house's windows were much too small to tell anything that was going on inside, except for the occasional light turning on and off. As it should be.

Selena was doing the crawl now. She was a fine swimmer. Good form. He wondered how easy it would be to kill someone who was a strong swimmer. You could use that as a double bluff, if the killer was known to be a weak swimmer, no one would believe she could drown a strong one, but if she'd secretly improved her swimming skills, then she might be able to get away with it. If he was going to write the scene before him, Selena would be the conniving villain slowly building up her swimming skills while plotting her enemy's demise. And Jake Wilton would have to follow all the threads painstakingly back to this moment.

He blinked. His hands felt itchy, as if they craved a pencil. The scratch of lead on paper. Words blossoming under his clumsy, calloused hands.

He wanted to write it down, the opening scene. The lovely criminal doing the crawl, plotting out the ingenious murder.

Warner's hand didn't move for a pencil, but to his chest. It was rising and falling quickly. He was breathing fast. What was happening to him? He felt shaky, but he wasn't drunk. He stumbled away from the window, recoiled when he saw his laptop on the kitchen island. He'd been paying bills earlier. It wasn't beckoning to him. He didn't want to sit down and write. Impossible.

He rubbed his hands over his eyes to keep them busy. This was ridiculous. He glared out the window.

Selena was still at it, oblivious to his minor crisis. Thank God.

This wasn't the first time he'd had this compulsion. But the urges seemed to be getting more common. Stronger. Stronger even than the impulse to drink. He'd mastered that desire sometime after the horrible first year, when he'd had no misgivings about cracking open a bottle of scotch in the middle of the day and finishing it by the next. He'd pickled himself for a year and then decided he didn't actually want to die and put away the bottle. All of them. Now he only let himself drink amongst company, when he couldn't get too sloppy.

But this wasn't drunk. This wasn't anything except the hankering to type a few words. What's the worst that could happen?

He cautiously opened the laptop. The screen woke to reveal his inbox. He had a new email. Joanna. Wanting to talk about the anniversary dinner, no doubt.

It all came rushing back to him like a cheesy movie montage or inelegant backstory dump in a bad novel. Meeting Angie at NYU, somehow becoming the odd couple, him a gawky kid from an L.A. suburb, her a true old-money Manhattan socialite who was bright and quick and self-assured and so convinced of his writing talent that he had to believe in it as well.

They'd married young, and he became absorbed into her life willingly, if not without a pang for Los Angeles, a place he wrote about while staring out the window of their Park Avenue apartment, made possible by Angie's more than adequate inheritance.

He remembered it all like slides from someone else's life: the two of them, their blond heads bent over his pages, her pointing out the weaknesses in the story, making brilliant suggestions, helping everything click into place in his mind. Her smile when he'd finally signed the contract for *Gunsmoke*, with one signature making more money than he'd ever had at one time. The champagne when it hit the bestseller list. The first time she'd shown him the listing for this house, him wondering where the hell Misty Harbor was. Driving up in her classic Mercedes convertible with the top down, the sea air whipping their faces as they crawled through the quaint downtown, past the harbor and toward the big estates with seventy-year-old oaks towering over them.

The confidence with which she moved them from the city to the small seaside town had been classic Angie. She wanted the project of the rental properties she was buying and going to fix up and manage, and she wanted him to be able to focus on the sequel to *Gunsmoke*. But then she'd gone and wrapped her car around a tree, and he'd seized the excuse to put away the manuscript.

How could anyone expect him to finish the book when his wife had died?

He was enough of a coward to use his wife's death to get out of his contract. And he wasn't quite done hating himself for it.

He'd been willing to accept the shame if it meant he didn't have to write. Now he'd lived with the shame for years, as much an old friend as this oversized house. In a way, the shame and the house were both his prisons. He'd built them for himself out of Angie's dreams. Sure, he could break out once in a while, but he'd always have to return to Misty Harbor, to live out his years doing penance for being alive, while Angie had been exiled forever.

But now, perversely, he wanted to write. That's what this feeling had to be, didn't it? The nagging desire to turn his thoughts into words, to turn the observations his brain couldn't help forming into sentences, one after the other until suddenly he'd have a paragraph, a page, a chapter.

He snatched his hand away from the keyboard as if it was burning him.

Fuck. He closed the laptop slowly. He looked in the direction of the pool. He couldn't see Selena from this vantage point, but it was enough to know she was there, an easy target to blame his discomfort on. He hadn't lived so close to anybody in years. But this wasn't her fault. She couldn't help being vibrant and nosy and *alive*.

He turned away from the computer, flipped on the TV to keep his brain occupied with thoughts other than death. Barbara Stanwyck was making big, sad cow eyes at Fred MacMurray. Oh yeah, big improvement.

The loud knock a moment later rattled the door and his nerves. The back door was mostly window, so he had no trouble seeing who the intruder was. Selena, of course, wrapped in a blue striped beach towel he had himself placed in the pool house linen cupboard. It was tucked under her armpits, covering her modestly. She still wore the bathing cap, and when he looked down, he saw a pair of gold colored flip-flops and pretty feet with tidy, unpainted toenails.

She was smiling, pink lips framing even teeth. "Hi! I finally found time to use the pool."

"Evidently."

Her smile dimmed, and he cursed himself for taking away her joy merely by existing.

"Anyway, I was wondering if I could use the laundry room." In one of their exchanges about the property, he'd told her she could use the washer and dryer inside.

"Of course."

"Great. Otherwise, I'd have to wear this towel to the laundromat. I'm completely out of clothes."

He liked her bathing suit, but she'd look terrific naked, he had no doubt. He blinked away the inappropriate image.

"I'll show you," he said.

"Thanks."

He opened the door wider, and she came into the kitchen, her flip-flops clacking noisily on the tile floor.

"Oh, wow," she said, sounding surprised.

He looked around for the source of her consternation.

"*Double Indemnity*. I love this movie."

She was looking at the television, which he'd forgotten was on. He tried not to be pleased that she liked one of the greatest films of all time, and one of his personal favorites.

"My house in L.A. is really similar to the Dietrichson house. You know that style? Terracotta roof and iron-work? When it came on the market, I made the association immediately, and I kind of had to have it."

Now she'd surprised him.

"You live in a villainess's lair?" he asked.

She smirked. "Hey, a villain is the heroine of her own story," she said. "And yes. I'm very proud of it. Want to see a picture?"

She had her phone clutched in her hand. He had to approve. She was a woman in a stranger's house. The phone was a security feature, he was sure.

"Okay," he found himself saying.

She unlocked her phone, tapped the screen a few times, then held up the device to show off an attractive 1930s-era hacienda style house. It was situated on a corner, like the one in the movie. It didn't have the striking octagonal shape of the movie version, but it was beautiful in its own right.

"Lovely," he murmured. He peered at the land-scaping in the front. She had the typical array of drought-tolerant plants, including a smattering of echeveria, her namesake. "Do you garden?"

She shook her head. "Sadly, I am not plant inclined. But I have a good crew."

"You miss it," he said, noting the wistful way she looked down at the photo, as if she was remembering a loved one rather than a house.

"I'm a little homesick," she said. Then she looked up, eyes wide. She wasn't wearing her glasses, and he could clearly see her brown irises matched the mole on the edge of her eyebrow. "Not that this place isn't—I mean, the pool house is super comfortable."

"I'm not offended, Selena," he said calmly. He resumed the trek to the laundry room. "Does it sit empty while you're in Misty Harbor?" A thought belatedly occurred to him. "Oh, your significant other must take care of it." A woman like Selena probably had an interesting, successful partner to come home to after a long day on the set.

"No significant other," she said cheerfully. "My mom and dad will come by and check on it for me if I ask. Last year I was in Canada for a few months, and it was fine."

He ignored the way his pulse sped up at the knowledge that she was single while he showed her how to change the settings on the washer and dryer and pointed out the detergent.

"I'll have to pick up some laundry soap," she said, frowning.

The laundry room smelled like the lavender-scented brand Angie always used. It felt like she was perfuming the air with her memory, perhaps watching him interact with this red rose of a woman. After a beat, he said, "Don't worry about it. I have plenty."

"Okay, thanks. I'll get my laundry bag, and then I'll be out of your hair."

He didn't want her out of his hair. The realization terrified him even more than his earlier inclination to write.

"No trouble," he said stiffly. "I'll leave the back door unlocked. Come and go as you like."

"Thanks."

Cutting sharply through the lavender, Selena smelled like chlorine. Soft black wisps of hair stuck out the sides of her bathing cap. He couldn't seem to stop himself from cataloging every tiny detail about her. There was no reason not to leave the little room, to return to the kitchen and see her out. But he found himself wanting to delay.

"Your house. In Los Angeles. What part?" He winced as the stilted words came out of order. He did actually know how to talk to people, even particularly intimidating people. He had once, anyway.

She didn't seem bothered by his speech pattern. "Echo Park."

"I grew up in Eagle Rock."

"I should have guessed you were an Angelino," she said, "since you write about the city so well. I've been wondering how you ended up in Misty Harbor."

She bit her lip after that, as if she'd revealed something she hadn't meant to. Interesting. She'd been thinking about him? The notion made his chest warm.

"I went to college in New York." There was no simple answer to her question. "I thought I'd go back to L.A. after, but I fell in love with a Manhattanite. When we—" He had to stop talking to take a steadying breath.

Angie had gotten into her head a romantic fancy to raise kids in a bucolic New England town. They hadn't had the chance to start their family. But Selena didn't need to know that. She didn't need to know any of it, but he couldn't seem to help himself.

"My wife used to summer here as a kid." It was an incomplete answer, but it was the best he could do.

"You're married?"

Selena didn't seem upset; only curious. She had a bottomless depth of curiosity, apparently.

"She died. Less than a year after we moved here. I ended up staying."

"Oh." Her brown eyes went instantly liquid, and she touched his forearm lightly. He shifted at the unexpected contact, and she dropped her hand immediately. "Well, it's really different here than Los Angeles."

He felt unaccountably relieved that she hadn't commented further on his marital status, though he was dismayed to still be able to feel the impression of her fingers on his skin. "That's an understatement. Do you hate it here?"

She laughed. "No, I like Misty Harbor. It's cute. It's nice to be able to get to work in ten minutes instead of creeping through rush hour traffic. But I do miss other things. Los Angeles is a very underrated city."

It wasn't as if he hadn't been back in the nearly twenty years since he graduated from Eagle Rock High School, but it had been a while, much to the chagrin of his parents and siblings. The city had for a long time felt more like part of his past than his future.

For a second, he let himself wonder what it would be like to be in the City of Angels with Selena. She'd know all the cool, secret places, no doubt. He had a few inside spots of his own, places to drive and park for a view of the sprawling metropolis. Places perfect for a makeout session when you'd had your fill of the view.

Selena licked her plush pink lips, and he felt a tug in his groin that startled him so much, he pushed past her to the hallway. He didn't wait to see if she was following him.

"I'm going to the nursery. Feel free to come and go."

"Okay." Her flip-flops sounded loud on the floor as she hurried behind him. "Warner, is everything okay?"

He turned to face her. "Of course," he lied. "I just remembered I have to—"

"Go to the nursery," she finished, but kindly, as if she didn't believe him but was letting him off the hook anyway. He should feel appalled at the pity, but he only felt relief.

"Right. Well. Bye."

He waited until she'd let herself out the kitchen door before he grabbed the remote. Fred MacMurray was bleeding to death in his office chair. He switched off the television, wishing it was that easy to switch off the swirl of attraction and unease churning around in his gut.

Chapter Six

The rain was still pelting down when Jake stopped at the liquor store on Victory. He got a bottle of the good stuff, then made it two. His wallet was still thick from the retainer he hadn't earned. He knew her estate wouldn't notice the pittance, but guilt was his default. Least he could do was drink it away in her honor. He glanced out the window to the foggy parking lot. A woman with coppery hair was peering into the passenger window of his car. He waited a beat, and she moved on. Just another ghost.

— *Gunsmoke,* by Warner Mathis

"So he's a widower," Cami said, sucking on her water bottle straw, eyes gone soft, "that explains a lot."

"What do you mean?" Selena asked. They were sitting in the break room at the soundstage a few days after laundry day, when she'd managed to learn something about Warner and yet somehow had come away with more questions about him than before.

"Well, he's so broody and tortured, you know? Like he's had some major trauma. Widower fits."

"I thought maybe he was just a stereotypically reserved New Englander." Selena remembered the way he'd made small talk about her house, her garden. How out of practice he'd seemed, how skittish. The way the air had gone out of the small laundry room when she'd caught him looking at her lips. "He's originally from L.A."

"He is?" Cami looked at her closely. "I know you're living in literally his back yard, but I have to say, I didn't see the two of you getting so chummy."

She patted her pockets for her roll of mints, drew it out, and offered one silently to Cami, who shook her head with a smile. Selena popped one in her mouth, craving the sting. "I thought he was a friend of yours, through Jay?"

"I've talked to him a few times, but even Jay doesn't know much about him, and he's been coming to The Cove for years. He was at dinner at Nash's a few weeks ago, but Danica's the one who told me he owned rental properties."

Selena felt slightly disloyal to her friend by not

mentioning that Warner also happened to be the author of *Gunsmoke*, but she'd told him she'd keep it to herself. Besides, they had to get back to the set in a minute, and she didn't have time to get into the whole bestselling author turned landlord mystery. Shooting had officially begun, and there were always a million and one things to do. Luckily, the director of this episode had everything well in hand. She believed in hiring good people and then letting them have the chance to do their jobs without her jumping all over them.

"So you guys are friends now?"

Selena considered the question. She hadn't seen Warner the rest of the weekend—he'd taken off in his minivan and hadn't returned until well after she'd tramped back to the pool house with all her warm laundry, which she folded while staring into space, trying to come up with the perfect take for the finale of the series. She needed to decide soon.

She and Warner had talked like regular people—well, close enough. And she couldn't deny she found him fascinating. Weirdly, they had a lot in common, even if their styles were different. She found herself wanting to get to know him better. She wasn't into rescuing people or anything—self-sufficiency was pretty much the biggest turn-on she could think of—but the way he seemed surprised when he shared something about himself with her...as if he'd forgotten what it felt like to connect with another person. As if he needed it. As if maybe he liked it. As if maybe he even liked *her*.

She shrugged. "I honestly don't have time for making friends. But he's interesting."

Cami hummed in response. Selena decided she didn't need to know what that hum meant.

"Any progress on the finale?" Cami asked as they gathered their stuff to head back to the set.

Selena grimaced. "I've gotten a few ideas down, but I'm struggling with it."

"Still?" Cami looked surprised, and a little worried. "What can I do to help? Should we set up another writers' roundtable?"

"No, not yet. I need a few hours to really focus."

"Have you thought about—" Cami cut herself off.

"What?"

"Reaching out to Ryan?"

Selena sighed. She wanted Ryan Saylor to like the revival. No, she wanted him to love it. But she also wanted to do it on her own terms. Ryan hadn't wanted to be involved on a creative level, and she'd been relieved. "No. Let's keep that as a last resort."

"Fair enough. Look, you've been going twenty-four-seven since you got here. Talk to Becca and make sure she puts some space in your schedule for you to actually do the thing you're best at—writing a brilliant story."

Selena hoped it was as simple as getting a few hours to focus. She had the feeling she couldn't just schedule her way out of this creative block.

Warner drove slowly up the road to the beach house he was currently renting to Nash Speedwell, one of the *Sawyer's Cove* actors. A couple of weeks ago, they'd had a big storm, and one of Nash's guests had slipped off the road in the ensuing mud. Warner had had the private road graded in the aftermath. Another storm was on its way, and he wanted to make sure it was safe.

His minivan made it up to the house fine, so he parked behind Nash's truck. The man himself, movie star-handsome in running shorts and a sweated-through T-shirt, came from around the back. "Warner, hey. Just got back from my beach run."

"Any problems with the road?" Warner asked.

"Nope," Nash replied. "I'm pretty sure the only reason Mimi ran into trouble the other night was that her tires were overdue for replacing."

"I hope she's seen to that."

"Don't worry, between Jay and me, she's had her fill of car maintenance advice." Nash grinned and lifted the hem of his shirt to wipe the sweat from his brow. "How are things going with Selena?"

All of a sudden, Warner felt hot. Well, of course he did; despite the oncoming storm, the air was thick with trapped heat and humidity.

"What do you mean?" he asked, annoyed that his voice had come out rather strangled.

Nash put up his hands defensively. "I only mean she's been living in your place. Everything going okay?"

Warner stared at his renter. Nash knew Selena, called her a friend, as well as a co-worker. If he ever wanted to get someone's opinion, now would be the time.

"Does she like sticky buns?" he asked.

Nash's friendly smile morphed into a confused one. "Uh, pretty sure everyone likes sticky buns."

"But she doesn't have a nut allergy or something?" Warner pressed.

"Not that I know of." Nash studied him for a second. "I saw her eating some baklava at the craft table—that has nuts in it. She's probably not allergic."

"Okay."

"You want to tell me why the obsession with sticky buns?"

"Oh, I'm going to the Bakeshop later. I thought I might pick something up for her. A neighborly gesture."

Nash was several years younger than him, and annoyingly good-looking, but he wasn't stupid. His gaze sharpened, and Warner was acutely aware he was being judged. An agonizing feeling, since he was pretty sure anyone in their right mind would judge him unworthy of Selena Echeveria.

But Nash just said, "Things are going that well, then?"

Warner struggled for a minute. "It's not—I'm not—"

Nash waited patiently for him to finish, his expression open.

"She's an intriguing woman," Warner said finally, as if that explained everything.

Maybe it did. Nash squinted at him, and his mouth quirked up at the side, but he didn't laugh.

"She's terrific," Nash agreed. "And it sounds like if you want to know if she likes sticky buns, you should ask her."

"Ask her?"

"Yeah, like, in conversation. Get to know her."

"I could do that." He'd been ruminating on their laundry room conversation since it happened. It had felt good to learn about her, to tell her a little about himself. So good, he'd run away and been avoiding her ever since.

He straightened his shoulders. So he was a coward. He knew that already. But he was a little sick of his own bullshit. He'd been a teenager the last time he'd wooed someone—that didn't mean he couldn't do it as a grown man.

"Storm's coming," he said to Nash.

"That's what I hear. Don't worry, I'll batten down the hatches."

"Appreciate it," Warner said. "Let me know if you have any more issues with the road."

"Will do." Nash made for his front door, and Warner retreated to his vehicle. "And Warner—good luck."

Warner nodded his thanks before going back the way he came and pointing the minivan toward town. Nash made it sound so easy, but talking to people was literally his job; he even had someone telling him what to say. Warner had no such advantage.

Then again, he was a writer. Words were something that used to come easily to him. Perhaps he needed to think of conversation as simply dialogue spoken out loud. And perhaps he needed the practice.

"Hey Warner, how's tricks?" Trevor, the preternaturally effervescent employee at the Misty Harbor Bakeshop, greeted him warmly when he walked through the door. The place was deserted. Warner liked to time his visits to avoid the breakfast and lunch rushes. The caffeine addicts looking for their afternoon hit hadn't yet made their way to the Main Street bakery.

"Same old," Warner said automatically, then stopped himself. Things hadn't been the same since Selena came to town, but Trevor didn't need to know that.

"Really?" Trevor said, perceptive brat that he was. "The *Sawyer's Cove* circus isn't bothering you? They're shutting down part of Main Street later this week, did you know?"

Warner, in fact, did not know. He'd made a point to ignore anything to do with the show unless it directly impacted him. Like when its showrunner went for an early morning swim in her red one-piece. Stuff like that.

"Anyway, what can I get you?"

"I know what he wants." Zelda, the owner of the Bakeshop and genius behind the mouthwatering creations in the display case, emerged from the back, holding a bag of coffee beans. Warner sometimes thought she was omniscient, as she always seemed to know what a given customer needed at any moment.

"You beautiful mind-reader."

Zelda handed him the package, amused. "Not a mind-reader. You're more predictable than you think. You come by for one of these about this time every month."

Warner frowned. He hadn't realized he had developed a routine. How easy would it be for her to poison the beans, perhaps with something slow-acting to confuse matters? But what wouldn't react with the acidity of the beans? What about the evidence after the fact? She'd have to find a way to get the beans from his house, replace his poisoned bag with a fresh one.

He shook his head. Not important.

She was looking at him, still amused. "You look like you're miles away."

"Just stuck in my own head," he said. He wanted to add, "The plight of a writer," but Zelda didn't know he was a writer. *Used to be a writer, that is.* God, he was a mess, if thinking about the best way to poison a bag of coffee beans made him the happiest he'd been all day.

Happy. There was a concept. For so long, survival had been the only goal.

He looked around the Bakeshop through fresh eyes. There was Zelda, unassuming Zelda, her straight black hair tied away from her makeup-free face. The air smelled like it always did, of cardamom and cinnamon. Trevor was ringing him up for the coffee, pushing his shoulder length blond hair behind his ears, biting his lip the way he always did when he couldn't find something in the computer.

He knew these people, this place. He liked them. His

stomach turned over. Selena said she missed Los Angeles, her home. The truth was, he'd missed having any sort of home since Angie died. But perhaps he'd found one accidentally.

He shook off the disconcerting thought equating Misty Harbor with home and looked at the pastry case again, this time with purpose.

"A loaf of sourdough and a sticky bun. Two sticky buns," he said. "Please," he tacked on, feeling self-conscious.

Trevor didn't seem fazed by his diffidence. "No problem. You want something to drink to go?"

A flash of red going past the Bakeshop window caught Warner's eye and made him turn his head, but it was only a jogger in a red windbreaker. The weather was turning, and clouds were rolling in. It would be the first storm of autumn. A heavy rain tonight would cause early turning leaves to abandon their trees and paper the ground with a sheet of yellows and greens.

Trevor was talking, as he always did, but this time Warner tuned back in. "And they're setting up a whole carnival down by the beach and inviting everyone in town to be extras. Selena Echeveria told me about it herself when she was in here this morning. Isn't it cool that I basically know a Hollywood player?"

Selena. His ears perked up at the mention of her name, but he didn't want to seem overly interested.

"A carnival? When?"

"In a few weeks, I guess. It's for one of the last

episodes." Trevor shrugged. "Anyway, you know what's the wildest thing about this TV show?"

Warner shook his head when he realized the question wasn't rhetorical.

"How freaking nice everyone is. Aren't Hollywood people supposed to be jerks? But seriously, every single one I've met so far has been cool. Weird, huh?"

Warner did have to agree that was, indeed, unlikely. But he knew Nash and Cami and Jay, and they were all good people. Plus, Selena was in charge. She wouldn't hire someone who wasn't also a decent human being.

Trevor popped the sticky buns in a big cardboard box he'd gotten down for Warner's order. "Anything else?"

"When Selena was here, did she say what she liked? Pastry-wise, I mean?"

Trevor's perfectly manicured eyebrows came together for only a split second before he recovered. "Salted chocolate chip cookie. She couldn't decide between that and a chocolate croissant. I think she likes chocolate."

"Chocolate." Angie had hated chocolate. His relief was surprising. "I'll take a couple of those cookies, then."

Trevor's hesitation was again only a few seconds, but he was a professional and simply added the cookies to the order. Should Warner explain that she was his tenant and—what?—he wanted to give her something she'd like? Why was he compelled to get her anything at all?

Okay, he knew why, but his brain skittered away from putting it into words.

He paid for his sweets and coffee, sticking too much money in the tip jar. No matter. Trevor had earned it.

Now he only had to figure out a way to give Selena the cookies that wasn't weird or stalkery. That perplexed him the entire walk back to the minivan. He still hadn't come up with a plan as the raindrops started falling on his drive home.

Chapter Seven

Jake regretted leaving his piece locked in his glovebox the second he saw his door was ajar. He could go down and get it or—he glanced inside the paper bag with its two heavy bottles. Shame if he broke one, but as a makeshift weapon, a fifth of scotch would do.

— *Gunsmoke,* by Warner Mathis

Selena's day had started with her sleeping through her alarm and gotten worse from there. It had been a chaotic day on set when, because of the coming storm, the second unit had to cancel their afternoon shoot in the woods behind the inn and switch the schedule around to shoot some interiors. Then she'd had a short but contentious phone call with Brad at the studio about the continued negative rumblings about the casting of the show, in which she'd tried to be diplomatic while Brad ranted about the studio's marketing people and how they were letting it get out of hand. She was hungry and cranky and snapped at Becca when she'd suggested she might need a break. Which meant she needed a break.

She pulled into the driveway next to Warner's minivan gratefully. Her little rental car had been buffeted by powerful gusts the entire way home. She grabbed her bag and made a blind run for it through the pelting rain, wind pushing her hair relentlessly into her eyes. Her inadequate jacket was wet through when she finally got her keys out and threw open the door to the pool house. Inside was dark. Unusually dark, and unusually cold. She was about to reach for the light switch when she heard a noise behind her.

She whirled around, stifling a yelp. It was only Warner, doing his best impersonation of the grizzled fisherman killer from *I Know What You Did Last Summer* in an olive green rain slicker and black rubber boots.

"Jesus, Warner. What's going on?"

"Power's out," Warner said shortly. "Wanted to let you know."

"Fuck me," Selena said wearily. She needed to work, and her computer was low on battery. Besides, she was wet and hungry and not looking forward to managing on the light from a flashlight for however long it might take to get the power back on.

"I've got a generator, but it's not hooked up out here. You're welcome to come over. I have soup on the stove."

"And a working outlet?" Selena said hopefully. Soup sounded nice, but power for her laptop sounded even better.

He didn't question her priorities. "Yes, and a working outlet."

"Okay. Thanks." She shut the door firmly behind her and followed Warner to his kitchen door. Once inside, she peeled off her sodden jacket. Warner hung it next to his slicker on a hook by the door. Her wrap dress was only a little damp, thankfully. She stepped out of her thin shoes and left them by his boots. He was wearing soft-looking thick gray wool socks, and she shivered in her bare feet.

Warner looked down and frowned. "I'll get you some socks."

He was gone before she could protest—and she really didn't want to be cold for the sake of not putting him out. She was already putting him out, though he didn't seem to mind overly much. She'd just use him for electricity until the power was restored.

First things first—she located an outlet and plugged in her computer, reassured that her lifeline to work and the outside world wouldn't be completely severed. Then she washed her hands in the sink. With the light on inside, she couldn't see anything out of the kitchen window besides her wobbly reflection. But she thought on a clear day this window would have a direct view of the pool, and the pool house beyond. Had

Warner ever watched her swim, the way she'd watched him?

She turned around when she heard him come into the kitchen. It seemed as if he was making noise on purpose, so as not to scare her. She appreciated it. She wasn't normally this nervy.

Warner held out a pair of cozy heather gray socks. They were smaller than men's socks. Somehow, Selena was certain they'd belonged to his wife. She took them and shivered as their fingers brushed. Did it bother her to wear a dead woman's socks? She sat down on the nearest kitchen stool and put them on. She would mind less when her feet were warm.

"Soup?"

Now that she was drying out, Selena could focus on her other senses. She sniffed the air—tomatoes and oregano—and spotted a Dutch oven on the big six-burner stove. "I'd love some. Can I help with anything?"

"There's a loaf of bread. You could slice it," he said, nodding at a knife block. A wooden cutting board was sitting next to it, with a sourdough boule on top. She slipped off the stool again, found the bread knife, and cut four pieces off the fragrant loaf, while he ladled the soup into two white ceramic bowls.

"Did you make the bread?" she asked, for something to say. He could probably get through an entire meal without conversation, but that didn't mean she wanted to.

"No. I'm not much of a baker. I got it at the Bakeshop."

"Oh, I love that place," she said. "I was there today for a work meeting. Best part of a crappy day, actually."

"Why was your day crappy?" Warner asked. He set the bowls on the table, went over to his big stainless-steel fridge, and brought out a white ramekin. When he set it on the table, she saw it had mouthwateringly yellow butter inside.

"Oh, work stress. Dealing with shortsighted people. The existential angst of creativity. The usual."

She didn't imagine the ghost of a smile on his mouth.

He finished setting the table with two maroon cloth napkins, spoons, and butter knives.

She sat on the nearest side; he sat on the other. As soon as he sat down, he got up again.

"Do you want something to drink?"

"What are you having?"

"I have sparkling water or tea. It's a bit late for coffee."

She'd been expecting him to offer her something alcoholic, given what she'd seen him drink at The Cove the other night. "Water, please."

She stared down at the bowl of steaming soup while he went back to the fridge and got out a large green glass bottle. There was a hiss as he broke the seal and poured water into two sturdy glass tumblers. Warner lived very well, everything simple but high quality. Not like her boho shabby chic style. Everything in her house was from Cost Plus or Ikea, not having had the time or inclination to invest in anything fancier.

"Go ahead," he said, setting the glasses down with a clink.

She took a careful taste. It was warm, but not hot. And it was the best tomato soup she'd ever eaten. She took a second spoonful, looked up. He was watching her, his blue eyes clear and maybe not quite so sad as she'd grown used to seeing them. "This is delicious."

"Thank you," he said solemnly. He started eating, too, and there was no need to talk for a while. Eventually, Selena felt her hunger ease, and she slowed down, buttering a piece of bread generously.

"You're a lifesaver," she said. "Even if the power hadn't gone out, I was facing a pathetic microwave dinner and a glass of boxed wine."

He lifted his water glass. "Good thing the power went out," he said casually.

"Good thing." She gave him a small smile, and he—miracle of miracles—fully smiled back.

The expression transformed his face; Warner looked completely different. His smile crinkled the skin around his eyes, carved out a dimple in his left cheek, but not his right. The asymmetry compelled her to take a second look.

She'd felt this same pull the moment she first saw him, when she thought he was the gardener hired by the owner of the mansion they sat inside that very minute. She'd found him intriguing from the start, but now she just found him...attractive.

She hadn't felt this way about anyone in a while—since her last boyfriend, probably. Neil had been handsome and fun, and she'd had a couple of sleepless nights over their breakup when his company had transferred him to Chicago. But she'd gotten over it. She had more important things to focus on. Honestly, there was always partially a sense of relief when her relationships ended. Working in television was her first love. Her true love.

She'd basically given up on finding a man who could compete with her job for first place in her heart. And she didn't mind that so very much. Her cousins would carry on the Echeveria name, while her legacy would be the stories she put out in the world.

But that didn't mean she couldn't have fun. She liked sex. It was awesome cardio. She had a feeling Warner would be an attentive partner. It wasn't usually her style to sleep with people she wasn't at least dating, but it wasn't as if she didn't know him at all. She knew *Gunsmoke* backward and forward, and the author of that book had to know his way around a woman's body. Jake had found time between finding clues and solving the mystery to take a character to bed. The sex scenes were surprisingly nuanced for the genre, which was usually a fade to black or perfunctory tab-a-in-slot-b type description.

She decided to run a little experiment.

Selena allowed a trace of soup to cling to her full bottom lip. She was well aware her mouth was her best feature. Her big hair and glasses distracted from the ordinariness of the rest of her face, but she liked her lips, plump and slightly pouty.

Warner had nice lips, too, sculpted and not too thin

or too thick. He was probably a good kisser. She suddenly needed to find out. She deliberately licked the soup off her lip with the tip of her tongue. She watched as Warner's gaze dropped to her mouth, stayed for longer than a moment. His grip on his spoon tightened.

Excellent.

She finished her meal in a heightened state of awareness. Warner responded to her conversational gambits about the soup—which he had made from scratch—and the generator—which would keep the lights and heat on all night if necessary. The storm was still going on—she could hear rain lashing against the kitchen window when the wind sent up a particularly strong gust.

It felt as if the air was charged with static electricity, the colors of Warner's well-appointed kitchen becoming extra vivid, the clink of the dishes as he cleared their bowls to the sink overly loud. She'd been so tired before, but the soup fortified her, and now she felt buzzy, needing an outlet for her energy.

She could just make a move. What was a casual come-on between landlord and renter? It's not like she had to see him continuously for the next two months— oh, wait.

She leaned against the counter, the thin cotton of her wrap dress clinging to her like a second skin she was desperate to peel off. What was happening to her? She felt like a noir heroine about to seduce the stoic detective. She frowned. Had Warner dosed the soup? She looked at the long line of him, shapeless jeans, woolen socks. He was wearing a sweater—cable knit. But she wanted him.

Bizarre.

And probably all in her head. He was simply showing her a modicum of human kindness by inviting her in from the dark and cold. He didn't necessarily want to have sex with her.

Then he reached for a bakery box. She recognized the Bakeshop's logo printed on the outside.

He turned to her, box open. "Dessert? Salted chocolate chip cookies or sticky buns."

If she'd been waiting for a sign, that was it. "What did you say?"

He looked slightly bashful. "Um. I got some sweets. Trevor said you liked the—"

"Warner."

He looked relieved at being interrupted. "Yes?"

But as he gazed at her with those keen blue eyes, his expression guarded but somehow hopeful, she couldn't make herself say it. They'd only started to be friends. Did she really want to derail that with sex?

She wavered. "How about that tea? And do you have a living room in this place? Or at least a couch?"

He smiled again, a polite version of the real smile he'd given her before. "There's a couch in the den. I'll give you a tour while the water boils."

She let out a pent-up breath, shuddering as all the carbon dioxide came out. As much as she wanted something physical, something simple, she knew there was nothing simple about starting something physical with this man.

Chapter Eight

The apartment was empty of anything living apart from whatever organisms were growing on the two-week-old pad Thai in the refrigerator. The mess of every drawer and closet emptied would take time to clean up, but nothing had been stolen. This invasion was a message. *Forget her.* Well, Jake wasn't good at forgetting.

— *Gunsmoke,* by Warner Mathis

"You've already seen the laundry room," Warner said, as he took Selena down the corridor away from said room. "Here's the dining room."

She whistled. It was a rather impressive room, taking up nearly the whole depth of the house. The twelve-person table was too small for the space.

"More like a ballroom," she observed.

Angie had envisioned them throwing big holiday parties, but he rarely even walked in here.

They moved to the foyer. This was the entrance he used more often than not except when he was unloading groceries or plants through the back. The side table that held his mail and keys was the only thing of note, and he wanted to move Selena past it quickly, to the promised den, but she stopped in front of the photograph.

"Is this you?" she asked, sounding truly shocked, as if the baby-faced towhead in the picture couldn't possibly be the weathered old man standing in front of her. Before he could answer, she bent down to get a closer look.

"And this is your wife?"

He tried to get a read on her thoughts from her tone, but she sounded like she usually did. Matter of fact. Asking for information.

He struggled with what to say, then settled on, "Yes."

She looked at the picture for another minute. He wondered what she saw in it. Was she feeling sorry for the couple in the photo, or envious, or happy she wasn't one of them?

"She's lovely," Selena murmured.

He noted the use of present tense and appreciated it. Angie would always be lovely in that picture, her blonde hair swirling, Central Park spread out behind them.

"What was her name?" Past tense, this time. Still, appropriate, however much it still hurt.

"Angeline," he said, his mouth carefully forming the word.

She laughed, short and loud.

His eyes narrowed on her.

"Shit. Sorry." She schooled her mouth into a line. "It's just a perfectly dramatic name."

He was appalled that his mouth wanted to twitch up into a smile. "I always thought it was a romantic name."

"Super romantic," she said, clearly trying to be serious. "And don't pay me any attention. I'm a cold-hearted bitch, everyone knows that."

"No, you're not." Selena was many things, but cold wasn't one of them. She was fire made life, bringing warmth and light and sucking up all the oxygen in the room. And the thing of it was, Angie not only would have liked her, she would have agreed with her about her name.

"I always called her Angie," he said to Selena's back. "But she hated that. She thought it made her sound like a Yorkie."

Selena's easy laugh bounced off the wood paneled walls as she moved past him down the hall.

"What about you? What's with the two last names?"

"Unimaginative parents. Warner is my mother's last name. Mathis is my dad's. They named my sister after my aunt Diane."

She stopped in the doorway to the den. "I found the couch."

He peered over her shoulder, seeing it through her eyes. The room was much smaller than any of the other rooms on this floor. There was a television and lots of bookcases, one large couch, and an armchair. A desk he never used. It had been his office for a few months, and technically he supposed it still was, but it had long since been more of a reading room than a writing one.

She walked in, looked over his bookshelves with interest but didn't touch anything. Instead she sank down on the couch. The flimsy cotton dress she wore rode up her thigh, exposing a lightly tanned stretch of skin. She tucked her socked feet underneath her and looked at him expectantly.

The couch was big, but she'd sat in the center, which meant he could either take the armchair or sink down next to her. In her space.

He backed out of the room. "I'll go get the tea."

She didn't look annoyed, called after him, "Don't forget the cookies."

He practically raced back to the kitchen. The water had long since boiled during their slow circuit of the ground floor, so he pressed the button down again, got out two mugs and a box of herb tea. He needed a reality check. There was no way she was flirting with him. Was there?

He wished he had someone to ask. Diane was useless—on the other side of the country, busy with her kids, no time for her idiotic older brother wondering if a woman might be trying to seduce him.

He pulled his phone out. He almost searched *how to tell if a woman is flirting with you*, but God knows what advice the Internet would supply.

Perhaps the fates were listening, though, because a text popped on his screen as he stared at the phone. Actually, four texts.

> FYI I just drove home and the road is fine.
>
> Thought you'd want to know.
>
> Some storm, huh?
>
> Hope you're staying dry.

Nash Speedwell had the habit of texting in batches instead of one comprehensive text.

> Thanks for the update.

He sent it and then after a moment's consideration added:

> Can I ask you a question?

The reply arrived in seconds.

> Go for it.

Warner made himself type out his question before he could overthink it. If Nash told him he was being stupid, he could simply bring the tea to Selena and sit in the armchair, and everything would be fine. But if his suspicions were correct, well then...he'd have a decision to make.

How can you tell if a woman is into you?

Sticky buns were a hit?

Damn it. Warner wasn't fooling anyone.

I think it was the salted chocolate chip cookies, but yes. Help me. I need a head check.

Okay. Well this isn't an exhaustive list, but generally a woman might be into you if she

Laughs at your jokes

Touches you

Draws attention to her body

Any of this ringing a bell?

Warner thought back. She'd laughed a couple of times and had seemed to be drawing attention to herself during dinner. Or maybe it was all in his head. Oh, God.

Helpful. Thanks.

He hoped Nash could hear the sarcasm oozing from his reply. He put together a little tray with two steaming mugs of herbal tea, a plate of cookies, and a couple of napkins.

He was picking it up to take back to the den when his phone buzzed again.

> Real talk—if you want to know if she's
> into you, you can always just ask.
>
> Good luck, man.

Warner decided Nash didn't need a response. He put his phone on the tray and walked deliberately back to the den. *Just ask.* That's right. He was too old to play games. He could just ask. Then she could respond incredulously and they could never speak of it again and he could avoid her until she moved back to California.

When he walked through the doorway of the den, Selena was still on the couch, but she'd evidently found the controls for the gas fireplace in the wall. The fire was blazing, giving off light and warmth in the small room. She was reading a slim, beat-up mass market paperback. He had dozens of them, covers creased, musty pages brittle. But she was being careful.

He came and set the tray down on the table next to the couch, and she looked up from the book and smiled. His entire body tightened in response. If this was a seduction, he was the hapless schmo who couldn't—or shouldn't—believe his good luck when the gorgeous mystery woman showed interest in him.

Then again, a curvy, intelligent, funny, understanding woman sitting on a couch reading a book would turn anyone's blood to fire.

He ignored the armchair, sat on the couch next to her. She looked pleased.

He passed her a mug. She bent her nose over the rim and inhaled.

"It's hot," he cautioned her.

"Okay." She set her mug back down on the table and held his gaze deliberately. "What should we do while it cools?"

Oh, dear. His heart thudded uncomfortably in his chest. "Selena," he started. Her name came out like an accusation.

She lifted her eyebrows.

"Leaving aside the inevitable awkwardness about our living arrangement, there are two things you should know—" he wanted to say, "before we do anything," but that might be too presumptuous "—if we—" Damn, he really did not know how to finish that sentence.

But calm as anything, she scooted closer. He swallowed against a dry mouth.

"Two confessions, actually."

"Confessions?" Her mouth curved saucily. "I'm all ears."

"I have to admit something, in case you find out later and it bothers you."

Her cheekiness faded. She was probably imagining all sorts of depraved things. "What's that?"

"I've never seen an episode of *Sawyer's Cove*."

There was a beat of silence, and then she laughed, free and clear and full of delight. She laughed so hard, her body tipped toward his, her arm grazing him, her breasts glancing off his chest and then away.

He shivered and smiled hesitantly. "You're taking it very well."

She hiccupped through her laughter. "That's amazing," she said, apparently quite honestly. "Thanks for telling me, Warner, really. Sometimes it feels like the entire fate of humanity rests on me getting this fucking show right. But there's a whole world of people out there who couldn't give a damn. I needed that reminder."

"So it's not a dealbreaker?" Warner said, uncommonly pleased with himself for making her laugh so hard, albeit unintentionally.

She blinked at him, thick black lashes sweeping across her dark eyes. "Do you know how hard it is to meet people who I haven't worked with in some capacity or another? L.A. is such a company town, and the sexual politics is complicated. And here—Misty Harbor is full of *Sawyer's Cove* people. And I'm their boss. I'm not saying the landlord/renter dynamic isn't slightly problematic, but I'll take it over an HR nightmare with a co-worker."

"I never thought about that before." Of course she'd stay completely professional with her co-workers. He'd never been so happy that he wasn't part of the incestuous *Sawyer's Cove* circle.

She looked at him expectantly with bright eyes. "The second confession?" she prompted.

"Oh. That. Well." He hoped this one didn't make her laugh. But then again, if it did, perhaps he'd have his answer and they could stop this nonsense before it went any further. "I'm attracted to you, Selena."

She leaned toward him. "That's not much of a confession. I'm attracted to you, too."

"No, that's not it." It took him a moment to register

the second part of what she'd said. "Oh. Thank you." He paused, digesting it. "Why?"

"Why am I attracted to you?" Selena asked, the humor back in her voice.

"Well—yeah. You're objectively attractive, but I'm—" He looked down at himself. He was wearing his favorite comfy sweater. Frumpy was another word to describe it. He ran a hand over his jaw. Had he even remembered to shave that morning? He was no prize.

"First of all, I hope you find me subjectively attractive, not only objectively so," Selena said. She'd moved even closer, and now they were definitely touching, her knee against his thigh. He could smell her. She smelled like mint, fresh and bright.

He reached out and palmed the curve of her cheek lightly, ran his thumb across the smooth, soft skin at the edge of her eyebrow. "Subjectively, I think your beauty mark is quite alluring."

She parted her lips in surprise. "My mole?"

"It's a punctuation mark on an expressive face," he said, rather nonsensically, but the room was so warm, and he was touching Selena, and nothing really made sense anymore. He wasn't drunk, hadn't let a drop of alcohol pass his lips since he was last at The Cove. He was glad he couldn't blame the syrupy fog of his brain on whiskey.

"Oh." She nuzzled her face into his hand, like a cat begging for more pets.

He touched the rim of her glasses. "Do you wear these all the time?"

In answer, she slid them off and set them on the table next to the tea tray. "They're mostly for the computer, but my eye doctor says it's easier to leave them on all the time. I can see fine without them."

Without the glasses, she looked even younger. "Can I ask your age?"

"I'm thirty-seven."

He was surprised, but it made sense she was no ingenue. "Me, too."

Her eyes widened slightly. He supposed the last few years had been hard on him. He certainly felt older than that.

He'd always wondered if her hair would be as soft as it looked, if perhaps the cloud effect was deceptive and it would be coarse, but when he gave in and stroked it, her brown curls were silky. He longed to tangle his fist up in them, to tie himself to her, to allow himself to be ensnared.

"Are we just going to ignore all the reasons we shouldn't do this?" he asked.

"I'm still looking to hear what else you find attractive about me. Subjectively, that is. Then we'll do you."

He left her hair to caress her shoulder. She was warm and firm under his fingers. He hadn't touched anyone like this in so long. It was like opening his eyes to the light after living in the dark. "Your ears are rather pretty. Like twin seashells."

"Okay." She quirked her mouth. "Thank you." She sounded like she might be getting impatient with him.

"And your body is...confusing," he said.

"How so?"

"So many curves, so much skin. I don't know where to look, where not to look. Where to touch. Where not to touch."

She moved his hand from her shoulder to her breast. "You can touch me here, if you want."

He fondled her for a moment, savoring the weight of her in his hand. God, he'd missed breasts. Which reminded him that he hadn't gotten to the second confession.

He pulled his hand away reluctantly and looked her in the eyes. Her lids were heavy, as if she'd been enjoying his sophomoric fumbling.

"So the thing is—"

"Wait, don't you want to know how I find you subjectively attractive?" she asked quickly, as if she was afraid whatever he might say would ruin the moment. Her instincts, as usual, weren't wrong.

"I'm all ears."

She shifted and got right up in his face. He'd be alarmed by how close she was if he didn't so desperately want her to simply keep going, to plaster herself to him. He wanted to absorb her into his skin.

She brushed her fingers through the hair at his temple. "I like how you're already going a little gray, but because your hair is blond, you can only see it in certain lights. It's like a secret, and you have to be paying attention to find it."

"Have you been paying attention to me?" It seemed she had.

She cupped his cheek the way he'd done to her and rubbed a thumb over the hollow there. "You get a dimple, but only on this side. And your eyes are the same color as the sky in L.A. in June after the marine layer burns off and there's nothing but blue overhead."

He blinked as the image of a searing blue sky crowded out everything else in his mind.

She stroked over his light stubble, scratching through the bristles there. "You don't shave every day, which gives you an absent-minded professor kind of look. Not to mention your clothes. But your body—" She left his face and squeezed his upper arm. Her hand felt small on his muscle. "All that gardening and swimming —it clearly does a body good."

He'd always been a skinny kid, but as he'd gotten older, he'd retained more muscle, used it to dig and lift and repair. He liked doing things with his hands, and since he could no longer use them for what he thought he'd spend his life doing, it made sense that he put them to work doing other things.

"Okay, so we're attracted to each other."

He'd spent the last few years thinking of his body as nothing more than a tool to carry out Angie's plans, as something he had to deal with to keep going and not lay down and succumb to the nothingness that seemed like such an appealing option immediately after her death.

But after years of dormancy, it turned out he was very much alive, everything still worked, still responded to the touch of a beautiful woman.

Selena's hands were on his waist now; she was practically sitting in his lap. It was now or never.

"Yeah, so—confession number two," he said heavily. "It's been a while for me. Since I did anything like this."

"Necking on a couch?" Selena asked, her hands stilling on his waist.

"Yeah, sort of."

"What, like high school?" she joked.

"No, since my wife died."

She was silent for a minute. She didn't move away, but she didn't move closer either. "So how long is that?"

"Five years."

Chapter Nine

Jules: One of my favorite things about this absolutely wild episode is that we discover that Lily Fine, town slut, hasn't actually had sex in, like, two years.

Erika: If you were paying attention, you would already know that about her.

Jules: Of course I already knew that about her, E. Who do you take me for? I have a tattoo on my ass of a lily in honor of the unparalleled Lily Fine. You should know— you were there when I got it.

Erika: That was an epic night.

Jules: It really was. The point I'm trying to make is that it's common for teenagers to have sex for the first time and then go years before they have it again, and I love seeing that representation on the show. Having a celibate period is nothing to be ashamed of.

Erika: Amen to that—I'm in one right now. [laughs] Oh, it's funny because it's true.

FROM *THE SAWYER'S COVE REWATCH PROJECT PODCAST: THE
MISTLETOE*

Five years without sex—without *touch*. Selena's mind raced, but she still found it incomprehensible.

The two of them were trapped in a tableau, so quiet and still, she could hear the hiss of gas in the fireplace across the room.

Whether it had been five years or five days didn't change how very much she was enjoying touching Warner now. But maybe there was a reason he hadn't done this. Maybe she was pushing him into doing something he didn't really want. That wouldn't do.

"Are you sure you want to?" she asked quietly, breaking the silence. "It's not—I'm not expecting anything from you. I can go home. Or I can go to the other end of the couch, and we can talk about our favorite Chandler novels." She pointed to the vintage paperback she'd been reading before. She was a *Lady in the Lake* stan.

Warner smiled sadly. His dimple didn't show. "Look —I'm a bad bargain. I know that. That version of me, the sad sack with his own stool at The Cove—that's not too far off the mark. But it's dark and stormy and you're beautiful and you like Raymond Chandler and I'd be a fool not to want to find out how you taste."

She shivered. He was so intense, but it wasn't a put-on. She was used to Hollywood posers trying to be Tarantino or Wes Anderson, mannered and quirky.

Warner was quirky all right, but it wasn't performative. He had no one to perform for.

She was the only one here. Her and Warner, and Warner's ghosts, all rattling around this absurdly nice house in the middle of Nowhere, Connecticut.

"All right," she said, "but Warner, truly, we can stop at any time."

"I know." And then he kissed her.

She wasn't expecting it, and he caught her mouth half-open. She dug her fingers into his sweater for purchase, adjusted the angle of her head to make it better, glad she'd taken her glasses off so she didn't have to worry about them getting in the way.

He wasn't a bad kisser, exactly, but he held himself away from her, his shoulders locked into a starched square. She didn't want to be aware of his posture—she wanted to be lost in the kiss, unable to think about anything except the pressure on her lips. So she took control, licked into his mouth, nudged him against the couch by bumping her chest against his and pushing. He went easily, his arms coming around her back perhaps instinctively, his mouth opening underneath hers.

It was easy from there. She straddled his lap, heedless of the way her dress rode up her thighs, kissing him for all she was worth. If he hadn't kissed anyone in five years, she wanted this kiss to be worth the drought.

When his tongue touched hers for the first time, she felt a jolt of electricity down to her core.

She must have made a noise or something because he did it again, and the effect was no less extreme. She pulled away from him, staring. His eyes were slits, his mouth open and chasing hers as she dragged herself a few inches away from him, still sitting on his lap.

She touched her mouth. It felt hot. She hadn't had this kind of instant physical attraction to anyone in— ever. It was like they were both giving off pheromones and those pheromones were having a good old time.

"Um," she said intelligently.

"Yeah," he agreed, then he hauled her back in for another round of deep, soul-searing kisses.

She'd planned to be the one in control. The one who picked up the cues and set the pace and moved things along in an orderly fashion. But he overwhelmed her, touching her every place he could reach, as if he was worried she'd disappear if he didn't anchor himself to her.

Sex was supposed to be enjoyable, a physical outlet, an impulse you acted on with someone you liked. It was entertainment, something to do when there was nothing good at the movies.

Sex wasn't supposed to sweep you away, disorient you with pleasure so you didn't know which way was up. It wasn't supposed to clear everything out of your head so the only thing you could think was "yes" and "more" and "please."

But as she kissed Warner—and Warner kissed her— that was all she had room in her head for.

He kissed the lobe of her seashell ear, and she moaned, "Yes."

His hands crept forward to cup her breasts,

thumbing her nipples through the cotton, and she begged, "More."

He obliged, tugging down the stretchy fabric, freeing her breasts, then slipped his thumbs under the cups of her utilitarian black bra to knead at the stiff, aching nipples. "*Please.*"

She rose to her knees, so her breasts grazed his mouth. He took the hint, latching on to one with speed. He sucked the tip, and she sighed in pleasure, until he took her nipple between his teeth and bit lightly, worrying it between his teeth. She was no longer blissfully submitting to him, now she was squirming to get closer, desperate to get some relief for the ache building up between her legs.

She reached for his other hand, stuck it under her skirt, pressed his fingers to her clit through her panties. He rubbed, but the angle was bad, and they both made noises of frustration. He let go of her breast, gleaming wet from his mouth, and the sight launched a fresh wave of arousal.

Selena felt debauched. And warm. That little fireplace gave off a lot of heat; they were both panting as if they had fevers. Warner's cheeks were flushed, his mouth bitten dark. Her breasts were hanging out of her dress, but she felt no shame. She needed to be more naked, not less.

Untying the knot at her waist caused the wrap dress to gape open, exposing her to the room. To Warner. She wasn't small. Her belly proudly rounded out under her generous breasts. Her thighs bracketed him, unapologet-ically thick.

He responded by tugging his sweater, and the shirt beneath it, over his head in one smooth move that was more coordinated than she would have given him credit for.

The clothes landed in a heap on the floor, leaving his chest on display. She'd seen it before at the pool, streaming wet, but now she could explore his lightly developed pecs with their dusting of hair. She touched the flat discs of his nipples, scraped her nail over the tiny bud in the center of each. He let out a gratifying hiss.

She glanced up. Warner's expression was tense, but he continued to let her study him to her heart's content. She slid her fingers across his abdomen, the hair around his navel, to the waistband of his jeans. He wasn't wearing a belt. Denim outlined his erection; it jumped a little when she unbuttoned his fly. He grabbed her around the wrist, hard, before she could peel down the zipper.

Her gaze flew to his face, surprised. Had she done something wrong?

"Are you—" He stopped. She waited. She was so wet, she felt herself soaking through her panties. She had to be soaking into his jeans.

She kissed him, her breasts pressed against his chest, the skin-to-skin contact pure pleasure.

"Am I what?" she murmured against him. All she wanted to do was lean back and pull him on top of her, so she could feel every square inch of his skin against hers. But she vaguely remembered why they were going slow. The longer he waited before responding to the question, the more reasons filtered in. He was her landlord, and he had been celibate for five years, since his enchanting, golden wife died and left him grumpy and lonely in this too-big house, where he occupied his hands with planting flowers and making tomato soup instead of writing the next Jake Wilton novel.

"Are you on birth control?" he asked, cheeks more pink than red now. "I don't have any condoms."

"Oh." The practical question cleared her head. But then she realized what it meant. He wanted to get inside her. He wanted—of course he did.

She wanted that, too. She kissed him again. "Yes. I have an IUD."

"Okay."

She stocked condoms in her toiletries kit, like anyone who had been a Brownie in third grade and had "always be prepared" drilled into their head. But the pool house was awfully far away.

Selena kissed him and shifted so her aching, wet core was pressed against that bulge in his jeans. She was thrilled, knowing that he'd be inside her soon, filling up the emptiness. It had been a while for her, too. Not years, but months, certainly. It was going to feel so good to have Warner inside her.

They had to get more naked first.

Reluctantly, she scooted off his lap to slither out of her dress, leaving her in her underwear. And the borrowed socks.

She frowned down at her no longer cold feet. There was no sexy way to take off socks, but then Warner came to her rescue, taking each foot in turn and sliding the wool off slowly, seductively, as if she was a Regency miss and he was removing her gloves in an act tantamount to foreplay.

But this was actual foreplay. Hallelujah.

Warner dropped the second sock over the side of the couch, looked at her.

She smiled. "This is fun."

"Is it?" He put a hand on her hip, spreading his fingers out possessively. "It's incredible. Unexpected."

"Second thoughts?" she asked lightly.

"Not when I'm touching you," he said, his grip on her tightening. She responded by letting her legs splay open in invitation.

"Don't stop touching me, then."

She slid her underwear down her thighs. As he had with her socks, he tugged them the rest of the way off, dropped them on the floor. He gazed at her, heavy-lidded, his eyes sapphire dark in the half-light of the den. She experienced a moment of self-doubt, lying there to be seen, moles, stretch marks, wobbly skin and all. She wasn't an actress. Her career didn't depend on her looking like an extreme version of idealized woman-hood. She took care of herself, but she wasn't plucked and polished. And Warner might have been living through a dry period, but that didn't mean he didn't have preferences. What if she didn't measure up to whatever fantasy he had?

It didn't help that he was as carelessly handsome as a Hollywood star himself. How was it fair that a guy could forget to shave, barely comb his hair, throw on an ancient cable knit sweater, and still look appealing?

Or maybe she liked him so much, she didn't care about any of the trappings of male grooming.

Before she could spiral too far out of the moment, Warner lifted his gaze from her body to her face.

"Gorgeous," he said before kissing her again. That was good, his body covering her, denim rubbing on her bare legs, his weight pressing her into the couch cushions.

"Your turn," she said when he let her come up for air.

"Yeah, yeah," he said, finishing what she'd started by undoing his jeans and then awkwardly shaking out of them. He was a boxers man, apparently, loose dark blue shorts revealed along with strong, lean thighs. The hair on his legs was darker than that on his head. She was starting to lose patience and reached for the waistband of his boxers.

"Come on, Warner, we're all friends here," she said, tugging at the material.

He allowed her to pull them down, yanking to get them over the jut of his erection. She bit her lip when she saw him in his entirety. He was uncircumcised, and his cock was rosy red and thicker than she might have guessed. Fuck. She was very much looking forward to knowing what it felt like inside her.

He kicked off the boxers, then stopped to do his

socks. Why on Earth had they been wearing so many clothes?

She realized she was still wearing her bra, even though it was pushed half-down her waist, so she hastily unhooked it, then finally, finally, there was nothing but skin and air between them.

"Come here," she ordered.

He obliged her, settling between her legs. God, he felt amazing, all that hot skin, his restless hands touching every part of her he could reach. His cock, hot and hard between them, pressed against the vee of her pelvis, so close and yet so far from where she ultimately wanted it.

He went back to work on her breasts, sucking and licking as if they were delicious treats. She luxuriated in the feeling of his strong, broad shoulders. She loved men's shoulders, the strength of the muscles there, the way they were so different from her own soft, round pair.

He did that nipple biting thing again, and she arched up into his mouth. "Fuck, Warner, I need—"

"Yes? What? Anything."

"I need you, come on, don't make me wait," she said, panting in her eagerness.

"Oh, God," he said somberly, as if she'd asked him to lay down his life for her rather than just give her an orgasm. "Okay."

"It's going to be all right," she said. "I promise. It's going to feel so good."

"Good," he echoed, raising up on his hands, looking

down their bodies to where his cock bobbed, grazing her skin with its hot, wet tip.

"Please," she said again, shifting her hips, reaching down to guide him in.

He sucked in a breath, as if entering her caused him physical pain, but it felt glorious to Selena, feeling the stretch and burn of him. He hadn't put so much as a finger inside her, and she was wet enough to make the slide easy, but it was still tight. She moaned at the welcome feeling of intrusion, and he stopped, searching her face with his gaze.

"No, it's good. So good, Warner. Don't stop."

He pushed forward until he was all the way inside. She looked at his face, turning pinker than ever. "Breathe, Warner," she said, and he gasped, as if he'd forgotten how.

"That's right. Breathe."

He moved, his breaths reassuringly noisy as he started up a rhythm. She felt the drag of every inch of him as her body stretched, getting used to him.

"How does it feel?" she asked after a moment.

He squeezed his eyes shut at the question. "Too good, Selena. I'm going to—"

She didn't know what he meant at first, but then he stiffened, groaned. Again, it was almost as if he was in pain, but she knew he wasn't hurt.

He was coming.

Chapter Ten

She glanced down his body, unabashedly looking at him. He must have met some unspoken benchmark, because she moved to make room for him on the narrow bed. Her lips hovered over his, their hips an inch apart. He could smell her, honeysuckle and money. She smiled as if she could hear what he was thinking.

"Do your worst, Jake Wilton."

— *Gunsmoke,* by Warner Mathis

"Shit, I'm sorry. Sorry." He didn't know what he was saying. The wave of pleasure he'd felt at releasing himself inside her mixed with a wave of shame. He'd been inside her for all of a minute when he'd gone off like a prematurely launched firework display, all flash and no substance.

"Hey, it's fine." Selena lifted herself onto her elbows.

He could barely look at her. And he probably should pull out. Fucking hell. He'd let himself get carried away. He'd let Selena's confidence bleed over and make him think that casual sex was something he could do, even as woefully out of practice as he was.

He pulled out, groped at the pile of their clothes on the floor beside them, found his T-shirt, still tangled with his sweater. He busied himself extracting it, barely hearing Selena's words.

"Hey Warner, look at me, okay?" She'd sat up, her hand on his arm. He couldn't refuse her, not when he'd messed up so spectacularly.

He raised his head. She looked at him steadily.

"It's okay, really," she said firmly.

He didn't respond. What could he say?

"It's been a while for me, too. And I'm really enjoying myself," she said. "Are you enjoying yourself?"

"Clearly," he said, his throat dry as dust. "I'm sorry."

"Please don't apologize. I'm happy I made you feel good." She brushed the hair back over his forehead, the casual intimacy devastating. "You made me feel good, too. We can keep making each other feel good, if you want?"

He realized what she was offering him. Another chance. God, he was such an idiot. He should have made sure she came before he even got inside her. He owed her at least one orgasm.

"Of course."

"So, maybe we could keep going?"

He faltered. The moment had passed. He could no longer pretend he had a handle on this situation. He wasn't writing this scene, no chance to revise the messiness out of it. They were living it, messiness and all. "I'm sorry," he said. "I don't know."

"Look, it's okay," she said softly. "Everything's okay." She seemed to struggle with what to say next. "I guess I rushed this."

He didn't want her to regret being with him, even if she should.

"It's not your fault," he said firmly. "I'm—there's a reason it's been years for me. It's nothing to do with you."

"I know," she said quietly. "But I'm in your life now, for a while anyway. You were inside of me a minute ago. So it kind of feels like it has something to do with me now."

"Shit." He sighed, looked at the tray he'd assembled with such naive hope. "Our tea's cold."

She didn't answer, just leaned over the side of the couch and grabbed her dress. She put it on without underwear. He found his boxers and put those on. He should probably walk her back to the pool house, swear to her he wouldn't bother her for the rest of her stay.

But she reached for her mug, took a sip. "It's fine. I like mint."

He hesitated, not sure if he should accept her absolution. "I thought so," he said eventually, taking his own cup. The tea had been over steeped, but it was refreshing after the unconventional workout.

Selena took a cookie. "You're really not playing fair with these." She took a bite, hummed. "Whoever made these is a genius."

With that, Warner could agree. "Zelda is an outstanding human being."

"Who's Zelda?"

"She owns the Bakeshop. She's the architect of these cookies—and the best sticky buns in Connecticut."

"Zelda's a cool name. I'm imagining a gray-haired hippie."

"She's about our age."

Selena's lips thinned. "Attractive?"

Warner thought about the baker, with her dark hair twisted up in a perpetual bun. She was thin and yeah, pretty, with clear skin and dark eyes. She'd moved to Misty Harbor around the same time Angie died. He'd always thought it a shame she'd never met Angie, because they probably would have gotten along well. Her wealthy Korean immigrant parents were Eastsiders, too, and she'd left the city looking for greener pastures, like Angie and him. They'd compared notes on New York restaurants more than once.

Maybe Zelda was almost a friend? The way Jay was, and, by extension, Cami and Nash. And since Selena was close to Cami and Jay and Nash, did that make them part of the same circle in a strange Venn diagram of Misty Harbor and *Sawyer's Cove*?

"She's attractive," he said belatedly.

Selena frowned. "I don't care how addictive her cookies are. I think I'm a little jealous."

"Are you joking?" How could Selena be jealous of any woman, when next to her they all seemed wan and derivative?

Selena sighed. "I'm being silly. I'm sure she's lovely." She bit off another piece of cookie. "So, if she's so great, why aren't you dating her?"

He didn't know how to tell her that until a couple of weeks, no, days, no, *hours* ago, dating a woman had been the last thing on his mind.

"Zelda has too much sense to get involved with someone like me."

Selena's frown grew deeper. "But I'm just senseless enough to do it?"

"That's not what I meant." He was floundering, and usually Selena rescued him when he was out of his depth conversationally. But this time she didn't rush in with a kind word. Maybe she was irritable because she hadn't come.

God, he was such a fuck-up. He set his tea and cookie back down on the tray. He took a deep breath. He was a thirty-seven-year-old grown man. Yes, he'd messed a lot of things up in his life, but Selena was not going to leave his house unsatisfied. He owed her that, at the very least.

He stood, trying not to feel vulnerable wearing only his boxers. He held out a hand to Selena, who was looking at him with unimpressed eyebrows.

"Come with me. You can bring your cookie."

"Where are we going?"

"My bedroom," he said, trying not to let his uncertainty bleed through his voice. "I owe you an orgasm."

She practically threw the cookie down on the table. "Now you're talking."

She took his hand and stood up. Barefoot, he could see how much taller he was than her. She wasn't tiny, but her head barely came up to his shoulder. He took a moment to turn off the fireplace but left their discarded clothes where they were.

A crumb clung to the corner of Selena's mouth. He leaned down, licked it off with a flick of his tongue. She gasped, and he swallowed the sound, kissing her deeply.

He could have stood there, kissing her, for infinity. Kissing Selena was endlessly fascinating. How much pressure she responded to, the salty sweet flavor of her mouth, her little sounds and breaths. He wanted to know every permutation of kissing her, but she stopped him with a hand to his chest.

"I'm about to leak your come all over your rug," she whispered.

It took him a moment to process the words. "Oh, shit." He'd cleaned himself up perfunctorily with his T-shirt, but not her. His embarrassment returned full force.

"Let's go to your room."

"Right. Yes. That. Okay." He forced himself to walk out of the den, took a left, and made for the back staircase, which led to the suite that took up an entire end of the second floor of the house. The hallway felt much cooler than the cozy den, and goosebumps rose on his arms. He picked up the pace, not wanting Selena to be cold. He no longer heard any noises from the storm outside, but maybe it was a lull.

When they got to the bedroom, he flipped a switch, and light flooded the room. His favorite feature was the balcony, which overlooked the copse of woods that abutted the house. It was too dark and wet to open the French doors to the balcony tonight. Instead, he turned on a light in the connected bathroom.

"Would you like to freshen up?"

Selena nodded gratefully and disappeared inside. She came out half a second later. "That tub is enormous," she said in awe.

"Would you like a bath?" He rarely used the tub.

"I shouldn't," she said, biting her lip in a way that meant she totally wanted to.

"Why shouldn't you?"

"I'm so conditioned against taking baths because of drought," she said. "But it's a guilty pleasure."

"Then you most definitely should take a bath," he said assertively. "I'll draw it for you."

"Are you sure? That wasn't the agenda item we came up here to check off."

"Making you come is an agenda item now?" He supposed he deserved that.

"Well, you can't tell me you aren't feeling a bit of pressure to even the scales," she said, with irritating accuracy.

"You tell me, would you rather get to come or get to take a bath?"

She looked at him coyly. "Who says I have to pick? Maybe you can give me an orgasm *while* I take a bath. Bath sex is a thing."

He imagined her soapy and slippery, cheeks flushed from the heat of the water. His groin tightened.

"Bath sex. I've heard of it." He and Angie had made love in the bath on occasion. But he didn't think they'd ever done it in this particular bathtub. The thought was comforting. He didn't want memories of him and Angie hanging over anything he did with Selena, more than they already did, that is.

"Challenge accepted," he said. "Let me start the water." He didn't have any bubble bath. Angie's had been lavender, of course, but he'd thrown it out long ago. He went to the walk-in shower next to the sunken tub and grabbed his shampoo, poured in a liberal amount to add some supposedly masculine woodsy fragrance to the water.

"I'll be back in a minute." He retreated to his room, turned on the bedside lamps, turned off the overhead light. He dug in his dresser for something Selena could wear to bed later and found a worn gray T-shirt. It might be tight across her chest, but it would work. She could wear a pair of his boxers, too.

It might be simpler to walk her back across the darkened yard to her own bed, her own clothes. Surely, the power would be on soon. But he didn't want her to leave. As bizarrely as events had unfolded, and as ineptly as he'd behaved this evening, one thing was certain. Selena was remarkable, and he hadn't felt this alive in years.

It was hard to imagine going back to his half-life after this night. He'd been able to subsist on crumbs since Angie died, because he'd had no alternative. But now Selena was cracking open his world like an overripe melon dropped onto the pavement, sweet, sticky juice seeping out over the ground, jagged edges of rind and fruit everywhere, getting on everything. He wouldn't be able to clean up this mess so easily.

A moment later, the door to the bathroom opened an inch. By the time he crossed the room and entered, closing the door behind him to keep the heat of the room in, Selena was slipping into the lightly scented water. He grabbed two towels from the cupboard under the sink, left them on a chair within arm's reach.

"You're very prepared. Except for the condom thing," Selena said.

Did the woman ever not say the exact thing she was thinking?

"I wasn't expecting to need condoms tonight."

"Surprise," she said dryly, startling a laugh out of him. "Are you coming in, or are you going to work your magic from outside the bath?"

In answer, he dropped his boxers. The tub was more than roomy enough for both of them, and he stepped into the water so he was facing her when he sat down. The water came to the tops of her breasts, but he could see the beautiful round swells of flesh clearly below.

"I'd be honored if you gave me a second chance."

She sat back, causing her breasts to jut tantalizingly close to his face. "Do your best, Warner Mathis."

Chapter Eleven

Jake wasn't prone to poetic language. He wasn't composing odes to her in his mind while he was inside her; they fucked. She seemed to like it okay.

After was when he let his mind drift, recalling the exact slope of the tip of her breast, the way her skin felt like hot silk, how his big, rough hand had seemed so much larger than hers as they gripped each other tight.

How fleetingly beautiful it all was, a handful of moments and then over, like the lifespan of a dragonfly.

But there he went, getting poetical. He got out of bed and started gathering his clothes.

— *Gunsmoke,* by Warner Mathis

The tub was huge—it could have fit another two people. The tap was still running, and Selena didn't think about how much water they were using. It was raining outside. Surely, they were allowed.

Besides, they were floating in a storm-induced bubble where the real world was a dream and the only thing that was real was the fantasy they were living out together.

The funny thing was, despite her general frustration at having been on edge since the tomato soup, the fantasy wasn't all about sex. She liked talking to Warner, she liked looking at him, she liked trying to read his expressions, to decode what was going on in that handsome, mysterious head of his, just as much as she liked having her hands on him.

She liked *him*.

For a guy who previously had one mode—grumpy, taciturn guy—Warner had shown her a plethora of sides tonight.

There was the cozy, domestic Warner who cooked and plied her with her favorite sweets. There was the tragic widower Warner whose wedding photo spoke of young love cut down in its prime. There was insanely good kisser Warner, who seemed to know every button to push and wasn't afraid of pushing it. Then there was the awkward, apologetic Warner, the one who made her suspect she'd taken things too far, too fast.

She couldn't remember the last time she'd slept with someone the same night as their first kiss, but it must have been years. She'd gotten into a pattern of sleeping with a guy on the third or fourth date at least. Not out of prudishness, but because it took her that long to feel comfortable with someone to take that step.

But Warner was different—everything about him was unlike any man she'd ever known, let alone slept with. He was an exception to all her rules. He made her want to be reckless and daring, as if part of her knew if she didn't push, she'd never get to experience him the way she wanted to.

Push she had, and she'd ended up here.

Here in the bath, Warner was showing her yet another side of himself. He took control, grabbing her by the waist and hauling her in close while he feasted on her breasts, slippery from the water. He used that to his advantage, pretty much going to town on them. The heat of the water warred with the heat of his mouth as her sex felt squirmy with need almost as soon as he started licking and touching her.

"Warner," she moaned. He responded by plunging two fingers into her straightaway, no fumbling, no hesitation. She liked being in control during sex, but this was good, too. This was very good, indeed. He seemed determined to make up for last time, to get her off before he went anywhere near her body with his cock.

Well, if that's what he needed to do, far be it from her to oppose the plan.

He bit down on a nipple and thrummed her clit with his thumb, and she ground down on his hand to get a bit more pressure, and then it was all too much—her body stiffened as she came in a rush of endorphins.

She opened her eyes, and he was staring at her intently, as if committing to memory what she looked like when she came. His eyes glittered as they reflected the water.

"You are stunning, Selena."

Slowly, he tugged his fingers free of her pussy and the water. They glistened, wetter from her than from the bath. He rubbed them together, his expression unguarded. Then he licked his fingertips. Tasting her. The sight sent a shockwave through her body.

With a little groping, she was able to find his cock, gratifyingly hard, under the water. She maneuvered onto her knees and sank down on him, her pussy still hot and sensitive. The stretch of him was as satisfying as before. As satisfactory as his bringing her off with his fingers had been, she wanted the pressure and fullness of him pumping inside her.

He didn't seem upset about being used; he lay back against the wall of the tub, cradling her ass in his hands while she bounced up and down, not hard enough to throw water over the side of the tub.

"Damn it." She wasn't going to be able to get the rhythm she wanted in this position. She'd noticed the thick, clean bath mat on the floor beside the tub. "Come here."

He slipped free of her pussy as she rose, then she stepped out of the tub and tugged him along after her. It was chilly outside the water, but she didn't care. They were both wet, bubbles clinging to their skin here and there. She pushed him to the bath mat, got back on top, his hands on her ass, and this time they could go as hard as they wanted. Her breasts jiggled distractingly, but she felt sexy, and she loved the way he filled her up. His gaze was glued to her bouncing breasts, his iron grip surely leaving imprints on her flesh.

"Yeah, come on," he gasped. "Do it, Selena."

Every slide was pushing her toward another orgasm, but she needed a little more—he squeezed her ass, she ground her pubic bone down as hard as she could, feeling the head of his cock as deep as it could go. She had one hand on the side of the tub for purchase, the other she moved to her clit so she could finger it herself.

"Please. Yes," Warner said. "Come, Selena."

She wasn't waiting for permission, she swore she wasn't, but when he said it, the orgasm overtook her as suddenly as the one a few minutes before. She shook with it, and he took over the rhythm, hoisting her up and down his cock with apparent ease. She let him do what he wanted, still riding the high of her release, and it was a few more strokes before he let out a choked cry and the space where they joined got even wetter.

They stilled, both out of breath. Warner opened his eyes. "Okay?" he asked, voice hoarse.

"Okay," she agreed. "I think we're getting better at that."

"Might get even better with more practice."

It was the first time either of them had mentioned the possibility of this continuing beyond tonight. She was too tired to think about how that would work, but if it meant more hot, aerobic sex, she wouldn't argue.

"I'm up for it," she said lightly, then she carefully lifted herself up. Now that the frenzy of their coupling and flush of multiple orgasms had passed, she was cold. She looked down. They were both messy with the evidence of their activities. Warner followed her gaze, touching the mix of come and her slick on his still semi-hard cock. He didn't taste it this time, but he seemed just as in awe as before.

She let out an involuntary yawn, and his gaze snapped to her face. He looked—guilty?

"I'm going to get cleaned up," she said, suddenly out of her element. They'd had sex, but she wasn't used to sleeping with someone she wasn't technically in a relationship with. He wasn't used to sleeping with anyone, period.

"Okay." He got to his feet, and she got back into the bath. "I'll—I'll take a shower, if that's okay?"

"Sure." She wouldn't have minded him getting back in the bathtub with her, but maybe he needed some space. Maybe she did, too.

The water was still warm, and while in another situation she would have liked to soak and take her time, she honestly felt as if she might fall asleep at any moment. She had no idea what time it was, but it felt late.

She found a bar of soap in a dish and soaped up quickly. She ignored her hair, though the tips were bedraggled and wet. She'd have to sort it out later.

Meanwhile, Warner hopped in the big glassed-in

shower stall and stayed for barely a minute before he was out and toweling off.

"I'll give you some privacy," he murmured before practically bolting into the bedroom.

Clearly she wasn't the only one who didn't know what happened now.

She took her time drying off, wrapped his predictably plush towel around her chest. When she peeked into the bedroom, Warner was dressed in sweats and a T-shirt. No socks this time. She spotted an alarm clock on one of the nightstands and gasped. "Please tell me it's not really twelve-thirty."

"I'm afraid so."

"Jesus, no wonder I'm tired. I haven't stayed up this late in a while."

He grimaced apologetically. "It's still raining, I checked. And the power's still out."

She bit her lip, remembering she'd only accepted his invitation hours earlier because she had work to do. Not only had she not gotten any of it done, she was also going to be short on sleep.

"Damn."

"What can I do? Would you like to go back to the pool house? You're more than welcome to sleep here."

Selena had no idea what would result in better sleep, but she didn't relish fumbling around in the dark. "I guess I'll stay here, if you mean it."

"Of course." He was back to formal, clipped Warner.

She looked down at her towel. "Um."

"Oh, here's something you can wear." Warner

handed her a shirt and pair of boxers. His underwear. Great. She was a smart woman, but right now she felt like the world's biggest fool. She'd let herself get carried away by romantic presumptions, and she had the feeling she'd be paying for it for a while. Starting with an awkward night's sleep.

"I'll go sleep in the guest room. It's down the hall," Warner said, taking a step toward the door.

"Warner, no."

He stopped in his tracks. She looked at the bed. It was huge, like the tub. More than enough room for them both. "I'll take the guest room. Or—"

"Or?"

"We could share."

He looked from her to the bed and back. "I—I don't think I can do that. I'll be down the hall if you need something. Goodnight, Selena."

And he left.

Chapter Twelve

Erika: I know this isn't considered, like, a classic episode, but I've always had a soft spot for it.
Jules: Me, too.
Erika: Really? I thought I was going to be alone here.
Jules: You think you're the only one who loves seeing a funny Sawyer? Spencer Crosby is an underrated comic actor. Yes, it's a goofy premise, but I like the message.
Erika: Sawyer gets a second chance to make a first impression. We should all be so lucky.
Jules: That's why TV is better than real life. They can write in as many second chances as the characters need.

From The Sawyer's Cove Rewatch Project Podcast: The Tag Sale

When the alarm went off, Selena jolted awake from her dream fighting for air. She'd been struggling against the current of the ocean, which was inexorably dragging her under. She let out a strangled breath as she oriented herself. Or tried to.

Where the fuck was she?

The room was dark, and her phone was—her phone wasn't there. The blare of the alarm was coming from the clock on the nightstand. She hit a few random buttons before it stopped yelling at her. She rubbed her eyes, trying to remember where she'd left her glasses when it hit her—she was in Warner's bedroom. Alone.

She let out a pained whimper. It was six in the morning. She'd set the bedside alarm when she couldn't face tiptoeing downstairs where she was pretty sure she'd left her phone, along with her underwear. Jesus. Then she'd tossed and turned before finally falling asleep in the wee hours.

She was exhausted and crabby and sore. Goddamn it.

What had she been thinking last night?

Warner must have bewitched her with electricity and soup. Otherwise, why would she have forgotten about the work she was supposed to do and the fact that as someone in her late thirties, she required a decent night of sleep to be functional the next day?

She made a quick trip to the bathroom, looking balefully at the evil, wonderful bathtub. She hadn't even gotten to soak in it properly. She glanced at the bath mat. It was just a bath mat—a nice, probably expensive bath mat—but a bath mat nonetheless. She shouldn't be getting turned on remembering how she'd ridden Warner to completion on that bathroom accessory.

Her dress was filthy, so she balled it up in her fist. She ignored the bed. No point in making it—he'd probably have the sheets burned after she left, if the swiftness with which he'd run out of the room was any indication of how Warner was feeling after fucking her.

As she crept down the hall, trying to remember where the stairs were, she mentally berated herself. She'd slept with a widower who hadn't had sex in five years. Not the simple, emotionally straightforward relationship she usually opted for.

She found the stairs, though she didn't remember the banister from last night.

Unless—the thought had her frozen halfway down the stairs—he'd been lying about the five years thing? Had he merely been trying to get her into bed? Was that a line he used on all the girls who haplessly stumbled into his kitchen on dark and stormy nights?

She rejected the concept almost immediately. He was odd, but in a genuine way. And the alacrity with which he'd sped to the finish the first time was some evidence toward it having been a while.

When she got to the bottom of the stairs, she was confused—this was the foyer, not the hallway by the den. There was the table with the photo of Warner and Angeline—she still couldn't get over his wife's name. Last night, the stairs had been at the back of the house. There must be two sets. Of course. Why would a house this size only have one set of stairs?

She rolled her eyes and looked at the photograph again. Angeline, with her angelic golden hair, looked so happy in the picture, but not happier than her new husband. This young Warner with his radiant smile bore little resemblance to the man she was growing to know.

Her heart ached, and she rubbed absently at her chest through Warner's shirt. She'd never lost someone close to her, let alone someone she'd been in love with. She didn't know how she'd react, how she'd cope. Warner had been dealing with grief in his own way, and who was she to judge? As difficult as it was to comprehend, she softened when she thought about how lonely he must have been. With another glance at the photo, she backtracked down the hall.

She found the den after poking her head through several doors and finding a linen pantry, a bathroom, and a room empty of everything but a couple of exercise machines. How many rooms did the place have? Finally, success. She pushed in the door to the den, which was dimly lit by a single lamp next to the couch. The couch on which she and Warner had sex last night. The couch on which her host now lay sleeping.

A flare of irritation overlaid her concern. He'd said he'd sleep in the guest room—the place probably had half a dozen—but here he was, on a leather couch, his legs bent at an awkward angle. He was wearing the same sweatpants and T-shirt from last night. His golden-brown lashes fanned over his face, and the lamp cast shadows under his eyes, or maybe the shadows were because he'd had as bad a night of sleep as she had.

Well, good.

The tea tray had been cleared away, and she didn't see any sign of her discarded underwear. Well, she had other pairs. She turned, determined to find the kitchen and her way out of this house, even if the path out of this situation wasn't nearly so clear.

She stopped at the sound of Warner's voice.

"I'll make you coffee." He sounded like he'd gargled with sand.

"It's okay." She didn't wait for him to respond, just retraced her steps to the kitchen, finding it with minimal confusion. There she saw her laptop still plugged in, presumably topped up with juice by now. There were two paper bags on the counter next to her work things. She peeked in one. Her clothes were neatly folded inside, glasses on top. She fought a wave of embarrassment thinking about Warner handling her soiled underwear. Oh, well. He'd been married. He'd probably been intimately acquainted with women's underwear at one point.

She put on her glasses and looked in the second bag. Two salted chocolate chip cookies. She let out a rather hysterical laugh.

"Coffee will only take a minute. The beans are already ground."

She whirled around, and a sleepy-eyed Warner with hair messier than usual stood behind her.

"You are unbelievable," she said accusingly. "Like, literally unbelievable. If I was writing the part of you, the audience would complain about such an unbelievable character."

He held her stare for a few seconds, then moved to the coffee maker and flipped a switch.

"Eggs?"

"Excuse me?"

"I could make you eggs."

She sputtered for a second before deciding that as much as she didn't want to encourage him, eggs were tempting. She was tired, and she was hungrier when she was low on sleep.

"Can you make toast out of that bread we had last night?" she asked.

"Sure."

She decided not to care that she was still wearing his clothes. Her feet were warm despite no longer having those woolen socks.

"Why is it so warm in here?" she asked as she went to her laptop and opened it up.

"Radiant heat in the floor. The power came back on a couple of hours ago. I turned off the generator and reset the heating system. Your place should be back to normal."

She looked out the window. The little light over her door was on, disrupting the morning gloom. The entire back yard looked wet. The pool itself was darkly foreboding.

"Are you going to close up the pool for the season?"

"Not until October," he said as he went about the business of getting eggs and butter from the fridge.

She listened to the background noise of him readying breakfast, and the hiss and hum of the coffee maker, while she checked her inbox. It wasn't the disaster she'd anticipated. It seemed the storm had kept everyone home and out of trouble. That, or Becca had done an excellent job of keeping everything at bay so she could focus on the script. Which she'd written exactly zero words of in the last twelve hours.

She groaned and tabbed over to her document.

"Bad news?" Warner asked, setting a steaming mug of coffee on the table next to her.

"No, everything's fine. Or as fine as it can be in the middle of production." She blew on the coffee but knew it would be too hot to drink. "I'm behind on the last episode of the season. I'm supposed to have a draft for the writers to flesh out, and I've been stuck. I'm not sure how to end this thing."

"Endings are hard," he said cautiously.

"I've never felt this kind of pressure on a project before. There was so much written about the ending to the original *Sawyer's Cove*. This ending has to be satisfying and yet leave the door open for another season."

"So killing everyone off is out," Warner said. It took her a second to catch that he was joking.

"Definitely out," she said, a beat late. "Though that would solve some issues."

"Well, I told you last night, I've never seen an episode, so I'm probably not the right person to talk to about this."

She chewed her lip. "Actually, you're the perfect person to ask. Everyone else has so much wrapped up in the outcome. Everyone has an agenda. Even me."

"What's your agenda?" he asked, swirling butter in the pan.

"I want the show to be so entertaining, the haters can't say a thing. It's okay if fans decide they like the old series better—we're not trying to replace the original. But I want to add to the canon. And I want it to be objectively good TV. I want Ryan to be proud of it."

"Ryan?"

"Ryan Saylor. He created *Sawyer's Cove*, and he gave me the go-ahead to do the revival."

"He trusts you," Warner said.

"He does."

"Sounds like you need to start trusting yourself," he said. "What's the series about?"

"Besides who's sleeping with who and who's pining for who?" she asked.

"Yeah. What are the themes?"

"Themes?" Selena considered. She was usually caught up in the minutiae of character development and witty banter. She didn't think in terms of themes, but in arcs. Episode-long arcs, season-long arcs. There were themes embedded in them, she just had to tease them out.

For one, this new version of the show was more multi-generational than the first one. They had the original Cove kids, all grown up and now in their thirties, plus a fresh batch of teenagers, each one connected to the original crew in a different way. The parental figures were all still there, older, not necessarily wiser. A lot of the original viewers of the show hadn't been teenagers at all, but their parents, and they were still one of the important target audiences.

She thought about the core of the show—the five Cove kids, Sawyer, Parker, Amy, Will, and Lily. They were the ones who everyone really cared about, and their arcs were the ones she'd concentrated most on.

Parker and Amy's romance was shaping up into a happily ever after that had been hinted at from day one and never been able to be paid off.

Lily was on a journey of self-discovery that didn't have her pairing up with anyone, but she and Sawyer were finally going to have the fling they'd been dancing around for a decade and a half in one of the later episodes.

Will was emerging as one of the most important characters this go-round. His arc was centered around Danny, a young kid he was mentoring and brought back to Cloudy Cove. Will was the unexpected heart of the show this time around, the way Parker had been the first time. And he deserved a truly happy ending—or at least a hopeful one.

They'd toyed around with bringing back his high school love interest, Noah, played by Darren Silverstein, but when they were making the schedule this summer, Darren hadn't been available. But that was then. Things changed. What if she could get him for the finale—even if for only a day? They could put a tag on the episode if nothing else, a surprise blast from the past, that would give uptight Will a reason to get flustered.

"You look like you had an idea," Warner said, sliding

a plate toward her. When had he finished making breakfast? She took a bite of silky scrambled eggs and moaned.

"An idea and eggs. Thank you."

"My pleasure. Want to talk it out?" Warner sat down next to her, his own plate of eggs in front of him.

"I'm going to try to get one of the guest stars from the original show to come back for the finale. Even if it's only a cameo, it would be something to build the episode around. You're right. The reboot has a bunch of themes, but the most important is second chances."

"Second chances," Warner repeated. "Don't get many of those in real life."

"This isn't real life, Warner, this is television. Soapy, episodic television featuring people too beautiful to be real."

"Ah, well then, second chances it is."

"You know all about them, don't you?" she said, her mind racing and blood pumping fast with the caffeine boost. "Isn't *Gunsmoke* all about second chances? Jake gets to solve the case that's haunting him, making it up to the dead client. It was too late for her, but he still took the second chance he was given to solve the case for real."

Warner snorted into his coffee. "You remember it differently than I do. Jake was a sap. He would have been better off leaving everything alone."

"But he couldn't do that, that's what makes him so compelling." Was Warner being willfully obtuse about his own creation? "Jake can't let well enough alone, that's what makes him human."

"So, you're good now? You can write your script?" Warner said, ignoring her comment.

"Why didn't you ever write another book?" Selena asked, still high from her story breakthrough. "Unless you have another one coming out and I didn't hear about it."

He stared at the toast crumbs on his empty plate. "No. No book is coming out. No book will be coming out. I haven't written anything in five years."

Chapter Thirteen

Jake glanced wearily at his watch. Twenty minutes, and he'd beat his personal best record for no sleep. Good thing he wasn't about to do anything important—like try to trap a killer and get them to confess before he ended up the next victim.

— *Gunsmoke,* by Warner Mathis

He hated being the reason the light dimmed in her eyes, but he couldn't lie to her.

"Five years—since—"

That was it, the final nail in the coffin of their short, rocky affair. He was being exposed as the pathetic fraud he'd been all along.

"I told you I'm a bad bargain, Selena. Emotionally

damaged. Creatively constipated. You might see a man living alone, but there are a lot of ghosts in here with me."

She shook her head. "It's too early for self-deprecation. I'm just sad, I guess. For me. Because *Gunsmoke* is one of my favorite books, and I always thought Jake would make a perfect series character. I always wanted to know what he'd do next."

"He was supposed to be a series character, but it's been so long, I wouldn't remember how to write him even if I could." He'd believed that for a long time, but this time saying it felt almost like a lie, the way he'd been unable to stop ideas from popping into his head and rumbling around until they formed a cohesive picture that wanted to be set free on paper.

Selena looked shocked, though, as if he'd said he'd been diagnosed with an incurable disease. "Wow—that's rough, Warner. I don't know what I would do if I couldn't write. I'd be looking for another job, I guess. My mom would probably hire me as a paralegal."

"Your mom's a lawyer?" As much as she seemed like an open book, he didn't actually know all that much about her.

"Civil litigator," she said. "Has her own firm in Century City. My dad's a lawyer, too, but immigration. He works for the government."

"And what do they think about having a daughter in the entertainment industry?"

"They've always been supportive. It helps that I've always worked, since before I graduated UCLA. Never had to ask them for a dime. They're proud of me. Also, my dad's a huge reader. He's who got me into mysteries, thrillers. He loved *Gunsmoke*, too. He's going to be so jealous when I tell him I know the author. Been too busy to call them lately."

Warner tried to imagine Mr. Echeveria being happy about his daughter sleeping with her landlord, who happened to write a book once upon a time.

"You're going to tell him about us?" he said, wincing directly after the words came out of his mouth.

She looked taken aback at his phrasing. "Us?" She looked down, as if realizing she was wearing his clothes, sitting in his kitchen. She shifted on the hard wooden chair.

He wondered if she could still feel him from last night. He still felt her, on his skin. He might have showered, but he'd never forget the sense memory of her full and luscious body astride him, like a beautiful naked warrior riding into battle.

"I mean," he tried to backtrack, "not that there's anything to tell, I suppose."

"I'm not in the habit of talking about my sex life with my parents, if that's what you mean," she said, with a little smile. "I don't have to tell them about the *Gunsmoke* connection if you don't want me to."

"It's fine," he said quickly. It was stupid to make her keep quiet like it was some sordid secret. He wasn't ashamed of *Gunsmoke*, and he wasn't ashamed of his behavior with Selena. Or was he? They were both adults. He'd taken something that had been freely offered to him, and given in return, or tried to, but he was still not convinced he shouldn't have tried harder to stop it from happening in the first place, if only for her sake.

"Look, Warner—" She closed her laptop, reached across the table, and took his hand. He flinched at the casual touch. It was somehow more intimate than what they'd done the previous night. She didn't seem bothered and held on lightly.

He let her hold his hand, the eggs and coffee swirling around in his stomach unpleasantly.

"I'm not going to say what we did was consequence-free," she said slowly. "But it's not a bad thing, okay? I'm—I actually really like you." She sounded like she'd surprised herself with the sentiment and laughed.

He wished he didn't like her laugh so much.

"And what I said last night still goes—we can leave it at that. I'm here for a couple more months, we can go back to our stilted poolside conversations and passing nods. Or..."

He held his breath, waiting for the follow-up. He'd never been so anxious to know what came after a conjunction in his life.

"Or we can keep the physical stuff on the table. My hours are long, but Becca's always telling me to take more time off, so I'm trying to set a healthy work example."

"Who's Becca?"

"My assistant. My right hand, basically. I'm sure

you'll meet her one of these days. You can be my non-work buddy."

"Buddy?" He got what she was saying, but he objected to the term.

"If you want to go back to the way things were, that's fine, too. I'm not here to screw up your life."

But she'd already changed it, perhaps irrevocably.

"Think about it," she said. "I like you, and it's nice to share a meal with someone, to have someone to talk to who gets how hard it is to write. And I think we're pretty compatible in other areas, too."

He thought about how hard he'd come last night—twice. It wasn't all pent-up sexual tension. She was right—they were compatible. Conveniently, they lived in the same place. He looked down at their joined hands. She wasn't offering a romantic entanglement, but companionship and sex. He hadn't meant to go so long without either.

Angie wouldn't have wanted him to be a monk for the rest of his life. But he'd slowly shut the door to that side of his life, and it had rusted over when he hadn't been paying attention. Now he was trying to open it and finding it sticky, but not sealed shut permanently.

Selena had come in, shoved her shoulder to the door, and a crack had appeared, letting in light and air and giving him enough space where if he applied some WD-40 and elbow grease, he might get that door opening more smoothly from now on.

"That is nice," he said finally. "Let's try it."

She smiled at him, bright and happy, as if she hadn't

expected him to agree. "Okay." She checked the time and let out a yelp. "I'm very late."

She stood up and gathered her stuff. He handed her the paper bags he'd put her things in late last night. He walked her to her door, after shoving his feet into his work boots. She had her sandals on, making a picture in his T-shirt and boxers, but she didn't seem self-conscious about it. He used his own key to open her door, since her hands were full. The inside air was stale, but the lights were working, and the heat was on.

"Thanks," she said, and he didn't know exactly what she meant the thank you for, but it didn't matter. "I'll see you—" She paused, thinking.

"Soon?" he offered. It was vague enough to keep the pressure off but indicated that he hoped it wouldn't be too long. She apparently agreed. She smiled again, and it was rather striking how addictive her smiling at him like that was.

"Soon," she repeated.

He walked slowly back to the house. It felt emptier than it had in a while now that she was gone. He cleaned up the breakfast dishes, not bothering to turn on the television for company. He imagined Selena getting dressed for work but kept himself from glancing out the window too often. He didn't need to see her leave. He had lots of things to do today, didn't he? He thought about what she'd said about second chances, about Jake and his penchant for not leaving things alone.

His computer was on the desk in the den. He went there, looked around the room. He could picture Selena on the couch, lit up by firelight. He imagined her reading, her glasses slipping down her nose, while he sat at the desk. Would he be writing? *Could* he write something again?

He slowly turned away and walked upstairs. His brain was all fogged up, the emotional roller coaster and lack of sleep catching up to him. Despite the strength of his much-loved coffee, he felt as if his eyes were filling with sand. He flopped down on his bed, the remnants of Selena's scent floating around him, a final middle finger from the universe, and fell asleep.

Chapter Fourteen

PLEASE JOIN THE MISTY HARBOR LIBRARY BOARD
FOR THE MISTY HARBOR LIBRARY ANNUAL FUNDRAISER
DINNER AND SILENT AUCTION
HONORING THE LEGACY OF ARTHUR RUSSELL
SATURDAY, SEPTEMBER 24
6PM
SILENT AUCTION
LIVE MUSIC
SEMI-FORMAL DRESS
TICKETS REQUIRED

"And this Saturday is the library fundraiser. I bought two tickets in your name, but I think folks from here are going to it as a group thing." Becca tapped at her tablet screen. "Do you have something to wear? It's semi-formal."

"I have a cocktail dress," Selena answered absently. They were in the conference room, and she was trying to do too many things at once. After she'd finally gotten to the set that morning, over-caffeinated and under-slept, it seemed like there had been one crisis after another and it was going on nine at night—way too late for her to keep Becca here, but it couldn't be helped. "Wait—two tickets? Are you coming?"

"Um, yeah, I already have a ticket. I'm going with Bo."

That was interesting. "*With* with?"

"I'm...not sure," Becca said, but she was blushing, which meant she wanted it to be a *with* with situation. "He was kind of joking around when we were talking about it. Makes it hard to tell when he's being serious."

"Well, you could just ask him," Selena said.

"Oh yeah, dandy idea," Becca said sarcastically.

"Seriously. If I've learned anything about relationships, it's that it doesn't pay to beat around the bush. Just ask for what you want." Isn't that what she'd done last night? And if it had gotten her in a confusing situation, it was only because the way she felt about Warner was a little more complex than your typical temporary fling situation.

"Well, if you don't have anyone to use the second ticket, I can donate it back to the library, or I can find someone from the crew to use it."

The fundraiser was in support of the Misty Harbor Library, where Jay Orlando's sister was the head librarian. He'd rounded up the troops from the *Sawyer's Cove* cast and crew and been persistent as a Girl Scout selling cookies about getting everyone to buy tickets and donate to the silent auction. Nash had been in on that, too, come to think of it, practically demanding that everyone connected to the show donate something of value to the cause. He'd gotten her to donate an autographed script, which she'd only done on the condition it wouldn't be delivered until after the show had aired. You couldn't be too careful about spoilers these days.

She wondered if she could get Warner to donate a signed copy of *Gunsmoke* but then remembered he didn't want anyone in Misty Harbor to know about his erstwhile writing career. She still couldn't believe he hadn't written in five years. There were lots of writers who famously wrote one book and never published again, but it seemed clear that his writer's block had a direct correlation to his wife's death.

He must have loved her so much.

Her gut clenched. He'd said there were ghosts in the house with him. Well, she wasn't one of them. She couldn't help feeling it was healthy for him to interact with someone flesh and blood.

"Selena?"

She looked at Becca, who was giving her a funny look. She must have been trying to get her attention for a while.

"Sorry. I'm tired. Didn't sleep much last night."

"Yeah, that storm was something else."

"You said it," she said, yawning loudly. "Okay, that's it. I gotta get some sleep. See you tomorrow."

"You going to be okay to drive? And what about that extra ticket?"

"Ticket?"

"To the fundraiser," Becca said patiently.

"Oh, right." Everyone she knew in Misty Harbor was already going to the fundraiser, except—what about Warner? Would it be strange to show up on the arm of her landlord? They had never discussed taking whatever it was they were doing outside the property lines. "Um. Give me a day, and I'll let you know."

"Okay." Becca frowned at her. "Are you feeling okay? You've been going pretty hard. You don't want to get sick."

"Sick? I'm fine. Tired. I'm going to go home and sleep, I told you."

She shooed Becca out the door, checked her phone. She'd missed a call from her dad earlier, so she tried him while she packed up her stuff.

He picked up on the second ring.

"Sí?" Victor Echeveria said tersely.

"Hi, Dad."

His tone changed instantly. "Is it true? Is my daughter actually returning one of my calls? It must be my lucky day."

She laughed at the gentle guilt trip. "I know, I'm sorry. I told you this shoot was going to be all-consuming."

"How is everything going?"

"Okay." She'd had another meeting with Brad and the marketing people today, supposedly about the press tour, but they had mostly talked about the online back-lash against the casting. Since her strategy was to simply make the show great, she had no time for Internet nonsense. But it was still a thing.

She sighed in frustration. "This job isn't exactly what I thought it would be. I have all this creative control, but I feel like I'm wasting it. I had a breakthrough on the finale, and I still haven't had time to sit down and flesh it out. There's a lot of politics. I thought getting the green light would be the hard part, but there are still so many battles, and I'm getting a little tired of fighting them." She yawned. "Or maybe I'm just tired."

She made her way out of the soundstage building, nodding at the security guy at the exit. She unlocked her car and switched the phone to speaker.

"So what's up with you?" she asked, pointing the car toward home.

"Hold on, back up, *beep*, *beep*, *beep*," her father said. "There's a lot to unpack there. I'm not a therapist, but I know deflection when I see it."

She laughed. Her dad was a great listener, which made him an amazing advocate for his clients who were trying to navigate the immigration system. "Fair enough. But I feel bad. I haven't talked to you or Mom in weeks."

"We're fine. Work's busy. We decided we're going on a trip at Christmas to Amsterdam, so you can do your own thing."

"Wait, I'm not invited?" Her parents were avid travelers, but they usually didn't leave her alone at the holidays.

"It was the only week we could both get off at the same time. But you can come over for Thanksgiving."

"Gee, thanks," she said sarcastically, but she wasn't upset. She'd probably still be working twelve-hour days on post-production anyway until the first two episodes dropped on Christmas Day.

This show was her baby, the cast and crew her family. She didn't really want any distractions.

So where did Warner fit in? Which reminded her—"There is one thing I thought you would find interesting about Misty Harbor. Guess who lives here?"

"Someone famous? Taylor Swift? Justin Bieber? Lizzo?"

"Not sure why your brain went there, but no. Let me narrow it down for you. Guess what mystery novelist lives here?"

"Dick Francis? Patricia Highsmith? Sue Grafton?"

She groaned. "Sadly, I'm pretty sure they're all dead, Dad."

"Michael Nava? Walter Mosley? Gillian Flynn? I can play this game all day."

"Okay, fine, no more guesses. Warner Mathis."

"Warner Mathis—*Gunsmoke*, right?"

"Yep."

"Oh terrific, did you meet him? Did you ask him where the sequel is?"

"I met him." She turned into Warner's driveway and killed the engine. There was no reason not to tell her dad that she was living in his back yard, but suddenly it felt like too much to get into. "I asked him. He says he doesn't write anymore."

"What a shame. I loved that one. Interesting detective. Tortured but not completely morally bankrupt. Not exactly an anti-hero. Complicated, though."

"Yeah, I agree." She yawned so hard, her ears popped. "I'm going to get some sleep. Talk to you soon."

"I'd tell you not to work too hard, but I know you will. Love you."

"Love you, too. Say hi to Mom."

They hung up, and she sat there for a minute. She couldn't go knock on Warner's door at nine-thirty at night. She needed a regular night of sleep; she needed her routine.

She needed to write.

She walked through the gate and past the pool, glancing over her shoulder at the house. There was only one dim light on in the kitchen, and she didn't see anyone moving around inside. Warner was probably in bed early, too. He'd gotten even less sleep than she had.

Telling herself she wasn't disappointed, just tired, she put herself to bed.

The next morning's alarm didn't feel quite so much like a torture device.

Selena got up and made herself a cup of tea, trying not to wish it was Warner's delicious coffee. While she was still in her pajamas, she forced herself to sit down in front of her laptop and work on the finale. She'd contacted Darren's agent yesterday, and it looked like there was room in his schedule to come for at least two days of shooting. She was banking on it, letting the episode take shape around the reveal, which would throw Will's storyline into relief.

She was also pleased with how the Lily/Sawyer arc was shaping up. The two had gotten a second chance to act on feelings they'd dodged for years. The writers were of two camps—those who felt it was a fling they were getting out of their systems, while the other camp wanted Lily and Sawyer to commit to each other, which would give each of them stability, as well as something to lose. Lily was notorious about protecting her emotions, and being with Sawyer would be high stakes enough to throw that self-preservation instinct into panic. Sawyer, meanwhile, needed someone to take care of, someone to remind him that he was his best self when he stopped navel gazing and turned his attention outward to the rest of the world.

Selena had been holding firmly neutral during the debate, but now was the time to put up or shut up. She'd made a decision—she hoped it was the right one.

She wrote until the sun was well up and her stomach felt like it was caving in on itself. She dressed, threw on some makeup, and pinned her hair up into a high bun on top of her head, wishing she had time for breakfast. Thank God for craft services.

Then there was the issue of Warner. She hadn't even texted him last night. Was that bad? He hadn't texted her either, so she guessed they were both operating under the terms they'd agreed on—that they'd see each other again "soon."

On her way to her car, she remembered the extra library fundraiser ticket. She felt a thrill when she saw Warner's silhouette through the kitchen window.

Not only could she see him moving around inside the kitchen, she smelled bacon. What was a better invitation than the scent of bacon frying?

She knocked.

It took him a minute to open the door. He was wiping his hands on a dishcloth tucked into the waistband of his jeans, and he made such a perfect picture of domesticity—like one of those jokey "porn for women" calendars featuring the underwear model who had dinner on the table in an immaculate dining room, an impossible fantasy.

She didn't want a fantasy, but she wasn't quite sure what it was that she did want from Warner. Besides mooching breakfast.

"Good morning." He didn't smile, but that was in character.

"Good morning. That bacon smells alluring."

"Would you like to come in? I'm making breakfast sandwiches."

Her stomach begged her to go in, but her pride made her want him to work for it. "I really have to get to work."

"I'll make it for you to go," he offered, holding the door open.

"If you're sure," she said, walking in. The space was familiar now, and she set her things down on what felt like her spot on the counter.

The bacon was already done, so all he had to do was toast the bread and fry the egg.

She reveled in his efficient movements. He really did look charming in the kitchen. She watched his ass for a minute while he worked at the stove. He turned around, and she raised her eyes quickly, hoping she hadn't been caught.

"Uh, so there's something I wanted to ask you," she said. "I'm going to this library fundraiser, and I have an extra ticket. It's Saturday night, and I thought maybe it would be fun to go together."

He checked the toast. "I donated a week at my short-term rental house to the silent auction."

"That was generous of you." She waited, but he didn't say anything else. She supposed that was her answer.

She was a little bit disappointed, and a little relieved. They weren't dating, so she probably shouldn't have proposed anything that resembled a date.

He took the toast out, slid the egg and a mouthwateringly crispy slice of bacon onto it, wrapped half of it in tin foil, then added a paper towel around that.

"Have a marvelous day," he said gravely.

She took the sandwich and, since there weren't any rules to this thing, pushed up on her toes to kiss his cheek.

"Thanks for breakfast. Sorry I can't stay to eat with you," she said, backing away. He had a cutely befuddled look on his face.

She was nearly at the door when he said, "Selena?"

She halted and waited, but he said nothing.

"Never mind."

She waited an extra beat. Her patience was rewarded, because he crossed the room in a few swift steps and paid her back with a kiss on the mouth, soft and lingering.

"You should go," he said, his voice low in a way that meant that he didn't particularly want her to go, but if she didn't, he couldn't be responsible for the consequences.

If she stayed for more of those kisses, she'd most certainly be disastrously late.

"Yeah," she said. "Bye."

"Goodbye, Selena."

She smiled the entire way to work.

Chapter Fifteen

He ran his finger along the bookshelf and came away with a layer of black grit. The dust in Los Angeles was the evidence of a culture built around cars, a blend of tire rubber particles mixed with dirt, oil, exhaust fumes. Throw in the ashes of a couple wildfires and the sloughed-off dead skin of celebrities, and you had a genuine California cocktail.

— Untitled work in progress, by
Warner Mathis

The house still smelled like bacon. Warner opened the back door to air out the kitchen. It was an unseasonably hot day—the storm had cooled things off temporarily, but now it felt like summer again, even though it was officially fall.

He was second-guessing himself. Should he have agreed to go to the fundraiser with Selena? He was so far outside of his comfort zone, he didn't even know what zone he was in half the time. He'd felt more centered after sleeping for several hours yesterday, followed by several hours outside doing storm clean-up at his various rental properties. Nothing like sweat and dirt to release stress.

And he had been stressed since Selena had left the day before. But not about her, not really. It was more the way his brain couldn't stop racing, couldn't stop thinking about a story.

He'd been having the urges more and more frequently, thinking in snippets of dialogue, contemplating character quirks, devising unique motivations and interesting ways to murder someone and get away with it. But he'd been able to repress it. To push the compulsion down and smother it with hard physical work, or a swim, or a visit to The Cove and a double scotch.

But since yesterday, the story wouldn't quit. Wouldn't be repressed. Wouldn't be stuffed under the mattress or buried in the yard. He didn't think it was something as simple as having sex for the first time in years that unblocked that part of his brain. That was ridiculous. But he supposed in having sex with Selena, he'd allowed himself to crack open more than one sealed-shut door. Five years' worth of pent-up creative impulses spotted their chance to escape and weren't giving up easily.

His mind was a roar of words, images, phrases. He had to get them out, or he'd explode. It would have been easier to take a hammer to his head, to crack it open and let the words spill out that way, but he couldn't do that to Selena, couldn't leave her with a mess that big to clean up. He forced himself to go to the den, to pick up his laptop and take it outside, where it didn't smell like bacon. He opened the device, ignored his email with a sort of manic glee, clicked on the word processing software. If his computer could have grown cobwebs, the app would have been coated in them. But after a moment, the program spit up a blank page. The cursor blinked. He blinked back. He felt a little faint. The sun seemed to be coming down extra hard. He should be wearing his hat. He should move to the shade. He should chuck the damn computer into the pool.

Instead, he thought about Selena, about her fearlessness, her confidence. He thought about second chances and how damn happy he was to be alive. He put his fingers on the keyboard and began to type.

Two hours later, Warner was a zombie. His fingers were as cramped as if he'd been pruning roses nonstop instead of typing. He stood up, and his back cracked in a few places. He hadn't eaten or drunk since breakfast, but he felt wired. He'd written, a messy, garbled dump of words, but they existed where before there had been nothing. It felt like a miracle. It felt like hard fucking work.

He saved the document. Who knew if it would turn into anything, but that didn't matter. He went inside, thinking that if he'd had any, he would have celebrated with an ice-cold beer. Perhaps he'd take himself out to lunch and get that beer anyway.

The house phone rang as he was grabbing his wallet. He answered before checking the number. Usually the only person who called him was his sister.

"Hello?"

"Warner, hi! You actually answered. I thought I was going to get voicemail."

"Joanna." Damn his distraction. He'd made a rookie mistake. No picking up calls from Angie's friends. He'd made that rule long ago.

"I know you got my email, and I'm not taking it personally that you didn't respond, but Daphne and Megan and I are talking dates for the dinner, and I'm going to make a reservation. Can you make it in early November?"

He thought about hanging up, pretending the call had dropped or his phone had run out of batteries, or an asteroid had hit Misty Harbor.

But he was trying not to be a coward, wasn't he? He cleared his throat. "I appreciate the invitation, Jo. Won't you have more fun if I'm not there?"

She sighed and spoke slowly and clearly, as if he was one of her children and she was explaining exactly why it was a bad idea to play tic-tac-toe on the wall with permanent markers. "We miss you, Warner. You're our friend, too. The three of us can get together anytime. We want to see *you*. And since it's easier for you to come to us, yes, we're pulling the 'we have small children' card and saying you have to come down here instead of us having to come up to Misty Harbor. But if you don't make it down here, then God help me, I will pile my kids into the Volvo, and I will drive up there and camp on your doorstep until you let us in. Is that what you want? I'll do it, Warner, I swear."

She sounded so fierce that he had to laugh or be turned to stone via the long-distance death glare he was certain she was giving him.

"I'll have to look at my calendar," he said finally.

"Let me know soon, okay? We can do it another night if that's better for you."

"Okay."

"So how's everything else? The house?"

"The house is fine. The power went out the other night, but the generator worked well."

"And your rentals? All full?"

"Oh, yes. Misty Harbor is full up at the moment with the television production."

"What production?"

"*Sawyer's Cove*."

"*Sawyer's Cove*? But that show was canceled, like, a million years ago. I was obsessed with it in college."

"They're rebooting it or reviving it or something?"

"Seriously? How did I not know about this?" Jo's voice rose an octave before she answered her own question. "Oh, probably because since Rory was born, if it's not animated and doesn't have crime-solving dogs in it, it's not on my watchlist. With the original actors and everything?"

"From what I understand." Warner was beginning to think he should watch an episode, if only for the context.

"I used to have the biggest crush on the guy who played Parker on the show. Jay Orlando, I think. He never did anything after that show, but whew. He was fine."

"He's a..." Warner stuttered over the word *friend*, "an acquaintance of mine. The woman in charge of the whole show is renting my pool house for the season."

Joanna let out a surprised noise, and he suspected he'd made another tactical error. "That's wild. Now I really need to get up there."

He ignored the four empty guest bedrooms upstairs and said, "Well, it's not a great time, what with having a tenant—"

"I promise I won't just show up. Unless you make me," Joanna said sternly. Then her voice softened. "Seriously, Warner, you sound good. And it's going to be okay. Text me or email me, all right?"

"All right." He had to admit that having a normal conversation with someone from before made him feel more human. "Give my best to Bruno and the boys."

"Take care, Warner."

He drove to Main Street and parked in his secret spot around the corner on Willow. As he approached The

Cove on foot, aiming for a mediocre hamburger and crisp draft beer, he was flummoxed by orange cones and a small army of people wearing headsets barring the way. Everyone seemed to have a purpose, and none of them was welcoming him in for a meal.

"You can watch from over there, sir," a woman wearing a security guard uniform told him in a firm voice as he approached the barrier. He looked to where she was pointing and saw a small crowd of people on the far side of the street, all avidly watching the front of the bar. As a group, they were non-homogenous, but they all had the same gleam of excitement in their eyes, and they all had their cell phones at the ready.

"I take it The Cove isn't open for lunch today," he said to the security guard.

She shook her head. "No, sir. Closed for filming today. Try again tomorrow."

He thanked her, shaking his head at the surreality. The weirdness increased when the crowd across the street began to make noise and he caught sight of Jay coming out the front door. But it wasn't the Jay he'd known as long as he'd lived in Misty Harbor, the one who knew his drink order by heart and never let him drive himself home if he'd had one too many. This guy was wearing an athletic shirt and basketball shorts, his very short, tightly curled hair damp, as if he'd gotten sweaty playing some hoops.

Jay played basketball? But no, this wasn't Jay. It was Parker—that was his character's name, wasn't it? There was another burst of activity, a woman dabbed at Jay's face, another woman on a headset talking to him, and a camera rig pushing up close.

The security guard caught Warner's eye and pointed silently across the street, and Warner walked slowly over to the crowd with the other spectators. Someone must have made a signal, because everyone got quiet at once, and the camera started moving along with Jay as he walked into The Cove, the door shutting behind him.

The group relaxed, and the noise level rose.

That was it? Three seconds of Jay walking into a building?

TV was weird.

He was about to leave and find an establishment that would sell him a meal when he saw Jay come back out of the building. The fans around him snapped back to attention. The entire process happened again—the dabbing at his face, the camera moving to its original position. The hush, and then Jay walked into the building again.

Okay.

He was walking away when he saw Selena. She was talking on a cell phone and looking at a tablet held in front of her by someone with a headset.

She looked in her element, completely confident. He wouldn't have expected anything else, but it was still strange to see her in work mode. She nodded at something, then she smiled. His stomach dipped oddly. He must really have been hungry.

She didn't see him, and he didn't want to bother her. He kept going up Main Street, passing the Bakeshop, but he was looking for more of an early dinner at this point. He ended up at Antonio's, the Italian place on a nearby side street.

The place was empty, and he took up an entire booth guilt-free, ordered too much food so he could take home leftovers. The single glass of wine he'd decided would substitute for the congratulatory beer was delivered, and he raised the glass to himself, wishing oddly that Selena was there to help him mark the occasion. He wasn't certain that writing again wasn't a huge mistake, or even something to celebrate, but it felt like something that should be honored.

The wine was tart and dry on his tongue. He savored the flavor, realized it reminded him of one of Angie's favorites. He'd been a humble beer drinker when he met her. She'd introduced him to wine, and whiskey, for that matter. Her parents had taken her on trips to Paris and Italy growing up. She knew all about varietals and vintages. He'd learned enough to keep up with her, but letting her order wine when they were out together was always a pleasure. He'd always enjoyed deferring to her, in everything from where they lived to what wine they drank. How he should structure the novel. What the ending should be.

He'd looked to her for guidance, and he'd come to depend on it. When she died, he was lost. There was no point in writing if he didn't have her to read it, to give him feedback. He had done the only thing he could think of, which was continuing to carry out her plans, her dreams.

But he was trying to get better, wasn't he? He could enjoy the wine and smile at the good memories, not feel a flare of hurt at the loss. He could order carbonara, even though Angie hated it.

He could take a lover, because he liked Selena, and she made him feel alive. He'd cut himself off from feeling anything, because to feel the entirety of Angie's loss might have truly finished him off. But his heart hadn't completely withered. It was more like a houseplant he'd forgotten in a dark room, stunted and pale.

Being with Selena was like pulling back the shades around his heart and letting the sun in. He only hoped he was strong enough to withstand the inevitable pain.

Sometimes the sun gave life, and sometimes it burned you to a crisp.

Chapter Sixteen

The ice around her throat matched the cold look in her blue eyes. Jake deferred to her—when your prospective client's jewelry was worth more than everything you owned—times two—you listened when she was dressing you down. Then you increased your fee by fifty percent.

— Untitled work in progress, by Warner Mathis

The rest of the week was so busy, Selena didn't have time to check in with Warner about anything, including the fundraiser. She was so tired by Friday night that she went to bed and let herself sleep until nearly noon. She couldn't remember the last time she'd slept that late. She must have needed it.

As she went about her Saturday, slowly taking care of personal business, she couldn't get the idea of taking another bath in Warner's fabulous bathtub out of her mind. She could soak and then get ready for the party. He probably wouldn't mind, but would he think asking to take a bath was code for sex? It would be a fair assumption, given what had happened the last time she'd used his tub, and, to be honest, sex wouldn't have been the end of the world.

But when she texted him to ask if he'd be okay if she borrowed his bathtub for an hour, he responded that he was out but the kitchen door was open, and she was welcome to it.

Maybe that was for the best. She grabbed her latest paperback read, cocktail dress, and makeup bag. Might as well make full use of Warner's generously-sized bathroom rather than try to get party-glamorous in the closet-sized bathroom in the pool house.

She let herself in, wondering about security. When she'd moved in, Warner had been very clear about the security system in the house and perimeter, but maybe he wasn't going to be gone long.

Should she ask him for a key?

The kitchen was immaculate, as always. She'd never seen a cleaning service at the house, but she had a hard time imagining Warner keeping a place this size clean all on his own. On the other hand, he seemed to thrive on hard manual labor, so maybe it was therapeutic for him. She shrugged, found the back stairs, then Warner's bedroom. It was strange that she'd slept there without him.

She went straight to the bathroom, hung up her dress, and set the other things down on a chair. She remembered vaguely that Warner had used something from the shower to make the bubbles the other night, but today she found a brand-new bottle of mint bubble bath, which she felt free to use liberally. Mint was her favorite. Soon she was sliding under a sea of frothy, fragrant lather.

Yesterday, Becca had gotten her into a local salon to get her hair cut and blown out. Her hair was so curly that to make it truly straight took a gargantuan number of products and effort, so she hadn't opted for that, rather the hairdresser had given her glossy, smooth curls, which she had carefully pinned to the top of her head before getting into the bath. It wouldn't do to get them wet.

The salon had been busy—apparently, the library fundraiser was the social event of the season. She'd shamelessly eavesdropped on a few conversations, using the writer's prerogative. The show had come up—one person was annoyed they'd closed lower Main Street yesterday for more exterior filming, but then another woman said she was happy because the production had sourced some of their wardrobe and props from her consignment shop. The locals seemed to be more focused on the production rather than the actual show. She wondered if they would watch it when it came out. Sometimes she worried no one would watch it—that this was a futile exercise in nostalgia and the only people who cared were the ones making the show.

But that wasn't true. By some mysterious metric, online chatter had gone up every week since they announced the reboot, for whatever that was worth. They'd released a few stills a couple of days ago, and they'd been plastered everywhere. The studio was sending reporters in batches practically every week to do interviews with the cast.

She'd been involved in some high-profile projects before, but this one mattered more than any of the others. What if she couldn't deliver? What if the audience hated it?

She felt her heart rate climbing, and she forced herself to take a breath. This event was coming at the perfect time; it would be healthy for her to have a night off, to blow off some steam.

She tried to read her book—a recent mystery—but it didn't hold her interest. She set it aside, slipped as far under the water as she dared without wetting her hair, and sighed. She could handle work stress. She could even handle disappointment if the reboot didn't turn out the way she wanted it to.

But she couldn't get a handle on Warner. They'd barely seen each other since the night she'd slept over. Yes, they'd kissed in his kitchen the other morning, and, yes, it had been good. But their schedules hadn't lined up, and she'd been sleeping alone in the pool house ever since.

It wasn't that he was avoiding her, she didn't think.

But he had his life, and she had hers, and there was nothing keeping them in each other's lives when the only thing that had brought them together in the first place was a power outage and salted chocolate chip cookies.

Still, there was something about him. As busy as she'd been, his solemn blue stare and the raspy way he said her name when he was coming had never strayed far from her thoughts. Was he almost melodramatically intense? Yes. Did she kind of dig that about him? Also yes.

But she needed to get with the program and acknowledge that perhaps they were at different places in their lives. Just because she was the first person he'd slept with since his wife died, it didn't *mean* anything. She was handy. Available. Their having sex was a combination of circumstances and timing.

She frowned. But she didn't go around sleeping with everyone she had late-night conversations with. And he didn't either.

So why hadn't they done it since?

As if she'd wished him into being, a soft knock came on the bathroom door.

She looked to see if there were sufficient bubbles still covering her, then remembered he'd seen everything before. "Come in." The door opened, and Warner leaned his top half through.

"Sorry to bother you," he said, keeping his eyes fixed somewhere on the wall behind her head. "But I noticed your car has a flat tire."

"What?" She sat up at that unwelcome news, her breasts bobbing in the water. "How could—" She stopped when she remembered seeing a light come on the dash during her drive home. She'd made a mental note to have Becca make an appointment at a mechanic next week, then ignored it. Maybe it had been the tire pressure sensor or something. "Shit."

"I don't have a jack, or I could try to change it. I don't think you should drive it far on the spare anyway."

"Triple A?"

"I called Ravi at the garage, but he's not there."

"Oh, thanks for trying."

"It was nothing."

"I'll get a cab or something." They had Ubers in Misty Harbor, she knew for a fact.

"How's the bath?"

She wished it had done its job of relaxing her, but her thoughts had kept her from truly unwinding. "It's nice," she said anyway. "Thanks for letting me use it."

"Of course."

He was still half-in, half-out of the bathroom. His gaze hadn't once slipped down to her naked, wet body. She supposed he was trying to give her privacy. She suddenly shivered, despite the warm water. She didn't want privacy.

She wanted Warner.

His gaze shifted inexorably as she slowly rose out of the water.

"Hand me my towel, would you?"

He came fully into the room, took the towel from the

chair, and walked it over to her. She stepped onto the notorious bath mat, and instead of simply handing her the folded towel, he shook it open, wrapped it around her shoulders, then tugged her forward. She smiled at being trapped against his clothed front, breasts pressed against him, getting his shirt wet. He didn't seem to care. His eyes were dark as they looked down at her, and he said nothing before sealing his mouth over hers.

Yes, her body sang as she melted into him.

The kiss turned filthily open-mouthed in seconds. The fabric of his button-down shirt caught at her sensitive nipples. She worked at the buttons for a few seconds with her bath-pruney fingers, then gave up as the towel fell to the floor and Warner grabbed her ass, digging into the flesh with his strong, calloused hands. They stumbled out of the bathroom, Warner only letting her go to scramble out of his jeans. He whipped his shirt over his head without bothering to get all the buttons undone.

She pulled the sheets back on his bed and climbed on. It was as comfortable as she remembered, but it was so much better to be there with Warner, to have the delicious weight of him settle on top of her, the hard line of him firm between her legs as he kissed her, searing hot.

If she'd assumed their first coupling was intense because it had been a while for him, for them both, this time was no less urgent, no less passionate. He kissed her as if he'd been wandering in a desert and she was the first green thing he'd seen.

They'd already done it without a condom, twice, and she didn't want to stop to talk about it when she didn't really want to use one anyway. Instead, she simply opened her legs in invitation. Warner plunged into her without preamble.

She gasped. The pressure on top of her, inside her, drove all of her worries out of her brain. She tilted her hips, and he rose onto his knees, lifting her ass to rest on his thighs as he snapped into her deep, his chest and abs rippling with the effort, his mouth open as he watched her take him. He looked younger like this, all his taut control redirected toward her body, her pleasure.

He grabbed her hands and put them on her own breasts, squeezing, forcing her to pinch her own nipples, and it felt so good, she was suddenly coming. He followed a moment later, shouting, driving into her so hard, she shot back, her head banging into the headboard, his cock buried deep as it could go as he shook through his orgasm.

Her entire body buzzed with aftershocks at being taken hard and fast like that. She felt floaty and slow, groaning as he disengaged, flopping over on his side, one of his arms around her middle. She turned toward him, slowly registering that she was damp all over, partly from sweat, partly from the bath.

She looked at his face; the blue eyes and serious mouth were becoming so dear to her. In the quiet after their coupling, the thoughts, the worries, the stress started to trickle back in, but she held them at bay by tracing a finger in a figure eight pattern on his arm. "Do you have a bathtub kink or something?"

His laugh was rich and warm and startled her. She'd never heard him laugh like that before.

"I don't have a bathtub kink," he said, still chuckling. "It's just *you*, Selena."

If she'd been worried this was merely about convenience, she couldn't feel that way when his beautiful eyes were on her, clear and focused and looking at her as if she was the only thing in the world that mattered.

She allowed herself to be pleased at his response, then froze when she caught sight of the alarm clock behind him. "Damn. I'm going to be late."

"Late?"

"For the fundraiser." She sat up, mentally cataloging all the things she had to do to get ready. She didn't particularly want to leave Warner's warm, cozy bed, where Warner currently sat, unabashed in his nakedness. But she'd said she would go, and she kept her promises.

Warner didn't try to talk her into staying anyway. "How can I help?"

"I brought everything over, so I'm going to borrow your bathroom again. If you can manage not to have sex with me for about fifteen minutes while I get dressed and do my makeup, I think this will work."

"Not have sex with you for fifteen minutes," he repeated seriously. "I will do my best."

It didn't take long to rinse off in the lukewarm bathwater, towel dry, then apply her simple makeup and let her hair down over her shoulders. She donned what she thought of as her fancy pair of glasses—black frames with rhinestones at the corners. Her underwear and bra were more supportive than sexy, but the cocktail dress she slid over them was sexy enough, knee-length with a slightly flared skirt. Red, of course. She stepped into strappy black sandals, and she was all set.

"Damn." She wasn't all set. She never wore much jewelry, and she'd forgotten to bring her nice pair of earrings from the pool house. Now she'd have to go all the way back, and she was already late.

She went to the bedroom. Warner stood in the middle of the room in his jeans, his shirt on but unbuttoned. He was frowning down at his phone.

"I have to go get my earrings."

He didn't seem to hear her. "Bad news—there aren't any cabs available. I think everyone is using them to get to the fundraiser." Then he looked up from his phone. His eyes grew gratifyingly wide as he looked her up and down in blatant perusal. "You look beautiful, Selena."

"Thanks." She appreciated the simple compliment. "I'll have to call Cami for a ride."

"Nonsense," he said. "You can borrow—"

"I'm not leaving you without a car," she interrupted, though it was sweet of him to offer his minivan. "What if there's an emergency? Cami can get me."

"I have another car in the garage."

"You do?"

"You said you need earrings?"

"I've got some at the pool house."

Warner opened a drawer in the wide dresser against the wall. He poked around and drew out a pair of deceptively simple square cut stones set into platinum studs. They looked like diamonds. From the size of them, they were probably worth the entire *Sawyer's Cove* wardrobe budget.

"These would look good with your dress," he said.

"These would look good with a garbage can." She wasn't a jewelry connoisseur, but she could appreciate an exquisite pair of diamond earrings. They glinted seductively in the low light of the bedroom.

"I'd be happy for you to borrow them," he said, holding them out.

She took them because they were beautiful, and it seemed easier than trying to explain why she didn't want to wear his dead wife's earrings. There was no doubt in her mind that these had been Angeline's.

She fixed them in her ears by touch, then crossed over to a small wall mirror over the dresser. She touched the little glints of white fire at her ears and couldn't help a smile. "They're incredible. Thanks, Warner."

He was looking at her with a funny expression on his face. When he realized she was looking at him, he shook out of the moment. He slipped on a pair of loafers and buttoned his shirt as he walked out of the room. "Come on, I'll get you the key."

She grabbed the small black evening bag she'd put together, left her other things behind, and hurried down the hall after him, her sandals clacking on the floor.

He led her down the front stairs, grabbed a key ring from the table that held the wedding photo. He looked at her critically before they went out. "You don't have a sweater or something?"

It had been another unseasonably warm day, and the event was inside. "I'll be okay," she said, "but thanks for your concern."

He looked like he wanted to argue but refrained, to her amusement. Instead, he picked up a garage door opener from the tray with the keys and went out the front door. She'd never used this entrance, always having come in the back. They crossed the driveway, where she could see her poor rental with its deflated rear wheel. His minivan was parked next to it. The garage was a detached building on the far side of the gate. He clicked the opener, and the door rose slowly to reveal a small red roadster. It looked vintage. She recognized the badge in the grill at once.

"A Mercedes?" She grinned in delight and appreciation of the car's trim lines.

"It's a nineteen seventy Mercedes two-forty SL."

"You won't believe this, but I have an SLK at home. This is like my car's grandma. It's even the same color."

He laughed unhappily. "Of course you do."

"Why on Earth don't you use this as your daily driver? What's with the minivan?" Then she realized. This was like the socks and earrings, only so much worse. "Oh, no."

He made a slightly apologetic face. "Full disclosure, Angie was driving this car when she had her accident. But it's been completely repaired, practically restored to like new in the process."

"No," she said, shaking her head. She could wear a dead woman's socks, even her earrings, but she was not going to drive the car she was driving when she was killed. "Nope, sorry, not going to borrow your wife's death car."

"It drives really well," he insisted. "And it could use the exercise."

"You drive it, then," she snapped. "I'll call Cami." She got her phone out, but he stopped her with a gentle hand on her arm.

"Fine. I'll drive you. Get in."

She eyed the car uneasily. It was a beautiful machine, but it wasn't just a car. It meant something. Why did he still have it? Then again, why did he have so many of his wife's things?

Her stomach buckled unpleasantly. Oh, dear. Had she gotten herself into some kind of *Rebecca* situation?

She dismissed the suspicion as quickly as it occurred to her. She wasn't the new Mrs. de Winter, and there was no obsessed housekeeper. Only Warner, troubled, complicated Warner, who was doing the best he could.

"Let me drive you, please. It's the least I can do for making you late."

He looked so hopeful that she couldn't say no. Besides, she really did need a ride. Practicality married with sympathy, and she gave in.

"Okay."

Chapter Seventeen

Jake took the curve too fast, but he steered into it and kept pace with the Mustang. His VW wasn't much to look at, but it had a solid engine. He had another advantage over his quarry—he wasn't afraid to die.

— Untitled work in progress, by
Warner Mathis

As they sped down Blue Bird Lane to the main artery that would take them to the Misty Harbor Inn, the location of the fundraiser gala, Warner couldn't help feeling this entire evening had been terribly surreal. Had he finally broken with reality?

He'd spent the day working. As the owner and manager of three rental properties, there was always something to do, from maintenance to paperwork. But always in the back of his mind was his story. He'd worked a bit every day this week. The damn thing had gotten its hooks in him, like a cat who'd clawed open one of his veins. Once he'd let the blood start to flow, he couldn't stop it. And what's more, he didn't want to.

It wasn't exactly a smooth drip of words onto the page. He sat there, typing in fits and starts. He was rusty, but it was coming back to him—the rhythm of translating his thoughts into sentences, watching the sentences form paragraphs that flowed together into some sort of coherence. It was a craft he'd honed once before, and his muscles had diminished but not disappeared entirely. He could build them back up again, he was sure.

If he didn't stop himself by going around the bend first.

He glanced at Selena. She looked like a movie star, her satiny hair flowing free, Angie's diamonds winking at her ears. Angie would be happy someone was wearing them. She'd always been cavalier with her possessions, giving things away at the drop of a hat. If someone in her life commented on her scarf or bracelet, she'd simply give it to them. She had the generosity of a poor person and resources of a rich one.

But it was fair that Selena didn't want to drive the Mercedes. And it probably wouldn't have been safe for her to do so in her strappy sandals either. He should drive it more, though. The car wanted to be driven. It hadn't even been that damaged in the accident. Angie had been unlucky—skidding on black ice, her side making direct impact with one of the grand oaks they'd so admired when they moved here. She wouldn't have wanted him to junk her baby. Instead, he'd found a shop willing to work on it for a premium. Money, he'd learned from Angie, could solve most problems.

"You okay?" she asked. "You seem like you're thinking harder than usual."

"I'm wondering why I feel like I'm in a surrealist painting. A beautiful surrealist painting, but still, strange."

"What's so surreal about driving your tenant who you just fucked to a party you won't go to as her date in the car your wife died in?" she asked, slightly hysterically.

Okay, so he wasn't the only one who found the situation bizarre.

Her voice continued to rise as she went on, "Why do you have this car anyway, and these earrings? And the socks? Did you keep *everything* of hers?"

The socks? It took him a second to realize she was talking about the socks he'd given her the night of the storm. "I bought those socks for me, and they shrank in the wash."

"Oh." She looked mollified.

"And I bought Angie the earrings when I got the advance for *Gunsmoke*, as a thank you. I couldn't seem to part with them. The car, too. I wasn't ready to let it go. Most of the rest of her things got donated or given to her friends. She didn't have much family."

"Oh. Well. I guess I can understand the earrings. But the car is kind of morbid, Warner." She let out a short laugh. "Then again, having read *Gunsmoke*, maybe I should have guessed you're a bit of a morbid guy."

She was back to her normal register, the tone of her voice matter of fact, as if she'd already forgiven him. As if she accepted him. The feeling of surreality returned. They were a few blocks from the inn, so he pulled over to the side of the road and turned to her. "I am so sorry, Selena."

She looked confused. "What are you sorry about?"

"Because I'm a fucking grab bag of issues, a variety pack of neuroses, and you're an amazing woman who should be with someone who can have sex with you without it being a huge deal, who can take you on proper dates and drive you to them in a normal vehicle. You're an impressive, successful, beautiful woman, and I'm a hack who's bad with change. Spending time with me somehow seems to be something you're doing out of choice, and being with you feels so selfishly good that I don't have the inner strength to tell you to stay away from me. I mean, it's obvious to both of us that you should be with someone in a better place than me. So, I guess that's why this feels surreal. We had sex—incredible sex, for me at least—and now you look like that." He gestured to her outfit. She looked so hot, he was afraid to touch her lest he get burned. "I'm such a schmuck to let you go to this thing alone. It would serve me right if Nash Speedwell—or Brad Pitt, for that matter—sweeps you right off your feet. I hope that happens, Selena, because you deserve it. This—" he waved his arm vaguely around the cabin of the car "— this fucking Dali mess is not what you deserve. So yeah, I'm sorry."

He stopped talking and found he was breathing heavily. It seemed the words hadn't only been loosed through his fingers. He couldn't remember saying that much at once since Angie died.

Selena was looking at him, her eyes wide behind her sexy glasses. He'd meant every word of his diatribe, but now he was petrified she'd take him at his word, that she'd get out at the inn and he'd never see her again now that he'd pointed out the obvious.

He didn't exactly know what was happening between them, but he was suddenly terrified of losing it. That was why he'd kept everything locked down for so long, this very reason.

But she didn't agree with him, or laugh at him, or get out of the car. Her voice was even when she said, "Nash Speedwell is dating Mimi Orlando. And Brad Pitt is too old for me."

He took that in. "Nash and Mimi?" That actually made a lot of sense.

"And I am choosing to spend time with you because you make me feel good, too."

He did? "How is that possible?"

She was smiling at him with a look he'd never seen on her face before. It took him a moment to select a vocabulary word that described the expression. *Fond.* She was looking at him with fondness.

"Warner Mathis, you don't even know, do you?"

"Know what?" he said stiffly, proving her point and touchy about it.

"I'm not going to tell you you're the most well-adjusted person in the world, but who is? Most of us are messed up in one way or another, but you don't hide it. You're just you, and the rest of the world has to deal. I like that. You're thoughtful, you're one of the least selfish people I've ever met. You've got a quick mind. You can keep up with me, but you aren't threatened by me, which I appreciate. Being with you is interesting. You help me see things differently. And we have a lot in common, which is unexpected, I'll grant you. Who would have thought I'd meet another writer who grew up in Los Angeles and loves mysteries and noir films and swimming out here in Misty Harbor?"

He didn't know what to do with the full feeling in his chest, so he kissed her. She tasted like mint and lipstick, so delicious he felt himself hardening in his jeans.

She kissed him back, her tongue exploring his mouth thoroughly. They broke off the kiss at the same time, as if by mutual agreement that to take it any further would be dangerous.

"Look," she said, her lipstick smeared and making him ache with the need to see her mouth stained red and stretched around his cock. Fuck. Next time. "I'm going to this event, I'm going to have a swell time, I'm not going to get swept off my feet by Brad Pitt or anyone else. And later, I'm going to get a ride back to your house, and I'm going to come in, and we're going to sleep in your bed. Together. And tomorrow, we're going to hang out. I have the day off, and boy, do I need a proper day off. All right?"

"Does hanging out involve sex?"

She did laugh at that. "If you want it to. Sex definitely qualifies as a hanging out activity."

"I do," he said.

"Here, you're all lipstick," she said, holding out a tissue. He swiped at his mouth, not really caring.

He started the car and waited for a break in traffic before pulling onto the road again. She fixed her makeup on the way, and soon he was pulling into the circular driveway of the inn.

"Have a good time," he said. "I'll be waiting for you at home."

It wasn't a slip of the tongue. His home was hers, tonight at least, and for the rest of her stay in Misty Harbor if she wanted it. He might have been messed up, but he wasn't delusional. He knew Selena in his bed every night was better than he deserved, and he wouldn't turn it down.

"Thanks for the ride, Warner," she said, winking at him. Then she got out of the car, swinging her hips as she walked to the inn's entrance.

Damn. She was a first-rate woman. And she was his, for the moment anyway.

Chapter Eighteen

MISTY HARBOR LIBRARY FUNDRAISER
SILENT AUCTION LOT #61
AN ORIGINAL SCRIPT USED DURING THE FILMING OF
SAWYER'S COVE EPISODE 101, "THE HOMECOMING," SIGNED
BY SELENA ECHEVERIA AND CAMILLE CORSAIR
BIDDING STARTS AT $300

The first thing Selena saw when she entered the ballroom and looked around was Jay Orlando planting a kiss on Camille Corsair's cheek. Her producing partner, star of the show, and friend's cheeks turned as pink as the blush-colored retro fifties-style dress she was wearing. They made a dazzling couple, Jay tall, dark, and handsome, with the blonde-haired, blue-eyed girl next door on his arm. Selena was happy they'd found a second act for their relationship after being apart for too many years, but she felt a blaze of jealousy, too. This thing with Warner was new, and fragile, but she would have liked to have spent the evening getting to know him better, if nothing else. She spent twelve hours a day, five days a week with these people.

Still, as she noticed Becca standing with Bo near the bar, both of them more dressed up than she'd ever seen them—Becca in a long flower-print dress, her dark wavy hair left long, and Bo in a snazzy blazer over a white T-shirt and dark jeans, his short black hair spiked with gel—she had to admit, it was fun to see them in a different context. When was the last time she'd had a conversation with Becca that didn't involve the production?

She found her assistant and gave her a hug. Becca drew back, looking surprised. "What? I'm not allowed to hug the best thing that ever happened to *Sawyer's Cove*?"

Becca rolled her eyes and looked pleased at the same time. "You're allowed. But let's all agree to take a break from talking about work."

"You read my mind. Bo, what are you drinking?"

Bo held up his watermelon-hued drink. "It's the gala's signature cocktail. I didn't ask what was in it, but it tastes fruity." He smacked his lips. "I like it."

Selena laughed, remembering being young and willing to try anything alcoholic once. "I think I'll get a glass of wine."

"I can get it for you," Becca said.

"You are off the clock, remember? God, are we all inveterate workaholics?"

"Only some of us," Bo said, glancing between her and Becca. "But I know how to party. And you need this punch to party."

He managed to sneak in at the bar and return with two more of the pink drinks. Selena smelled hers. It was, as described, fruity. She shrugged and took a sip. It was sweet and tart and didn't taste a thing like alcohol. Maybe Bo was on to something.

She was on her second signature cocktail when Spencer Crosby, known simply as Crosby, who played the eponymous character Sawyer North, joined their little group. He was resplendent in a shiny suit and silver shirt, an outfit that jeans-and-flannel-wearing Sawyer wouldn't be caught dead in. With him was a handsome young man dressed all in black, except for his ostentatious yet elegant purple eyeshadow. It took Selena a minute to place him.

"Trevor, from the Bakeshop, right?" she said, waving at him.

He put his hand on his chest. "Oh my God, Selena Echeveria knows my name."

She laughed. "I think everyone in Misty Harbor knows your name, Trevor."

"So, how are you enjoying our humble burg?" Trevor asked. "Are you pining for glamorous Hollywood?"

"Misty Harbor's growing on me," she said. "Despite the fact that you can't get a flat tire fixed at five o'clock on a Saturday night."

"You got a flat?" Becca asked. "Do you—"

Selena stopped her. "No work talk. You aren't my assistant tonight, remember?"

Becca looked sheepish. "I'll try."

Crosby frowned. "What are we supposed to talk about if we can't talk about work?"

Trevor held up three long, pale fingers and ticked them off one by one. "One, the weather. Two, the latest streaming show. Three, we gossip about who our friends are here with, and/or their outfits. By the way, I love you in florals, Becca. And you are ravishing in red, Selena. Not to mention those earrings are stunning."

Selena touched one of the diamond studs. She'd forgotten she was wearing them. Instead of dwelling on their origin, she smiled at Trevor. "You look great, too."

"What about me?" Crosby asked. "Is this a hit or a miss?" He ran his hands up and down his flashy lapels.

"You'd look handsome wrapped in tin foil, which is lucky, given your choice of suits," Trevor said, with a cheeky grin.

Selena was surprised when instead of getting defensive, Crosby smiled, snapping his fingers ruefully. "And I almost went with the tin foil suit—next time, I guess."

Trevor laughed and bumped Crosby with his hip. They were cute together, and it was nice to see Crosby relaxed and happy. He was always so serious on set, both because his character was kind of a serious guy and because Crosby was one of those actors who took his craft seriously, even when he was acting in a frivolous teen show. He always showed up and brought 110%. It made him a little intimidating and hard to get to know, but Selena had enjoyed working with him these past few weeks.

Still, as the evening progressed and Crosby and

Trevor stayed glued to each other's sides, Becca and Bo casually flirted with each other, and Jay and Cami made heart eyes at each other whether they were across the ballroom or sitting right next to each other, Selena was beginning to feel like the odd woman out. Had literally everyone come to this shindig with a date? Even Jeff, the sound guy, seemed to be here with Ariel Tulip, who looked ravishing in a green silk evening dress.

She sucked down another cocktail and wandered into the room where the silent auction items were set up. The sheer number of items was bewildering. She spotted tons of *Sawyer's Cove*-related lots, including the script she'd donated, and a day on the set as an extra Cami was arranging. There was the week at Warner's rental house he'd mentioned. She bid on a gift certificate to the salon where she'd had her hair done yesterday, and then on a basket of books donated by the library. After her third cocktail, she also bid on a Galapagos cruise and a week at a vacation house in Montauk, which she vaguely thought was somewhere near New York. She tossed her name on a few other items for the heck of it. It was for a good cause, after all.

Dinner helped make the floaty feeling in her head recede, but then Nash Speedwell unexpectedly took the stage to perform songs from his alt-country album, and she whooped and hollered so hard, she needed another drink to soothe her overworked vocal cords. His set was amazing, and the energy in the room was unreal. Why didn't he perform live more often?

"Cami!" She snagged her friend's hand in line at the

dessert buffet. "Why don't we have Will singing or playing guitar in the show?"

Cami tilted her head. "I can't think of an episode where it would make sense."

Selena groaned. "Missed opportunity!"

"Something for the second season," Cami said, patting her hand and grabbing a passionfruit eclair with icing as pink as her dress.

"If we even have a second season," Selena said darkly.

Cami frowned. "Why, did you hear something from Brad?"

"No, no." Selena waved a hand in front of her face. "He's being cagey. Just, what if we don't? What if we're one and done and Ryan hates it, and the fans hate it, and—"

"Selena, stop." Cami put down the eclair and wrapped her in a hug. "First of all, you're drunk."

"I am not," Selena said, with dignity. Then she giggled. "Well, yes, I am."

"Second of all, it's hard to see it when we're in the weeds like this, but we're making excellent television. I can feel it on set, I can feel it when we're watching dailies. I've been in crappy stuff, and I've been in good stuff, and we're making good stuff. Believe me."

"I want to believe you," Selena said, only half-facetiously. "I want to believe you" was an oft-quoted line from the show, and its unofficial motto.

"There you go." Cami smiled and dropped a mini

chocolate cheesecake into her hand. "Here, eat some chocolate and drink some water."

"Fine," Selena said around a mouthful of cheesecake. She turned to the dance floor in front of the stage as an 80s classic started playing on the sound system. Ariel pulled Crosby onto the dance floor, and soon it seemed like everyone at the party joined in, enthusiastically gyrating to Madonna.

She finished her cheesecake slowly, then dutifully went to the bar to ask for a glass of water.

Trevor was there and lit up when he spotted her. "Hey, I think you won that Montauk vacation. I'm jealous."

"Oh, God," she said, covering her eyes. "I don't even want to know how much money I accidentally spent. I was signing my name to those auction items like it was my job."

"Well, the library thanks you," he said. "Too bad Warner couldn't come tonight."

Her heart unaccountably started beating faster at the mention of his name. "Warner?"

"He's not the most sociable guy in the world, but I thought—" Trevor stopped, pressed his lips shut for a second, then went on, "Never mind what I thought. I'm trying not to gossip so much."

"Oh, well, that's admirable," Selena said, slightly disappointed. There weren't many people she could talk to about Warner. She sipped her water. It wasn't as yummy as the pink drink, but it was probably for the best. "But is it really gossip if it's just two people talking about a mutual friend?"

Trevor smiled slyly. "Totally not gossip. So, did you get your cookies the other day?"

"I got them," she said, her face heating up, which was silly because she was probably fifteen years older than Trevor and had nothing to be embarrassed about. He didn't know what those cookies had led to unless he was a telepath.

Her blush said more than her words, and Trevor rubbed his hands together gleefully. "Awesome. You know, it's about time someone got him out of his shell. He's a really cool person underneath that gruff exterior."

"How do you know?"

"Well, he knows a ton about plants. He gave Zelda advice about what plants would work well indoors at the Bakeshop. And he always gives money to all the local fundraisers. I think he must be loaded, but you wouldn't know it to look at him. That man could seriously use a makeover."

Selena kind of liked his casual beachcomber look, but she knew what Trevor meant.

"You can tell he has his good days and his bad days, but no matter what kind of day he's having, he doesn't make it your problem. Plus, he's a great tipper, which says a lot about a person."

"Definitely."

"Anyway, if you guys are hanging out, eating cookies together, I think that's awesome." He put a slight emphasis on "eating cookies," making it sound as if the phrase was code for something entirely different. Fair.

She hadn't exactly been waiting for his opinion on the matter, but she couldn't deny it felt nice to have the approval of a third party. Sometimes Blue Bird Lane felt so isolated, like she and Warner were the only two people in the world. Someday, she might like to see if their connection could be maintained outside the walls of his lovely house.

In the meantime, she'd do her best to sober up before she caught a ride home. Wham! came on, and she held out her hand to Trevor. "Wanna dance?"

"Absolutely."

Chapter Nineteen

"Gimme another."

The bartender hesitated, and Jake deliberately showed the guy his teeth. He concentrated on not slurring his words.

"What, you think I'm wasted? Believe me, pal, I've been a hell of a lot more in—ineb—inebri—*drunker* than this."

— *Gunsmoke,* by Warner Mathis

Selena woke up disoriented, with a headache spiking through her right eye and her mouth dry like something furry had died in it. She wasn't in the pool house, she knew that much. It took her a few seconds to realize she was in Warner's bedroom. In his bed. Alone.

"Warner?" Her voice was a croak. Why were her eyes sticky? She blinked a few times to clear the gunk out of them, as the reason for her misery filtered through her brain fog. The fundraiser. Those fruity pink cocktails. How on Earth was a library fundraiser the best party Selena had been to in ages?

She considered turning over and going back to sleep, but she was too discombobulated. She cautiously sat up and eyed the bathroom door. She could make it that far, she was pretty sure. The alarm clock showed the time as ten thirty-two, but the shades around the windows weren't letting in any light. She didn't *think* she'd slept through an entire day and into the night. Wait— blackout shades. That explained it.

A glass of water on the nightstand glowed faintly blue by the clock's light. Her thirst was suddenly enormous. She gulped down a third of the water, then saw the small bottle of generic painkillers next to it. Warner, bless him.

She only vaguely remembered Cami and Jay dropping her off last night, but Warner must have put her to bed. She was wearing one of his T-shirts again, and her own underwear. She touched her earlobes and felt the diamonds. She carefully unfastened them and left them on the nightstand, feeling lighter without them.

The water and promise of painkillers kicking in gave her the strength to make it to the shower, where she scrubbed her hair and face, removing all traces of her night out. She was flummoxed about what to wear when she stepped out of the bathroom—she didn't especially want to go rummaging around in Warner's drawers. Who knew what she'd find in there?—but then she spotted a fluffy gray robe in some sort of ultra-soft material hanging over the back of the door. She sniffed it experimentally, and it smelled clean, like the lavender laundry soap she'd seen in the laundry room downstairs, not like Warner, so she figured it was a guest robe. She wrapped herself in the luxe material and steeled herself to go find Warner.

She found him in the kitchen, the remains of his breakfast next to him. He was typing on a laptop and looked up, his expression flitting from surprised to—guilty?—before he shut the computer quickly and got up to greet her.

"Good morning."

"It is morning, isn't it?" she said, her voice still embarrassingly croaky.

He glanced out the kitchen window. Blue sky and sun. "Last time I checked."

"Sunday morning?"

He smiled at that. "Sunday morning," he confirmed.

"Thanks for the water and..." she lost her energy to elaborate and made a waving motion in the air, "...stuff."

His lips twitched, but he simply said, "You're welcome. Seems like it was quite a party. Did you have a good time?"

She sat down heavily on one of the high-backed chairs at the bar. "Open bar. Signature cocktail. Nash performed. I got carried away and spent way too much money on the silent auction."

"The library is grateful, I'm sure. Nash performed?"

"Yeah. He did his singer-songwriter thing up on stage. I was impressed."

"Remarkable."

"Sorry for being out of it," Selena said haltingly. "Cami told me to stop drinking, and I did, but then we were dancing to Madonna, and they said last call, and somehow I ended up downing a couple of shots, and—" She clutched her stomach. *Shots.* What had she been thinking? She wasn't twenty-five anymore.

"It's okay. You're really cute when you're drunk."

Selena groaned and buried her face in her arms folded up on the table.

She heard Warner's steps on the tile floor, then felt the pressure of his lips on the back of her damp head.

"Think you could manage something to eat?"

She lifted her head to peek at him. "Like what?"

"Grease is the best cure for a hangover I know. Bacon and eggs?"

"And coffee?" she added hopefully.

He made her a fresh pot, and too much food, which she picked at at first, but as the pills and coffee kicked in, her appetite did, too.

"It was nice to be around my coworkers but not working. Made me realize one of the best parts of this whole *Sawyer's Cove* reboot experience is the people. I didn't really know them that well back in the day and everyone's awesome."

"What do you mean, you didn't know them?"

"I was a writer's assistant, eventually a staff writer.

But the writers were based in L.A., and only Ryan flew back and forth regularly. I think I came out here twice in three years, maybe?"

"I didn't realize the writers were so isolated."

"Not only the writers. Some of the producers, the editors, the composers. The only ones who actually need to be on set are the director, crew, cast, the EPs some of the time. Once we finish up here, there's just as much work to do back in LA. There's another team already starting on post-production for the episodes we've finished shooting."

"Fascinating."

"Anyway, now I have another reason for wanting a second season order from the studio—I'd like to keep working with these folks." She pushed away her empty plate, along with her anxiety that if they didn't get a second season order, it would be all her fault. "What about you?"

Warner shrugged. "What about me?"

"Did you have a nice evening?" She wondered if he regretted not coming to the party with her even a little bit.

He glanced at his closed laptop, that slightly guilty expression edging onto his face again before he met her gaze. "Uh. Yeah. Quiet."

She narrowed her eyes. Far be it from her to judge him—what had he done, spent the whole night watching porn on that thing? He'd been celibate for five years; his porn habits were probably well-ingrained by this point. She decided to change the subject, but he spoke first.

"Writing. I was—writing."

It took a moment for her to process why he was saying it in that disjointed way. *Writing.* Warner Mathis had been writing.

She sucked in a breath. Her first instinct was to exclaim and gush and tell him how huge that was. But he already looked a bit like a spooked kitten, and she didn't want to scare him under the proverbial bed.

"Okay," she said calmly.

"Okay?" he repeated, looking a bit incredulous. "That's it?"

She smiled. "Well, do you want to talk about it?"

He thinned his lips into a flat line, his eyebrows coming together harshly, before his entire face relaxed again and he sighed. "That's how it worked with Angie. I wrote, she'd read and give me notes, and I'd fix it. I wrote the whole of *Gunsmoke* with her at my side."

"Wow." Selena was beginning to understand why he'd been blocked since Angeline died. If that was their system, yeah, that would be hard to lose. Not to mention losing someone you were planning to spend the rest of your life with.

"Not that I'm asking you—" Warner looked uncomfortable. "I'm just—it's all really new. I'm still finding my legs."

"Totally. I get it." She did. She'd never had the luxury of waiting around for a muse—she'd been writing on demand and making a living doing it for fifteen years—

but that didn't mean sometimes the words just wouldn't come if the conditions weren't right.

She was intensely curious about one thing. "Is it a Jake Wilton story? If it's okay to ask."

He looked at the laptop again, as if it held the answers they were both looking for. "I was thinking about what you said the other day, about second chances. About Jake, in particular. And so it is a Jake story, in a way, but I started with another character. I'm playing around with the point of view." He grimaced. "It's probably going to need major revisions, but I can't worry about that right now."

"No, definitely don't worry about that," she said. "It's wonderful you're writing at all."

"Yeah," he said flatly. "It's good." He said it like a question. "And fucking terrifying."

"Sounds like writing," she said lightly.

"Did you ever finish your script?" he asked.

"I turned a rough draft over to the writers, they'll flesh it out more, then I'll do a last pass on it. But yeah, I'm happy with it, for the most part."

"What's bothering you?"

She wondered what part of her body language betrayed that she still had some reservations about the ending.

"I don't know yet if this is it for the entire series, or if we'll be coming back for a second season. I think I would make some different choices, depending on the future of the show."

"So write both."

She had thought of that, but she'd been a little bit afraid to write the forever ending in case she manifested that accidentally. "Not a bad idea," she said. She'd think about that when she wasn't hungover. "So, you were writing this morning before I interrupted you. You want to get back to it?"

He looked surprised at the suggestion. "How are you feeling?"

She checked in with her body. "Actually, not bad. I should probably go to bed early tonight if I want to be functional tomorrow, but I'm good. Why, you got big plans?"

"I was thinking we could curl up on the couch in the den and put on a movie."

"Warner Mathis, you are a genius."

Seeing his dimple show made her feel better than the painkillers had.

They made a nest of blankets on the couch. Warner had cable, the freak, so they turned on the classic movie channel and caught *The Thin Man* almost from the beginning. They'd both seen it before, but it had been a while for Selena, and she reveled in the banter between Nick and Nora.

By the time Nick Charles had revealed the murderer and was climbing into the train bed with his wife, Selena was so snugly warm nestled against Warner's side, it was nothing to fall asleep. She woke up some time later under a blanket as Warner came into the room with a plate of sandwiches and pitcher of iced tea.

"You'd make a great husband," she said sleepily, the

movie tangled up with the dream she'd been having in which Warner was giving her a massage in a field of wildflowers.

She sat up so fast, she winced at the head rush. "I mean—"

"It's okay," he said, setting the food down on the coffee table. "I was a pretty good husband, I think."

She smiled at him, grateful he wasn't making it weird. The food was appetizing, but he was even more appealing. They spent the rest of the afternoon wearing each other out by having sex three times.

And the bathtub wasn't involved in a single one.

Chapter Twenty

"Hey stranger, where you been? Thought maybe you'd found a better watering hole." Danica, the manager of The Cove, and Warner's favorite bartender, greeted him warmly when he took up his usual stool.

It had been a while since he'd been here. He shrugged at her, suddenly self-conscious. "Been busy."

"Well, glad to see you back," she said. "The usual?"

"Let me start with a beer. Whatever's good on tap."

She took the change of order in stride and poured him a pint before going to wait on a group at the other end of the bar.

He sipped his beer slowly. It was true—he had been busy. He'd turned over one of his rental units, using the time between tenants to do some repairs and paint some of the rooms.

He'd also been writing. Not hours at a time or anything, but he'd made a point to write at least a few hundred words every day, just to work the muscle. It helped that it didn't feel like high stakes. His former agent, Doug Lemieux, had given up on him years ago, and he'd long since bought out his contract with the publishing house. This felt more like the early days, when he still worked a crappy daytime office job, writing at night and on the weekends. There was something freeing about not having a deadline over his head.

He thought about going back to the draft he'd been working on when Angeline died, but he hadn't quite had the emotional energy for that yet. Her fingerprints would be all over it, and right now he was happy to be working on something fresh.

Selena had been keeping him busy, too. She'd slept over nearly every night since the fundraiser. He'd slipped back into the routine of sharing his space with another person ridiculously easily. Selena was an undemanding housemate. She wasn't messy, probably because she didn't have much stuff to begin with, and she was gone twelve hours a day. If he didn't wake her with coffee and breakfast or have tea and a late supper waiting for her at the end of the day, he'd never see her.

She had a night shoot tonight, so he was on his own. He'd fallen back on The Cove out of habit. He'd been cooking more now that he had someone to cook for, and a mediocre hamburger wasn't as appealing when there was leftover pumpkin stew in the fridge.

"Can I get you something to eat?" Danica was back, sliding a piece of paper in front of him. "We've got some new stuff on the menu."

He peered at the addendum to the usual generic bar food. "Beet salad? Steak skewers? What's going on?"

She gave him a bright smile. "The new menu we're having designed. We're testing things before we decide on the final line-up."

The Cove's unexceptional food had been one of the things he'd liked about it. It was dependable. And now it was changing.

"You look different," Danica said, before he could decide if he wanted an experimental beet salad.

Change was in the air, it seemed.

He looked down. He was wearing sneakers and jeans, like always. Fall weather had finally arrived to stay, so he was wearing an old knit sweater with a hole in one elbow he'd been meaning to patch.

His clothes might not have changed, but he didn't feel the same. Six weeks ago, he'd been going through the motions of his life. Lately, he felt like what he did mattered, that he could make choices about his future.

He'd woken up after a long, dark night, and the dawn was more beautiful than he could have hoped for.

She frowned at him, searching his face, as if she could find some evidence to back up her claim. "New haircut," she declared.

He touched his temple. Oh, right. "Well, it was getting pretty shaggy." He'd had it trimmed earlier that day at the barbershop, and Maurice had convinced him to go with a slightly different look—sleek and clean around his ears, a little longer on top — and he'd acquiesced because he'd gotten tired of looking disheveled next to Selena's seemingly effortless professional polish.

"Suits you," she said. "Now, what's it going to be?"

He bravely ordered the beet salad and a burger, too. He'd forgotten to bring a book, so he got out his phone. His nephew's birthday was coming up, and he'd had the idea to text his sister to see what gift might be welcome.

He sent the text, noticed a missed one.

JOANNA

Dinner's on for the 9th. Be there. Dress nice.

He'd forgotten all about the dinner. Being busy had other perks. He'd banished the entire event to the back of his mind.

"Now there's the Warner I recognize," Danica said as she slid a surprisingly appetizing beet salad down the copper bar. "Your gloom cloud came back."

"My what?"

"You know that little shadow that follows you

around? It's like you travel with your own micro-climate."

"I do not have a gloom cloud," he snarled. "Don't you have someone else to wait on?"

"It's pretty slow tonight," she said breezily. "Our opening hours have been messed up lately with the show, and it's chased away our regulars. They'll come back when the *Sawyer's Cove* stuff dies down. So, what's up?"

He picked up his fork. Danica was one of the rare Misty Harbor residents who remembered Angie. They'd eaten a lot at The Cove while the kitchen at the house had some work done to it. Danica had been a bartender then, not the manager, and since she grew up in Misty Harbor, Angie always wanted to pick her brain about neighborhoods when she was looking at properties to buy.

Danica had even come to the funeral, the only one from Misty Harbor to do so, though they'd held it all the way down in New York so Angie could be buried at her family plot along with all the other Verdons who'd predeceased her, including her parents. There were a handful of Verdon cousins scattered around, but Angie had been on her own for a long time.

"Angie's friends are having a dinner next month in the city, and they've been hounding me to come. I know they mean well, but it puts me in a bad mood," he said.

"Ah," Danica said neutrally. "I gather it's not just any dinner."

"Joanna called it the anniversary. Five years since she

died. But aren't anniversaries supposed to be celebrations? It's like she wants to bring everyone together to say, 'Hooray, it's been five whole years since Angeline died in a car crash. My, how time flies,'" he said sourly.

Danica's expression hardened. "Warner, you know they want to celebrate her life, not her death."

She was right, he knew that. But he was confused. When all he had to do was mourn his wife and give in to the gloom that followed him everywhere, at least he knew what he was supposed to be feeling every minute of the day. Feeling like shit as a default made sense.

But since he'd allowed himself to feel something else, to be a different version of Warner who didn't constantly have a rain cloud over his head, things weren't so simple. He didn't know what to feel half the time. He didn't know how to feel happy and miss Angie and look forward to being with Selena and trust that things could maybe be better.

Could he be someone who remembered his wife with fondness, with love, and also someone who moved forward, opened himself up to new feelings, new experiences?

Maybe he'd been so on the fence about this dinner because it felt like a litmus test. It was either going to be the cap on a painful period in his life, or it was going to remind him how little progress he'd actually made. And he was afraid to find out which it would be.

· · ·

Late that night, he was in bed but awake when Selena tiptoed into the bedroom. He knew she liked to shower when she got home; he waited for her to get cleaned up for bed, and when she crept toward the dresser where she'd started keeping some of her clothes, he stopped her.

"Selena."

He flipped the sheets down, showing her his nakedness. Her gaze traveled over his body slowly. She bypassed the dresser and got into bed next to him, skin warm from the shower.

They said nothing. He kissed her pomegranate pink lips. She tasted, as ever, like mint. Would he ever be able to smell it again without thinking of her, the way lavender haunted him? He concentrated on the mint. He didn't want to think of Angie, not when he was with Selena.

He kissed her harder, rougher. When he was near Selena, her energy seemed to envelop him, turning him into someone else. Someone better. How did she do it? There was some strange alchemy at work, where Selena took all of his neuroses and calmed them, made him a man who was worthy of her.

It was a lot to put on her. He'd tried not to make this affair all about him. All about his healing, his heart. He'd tried not to make it about his heart at all.

But that was as futile as trying not to breathe. He'd slowly and surely been falling deeper and deeper into... something with Selena.

It wasn't love. It couldn't be love.

He knew what love felt like. He'd been struck by it, swiftly and irrevocably, when he'd met Angie and her sunshine golden hair had practically blinded him to anything, anyone else. There had been no one else for him after her. He'd been quite happy that way. It hadn't always been perfect, nothing ever was. But he'd loved her, her small quirks, her generous spirit, her ability to tackle any problem with grace and tenacity. The gobs of money she always had to throw around didn't hurt either. But he was certain even if she'd been raised without all the privileges of life on the Upper East Side, she'd have been the same at her core.

He'd loved Angie, and that's not what he felt for Selena. He liked Selena, he found her refreshing, a great challenge, light yet not insubstantial. She was serious about her work, took a frivolous thing very seriously because she knew it meant a lot to a lot of people, not only those who depended on the work she was creating to pay their rent, but to the millions of people who watched and loved the show.

Selena was impressive and imposing and approachable and fun. And she was like liquid fire in his hands, her hair sliding around the pillow as if it had a will of its own. Her body molded to him—everywhere he reached, he pressed into her flesh, and it gave satisfyingly. Her round hips, her thick thighs. He dipped his fingers into the soft, sweet well of nectar between her legs. She moaned and jerked against him, so he did it again, and again and again until she was a writhing mess.

"Please," she choked out. "Please. Warner. Take me."

"I'm going to," he promised. He arranged her the way he wanted her, and she let him, opening her legs easily. Her thighs were shiny and slick, and he bent his head down to lick at them. She shook under his mouth when he sealed it over her opening. She got so wet for him always, and he tasted it now, hungry for it, for her, until she was sobbing again.

"I need it," she said. "Please."

She said his name a final time, and he couldn't deny her any longer. He lined up and filled her in one stroke.

"Yes...yes..." She arched her body into a quivering bow. "There...right there."

"Here?" He plucked her clit ruthlessly.

She screamed, and he knew she was coming.

He rode it out until she pushed his hand away from her overstimulated clit, then he let himself go. One second he was holding on by a thread of control, the next he let the thread snap as a vicious orgasm burst through him, transferring all of his energy into the lovely, soft woman beneath him. He emptied himself into, felt her fill up with him, the sticky evidence of both their orgasms dampening the sheets.

Breathing hard, he got himself under control, cleaned them up with a handful of tissues.

She shimmied up the bed on what was becoming her side. He was being pushed to the left side after years of intentionally choosing the middle. Her head hit the pillow firmly.

"Holy fuck, Warner, that was intense."

He grabbed a pair of boxers from the dresser. "Want

anything?" He meant clothes, or water, or the entire world.

"I'm good," she said, sounding on the edge of sleep.

His stomach flipped realizing she was going to sleep naked. He turned off the light and got into bed next to her.

She sighed softly, a sign that she was about to fall into dreamland. But then she opened her eyes a crack. "I like your haircut."

"Thanks."

He'd never been a touchy-feely sleeper, but he found himself snuggling up close to her seductive collection of curves, a hand on her hip, reassurance that she was real as they fell asleep.

Chapter Twenty-One

ERIKA: According to my sources, they're going to wrap shooting in mid-November, and we're already seeing promos for the first episode, which drops on Christmas Day.

JULES: I think they're dropping the first two on Christmas Day, then doing one a week for eight more weeks.

ERIKA: So I should tell my family I'm not available that day, right? I'm going to be too busy freaking out and watching those first two episodes on repeat to open presents.

JULES: Oh yeah, Christmas is definitely canceled in my house this year. I'm already getting the only present I want—more *Sawyer's Cove*.

ERIKA: So I should return the convertible I bought you?

JULES: We live in Seattle. Forget the convertible. I'd take a Range Rover, though.

FROM THE SAWYER'S COVE REWATCH PROJECT PODCAST: HALLOWEEN REBOOT NEWS DEEP DIVE

October seemed to pass in a blur of long days on set and short nights in Warner's bed. Weekends were a mix of catching up on work and getting cozy with Warner in his den, which often led to more time in bed. As November got underway, Selena was feeling the consequences of burning the candle at both ends. She'd gone into this shoot knowing it would be intense, but she hadn't counted on getting a boyfriend for the duration. Men were time-consuming, which was one of the reasons she didn't have a dedicated partner. The fact that Warner was temporary—he'd stay in Misty Harbor when she left in a few weeks to go back to Los Angeles and her real life—only made it seem imperative that they spend as much time together as possible now.

He wasn't officially her boyfriend, but when they were within the walls of his house, he certainly acted the part. He cooked for her, asked her about work, told her funny stories from his childhood. They had sex almost every night. She supposed he was making up for lost time in that department, but she wasn't complaining. The downside to not having time for a romantic partner was the lack of regular sex. There was nothing like an orgasm to give her a good night's sleep.

Suddenly, she had another reason for wanting the show to get picked up for a second season. That would bring her back to Misty Harbor. Back to Warner. Perhaps they could do some sort of long-distance thing in the interim. Cami sort of lived here now, too, so it wasn't so wild to think she might come here for business meetings and brainstorming sessions.

But Warner hadn't said anything about the future, and it hadn't been part of their original bargain. It wasn't like her not to be direct and just ask, but still, she held her tongue. She told herself it was because she had more pressing things to take care of, but she was worried it was because she wouldn't like his answer.

One of those pressing things was the next batch of journalists the studio was sending to set. They were coming later today, and she wasn't looking forward to having to deal with them when they had a really complicated scene to shoot, but Becca assured her she had everything under control.

They were coming closer to locking the script for the finale. She and Cami had decided if they had time, they'd shoot an alternate ending they could hold in reserve once the verdict was in on the second season.

She had hoped based on the strength of the early cuts of the first few episodes, which she'd been working on remotely with the editors back in L.A., the studio might take a leap of faith and order the second season early, but they hadn't. She was trying not to take it personally.

Another thing that crept up on her was the weather. Gone were the warm humid days of late summer, as well as the crisp sunny mornings and rainbow colors of October. November had brought the cold.

She was freezing as she walked from the main house

to the pool house, where she'd left the warm coat she'd brought but hadn't yet needed. She'd worked in cold climates before, and she despised being cold, so she'd made a point to bring her warmest coat. Her thin sweater wasn't enough to ward off the chill by the time she got to the pool house. It was dark and still inside. She'd barely been there in weeks. She didn't miss eating microwaved meals from the mini fridge, but it was strange to think she was technically paying for a space she wasn't using. Or rather the studio was, since she had a housing stipend.

She found her jacket in the bedroom, realized she hadn't brought gloves or a hat to Connecticut, and wondered if there'd be time to run to the drugstore today to get some. She passed back into the main living space, looked out the window the way she used to when she first got here and was so full of questions about the mysterious man in the big house.

She smiled to herself. He was much less mysterious now. She knew how he liked his coffee, his weakness for sticky buns—anything caramel, in fact—how he took care of her, and his home, and the homes of the people he rented to. He was good with his hands, not only in the garden or the kitchen, but also when he was touching her and bringing her pleasure.

He was writing again—that was the most interesting thing of all. They'd even spent a couple of Sundays on their computers together, working silently in tandem, the soothing twin *clacks* of the keyboards the only sound in the room.

But there was still so much she didn't know about him. Was he over his wife? Was their affair all about expedience? Would he even care when she left?

When Warner was simply a fascinating mystery man with intense eyes and a swimmer's body, she wouldn't have cared about any of those things. But now that she knew what a good person he was, knew how good he made her feel, well. She might have gotten in a little bit over her head.

She locked up behind her, returned to the house to get her work stuff. Warner was writing in the den.

"Dinner later?" he asked when she came in and gave him a goodbye kiss on the cheek.

"I probably have to do dinner with those journalists."

"All right. That reminds me—I have to go to the city next week."

That stopped her. She'd never known Warner to go anywhere farther than Southville, the town next door. "The city? As in New York City?"

"The very one," he said. "Some of Angie's friends are getting together for, well, it'll be five years next Wednesday. They want to mark the date."

She swallowed. That was a big date to remember. She looked hard at Warner, but his face didn't betray any emotion about it at all. She visualized her calendar. They were filming the big carnival scene. A real-life carnival company had been contracted to set up a Ferris wheel on the boardwalk by the beach at the end of Main Street. It was going to be the biggest set piece of the series, the backdrop for the comedy of errors that was to be the penultimate episode before the threads all got tied up in the finale.

"I'll be shooting the carnival next Wednesday," she said.

His eyebrows drew together slightly, and she realized it hadn't even occurred to him to ask her to go with him. Which was fine. They weren't in a relationship, not a traditional one anyway. She had nothing to do with his dead wife, except for taking up the same space in Warner's life, wearing Angeline's earrings and bathing in her tub. Sleeping in her bed, next to her husband.

"Never mind," she said, pulse suddenly racing. She had no claim to him, but she could have given him moral support. But why should he ask her to come with him on a hundred-and-fifty-mile journey when they'd never so much as gone out for lunch together?

She hadn't quite realized it, but except for the time she'd accidentally run into him at The Cove, which was before they'd started up, she'd never even seen him outside of his property. Oh yeah, there was the time he'd driven her to a party and let her attend alone.

There were rules to this game. And she'd forgotten the main one. That this was temporary. That either of them could walk away at any time and no one's feelings would be hurt, because they weren't supposed to be feeling anything for each other in the first place.

She tried to shove a smile on her face by force of will. She hadn't gotten this far in Hollywood by throwing tantrums. She showed up, she did what she had to do to get in the room, and then she worked harder than anyone else to stay in the room and get invited to the next one. She had lots of practice pretending to be okay with shitty situations.

She just never thought she'd have to pretend around Warner, the only man she'd ever felt she could be her entire self with.

"I'll see you later," she said, putting her head down and walking out of the den.

"Selena, wait." He'd left his computer and was following her to the kitchen door. "What's wrong?"

"Nothing." She gathered her things, including the travel mug of coffee Warner had prepared for her. He could make her coffee, but he didn't want to be seen in public with her. Was it sick that she'd accept those terms because she liked him so much?

"It's not nothing," he said, surprising her by pushing back. They were experts at giving each other space, at leaving things alone.

She sighed. Perhaps she was being melodramatic. She'd always been able to say anything to him, so why was she censoring herself now?

Because I don't want to lose him. The thought surprised her, but she knew it was true.

"I have to go to work," she said, unwilling to start off on the wrong foot with the journalists by being late. "But think about this, Warner. I'm flying back to L.A. as soon as the shoot ends. You never have to see me again, because I literally won't be living with you anymore. But what if you do want to see me? How would that work?

I'd be willing to talk about it, but we've never even gone on a date. Something tells me a cross-country relationship isn't exactly on your mind. Which is fine." She rubbed at her chest, which had gotten suddenly achy at the thought of never seeing him again. "But I guess I was hoping—or not even hoping—I didn't expect to feel this way. And it's okay if you don't feel the same way. Just something to think about."

She waited a beat, but he didn't say anything. He was processing, but she didn't have time to wait around for him to let her down easy. She had work to do.

She walked out the door, and he didn't stop her.

Chapter Twenty-Two

Those involved in production on revived teen soap *Sawyer's Cove* are keeping the possible storylines of the reboot tightly under wraps, but fan speculation centers on the newest cast members, played by Stephanie Mae, Glen Michaelson, and unknown Henry Yu. Some fans are wondering if the casting of Mae and Yu is an effort to balance out the largely white original cast, and some are wondering if freshman showrunner Selena Echeveria is going too far to modernize a beloved classic.

— "Cove Casting Causes Controversy"
by John O'Toole

The journalists were driving Selena a little batty. Hillary, from an established entertainment website, was all right. She seemed like a genuine fan of the show and asked intelligent questions, but John from the television blog was a different story. He was snarky from the get-go. Selena bristled at some of his remarks but had so far held her tongue, sucking hard on her mint instead of taking his bait.

Becca ushered them from the office to the stage, where they were scheduled to watch some filming before doing a few sit-down interviews with the cast. Selena had asked Nash and Ariel to spend the most time with them. Jay's return to acting after twelve years was big news, but they were saving the big story on him until closer to the premiere date. Cami was shooting on location today with Crosby. Stephanie, Henry, and Glen were in the scene that was shooting today. It was the first scene of the season with all three of them, so Selena was interested in how this would play out. The three new Cove kids, as they'd come to be known, had immense off-screen chemistry. They were all around the same age, and even though Henry was new to TV acting, he'd easily adapted, with the more experienced Steph and Glen helping him out.

"This scene is in the third to last episode," Selena said as they approached the stage. "Grace and Kai and Danny are scheming. They feel like it's their fault that Parker and Amy are fighting, and they want to fix it."

"Are you mostly shooting in order?" Hillary asked.

"We're shooting the episodes consecutively as best

we can, but because we're doing the entire series at once, we have a tiny bit of leeway if we needed to go back and reshoot something from an earlier episode. That's the benefit of having all the actors here for an extended period of time. Scheduling is easier, and they develop a real camaraderie on the set."

They watched the actors work with the director on blocking for a little while. Selena was able to ignore her feelings about Warner and focus on her job because she loved seeing how smoothly things were going. By now, production was a well-oiled machine.

"What about Henry Yu? What's the story with him? A complete unknown. Did you simply not want Stephanie Mae to be the only Asian American in the cast?" John asked bluntly.

She stared at John. "Henry was the standout of those we auditioned for the part of Kai. And as you know, *Sawyer's Cove* has a history of casting unknowns." Jay Orlando had been a complete novice when he was cast almost as a stunt in the original show.

"What about Hispanic representation?" John added. "You're a Hispanic showrunner, why didn't you include any characters with that background in this show?"

There was a silence as Selena tried to figure out what to say. She wasn't normally at a loss for words, but she felt her face heat uncomfortably as the guy waited for his answer.

"Representation in casting isn't about ticking off boxes and making sure you have one from column A and two from column B. We cast the best people for the roles," she said. It was true, and it wasn't true, which everyone in the room knew. More than sheer talent went into casting. There was lobbying from everyone along the food chain, from the studio executives to the agents, to the casting directors, to the actors themselves. Stephanie Mae had a resume a mile long—her name recognition was a big reason she got the part. Henry Yu happened to have that boyish appeal, Parker Wild 2.0, they were looking for. And since Stephanie had name recognition, they could afford to go with an unknown for the other part.

She could have told John all of this, but she didn't feel like explaining herself to him when she knew he was purposefully picking at the casting.

"Besides," she added, "representation is important behind the camera, too." She'd said there were no boxes to check, but she had made an effort to hire people with different backgrounds and levels of experience below the line.

"It's just sad to see a show like *Sawyer's Cove* feel like it has to twist itself into something it's not to appease modern-day cancel culture," John said loudly.

She narrowed her eyes at him. "What does that mean?"

"I mean, identity politics has gone too far when a show about Connecticut teenagers feels like it has to cast diverse actors in order not to be canceled."

She was starting to get mad now. "You think Connecticut small towns aren't diverse?" She'd lived in Misty Harbor for weeks now, and she'd met people who'd grown up there, had moved there, had moved away and then come back. There were people who looked like the original Cove kids, mostly white, mostly straight, mostly rich. And there were some who looked like her, and Becca, and Bo, and Jay. Misty Harbor wasn't Cloudy Cove, but it was full of good people who'd opened their arms to the production, even when it meant delays and interruptions to their normal routine.

John didn't answer her; just stood there and smirked. Vaguely, she registered Becca's worried frown and the other journalist's sharp gaze.

"We're telling a story about growing up, about second chances. Those are universal stories. Is representation important? Yes, of course. But one TV series is not going to fix all of Hollywood's problems. Teen shows are about figuring out who you are. They're a product of their time. That's what makes them special. Has *Sawyer's Cove* changed? Yes. But that's because the culture has changed. We wouldn't be much good as a cultural touchstone if we lived in a bubble. *Sawyer's Cove* always addressed hard questions about identity and belonging, and we're still doing that. I'd invite you to watch the original show. Was it perfect? Do some things we thought were good ideas fifteen years ago seem cringy now? Yes. But that's life. I'd rather us keep trying, imperfectly, than to give up and pretend change isn't possible. Things have changed, thank God. And they'll keep changing. This reboot will probably seem cringeworthy in another fifteen years. And that's okay. We're making something that's both a reflection of culture and an attempt to improve on reality. And if you don't get that, or you think we cast Steph and Henry out of some cynical attempt at diversity, then you are wrong."

Becca, dear, sweet Becca, was trying to clap while not letting go of her ubiquitous tablet. Hillary looked serious, scribbling notes in her notebook. John's smile looked forced; his lip curled unpleasantly.

She wanted to know how much trouble she'd be in if she threw him off set. His mind had been made up before he stepped foot in Misty Harbor. What had the studio's marketing people been thinking sending him here? But in the end, she gathered her composure.

"Becca will take you to do some one-on-one interviews. I have a meeting." She left with her head held high and walked to the door as fast as she could without it seeming like she was running away.

Her heart was beating fast, and she decided to get her shit together in the conference room. She knew Becca wouldn't bring John or Hillary back there.

Cami was there, though, looking at her laptop. She wore street clothes, but her face was still fully made up.

"Are you and Crosby done already?"

"Nailed everything in two takes, baby," Cami said, looking up from her computer. "What's wrong?"

"Nothing. That stupid blogger got under my skin."

Cami made a sympathetic face. "Let me talk to the next one."

"It's not only that. It's Warner." Cami was the only person in her life who knew how far things with Warner had gotten.

"What about Warner?"

"Remember how I told you his wife died and he's still kind of hung up on her, or not hung up on her, just out of practice with normal human interaction?"

"Yep," Cami said.

"It'll have been five years since she died next week, and her friends are having a dinner in New York. Warner's driving down for it. He didn't ask me to go, and it's not that I necessarily want to meet all his wife's friends, but don't you think he'd even consider asking me? Am I delusional? Am I one of those women who ignores red flags thinking she can change the guy into someone who's capable of a real relationship?"

"Okay, hold on. First of all, it's tough to be in a relationship with a person who's lost someone they loved so tragically. I don't envy you that."

"Thanks." Selena suddenly felt bad for complaining. It wasn't Warner's fault he was a widower.

"Second, do you want to change Warner?"

"No. I like him the way he is. That's the problem. I like him so much, and no one except you even knows we're seeing each other."

"Then maybe you should talk about going public. The sneaking around secret affair thing can be fun— Jay and I got a lot of mileage out of that when we first got together—but eventually, you're going to have to move your relationship into the open. If he's not able to do that, then you have to decide if that's a dealbreaker."

"Honey, you and Jay might have thought you were

keeping things on the DL when you got together, but I'm pretty sure the entire cast and crew knew by day two."

"Really?" Cami's rouged cheeks turned pinker. "Well. That was a long time ago. We were dumb kids."

"But I think you're right. I need to find out if he's ever going to want to take this to prime time."

"All you have to do is ask."

Selena sighed. "I only wish I knew what the answer would be."

Chapter Twenty-Three

In a candid look behind the scenes of the new, but perhaps not improved, *Sawyer's Cove*, showrunner Selena Echeveria had some choice words for fans of the teen soap. Calling the original show "cringeworthy" and confessing to the way this franchise aged poorly, some are left wondering, why even bother to revive this property at all?

— *"Sawyer's Cove's* Echeveria: 'This reboot will seem cringeworthy in fifteen years.'" by John O'Toole

She and Warner didn't talk about that morning's conversation when she got into bed that night. She still felt raw after her rant to the journalists, and he didn't ask her any questions, simply folded his arms around her when she burrowed close to him, asking him wordlessly for comfort.

The next morning, she woke up before Warner, a rare occurrence. She'd slept well and was thankful work stress hadn't resulted in a barrage of bad dreams. She still needed her coffee, but she felt rested. The blackout shades always made it hard to know what time it was when they woke up, but there was weak gray light coming through the door to the bathroom, enough to see Warner's face by.

He looked younger in sleep. Untroubled. She wondered if he dreamed of Angeline at night. Was he still married to her in his sleep, and when he woke up in the morning did he have to remember all over again that she was gone? Selena had never set out to compete with a dead woman, but she felt a little frustrated that she'd never win an argument against her.

She didn't want Warner to suffer. She knew he'd always have some feelings for his wife, but that didn't mean he couldn't give her what she needed. There was no cap on love.

But that presumed he loved her at all.

She zipped her lips together, repressing a scream. She did not need this right now. The show was more important than anything going on in her personal life. She had shit to deal with on the set, with the studio. They were suddenly half a day behind on this episode. They were running out of time.

She was running out of time with Warner. Did she

really want to spend the rest of her stay in Misty Harbor fighting with him over something he probably wasn't capable of giving her?

She took a deep breath to steady her resolve. She wasn't going to lie to him; she respected him too much to do that. But she didn't have to push the issue, despite Cami's advice just to ask him. She would keep things between them status quo. They could enjoy their last couple of weeks together. They could make memories she'd take with her back to L.A. Maybe she'd call him when she saw his next book on the shelves at her favorite bookstore, because she had no doubt he was going to finish his book, and that it would be as entertaining and re-readable as *Gunsmoke*. She'd read it and remember their brief affair with fondness. It was more than a lot of people got.

Warner shifted, his eyes slitting open.

"Morning," he mumbled. His hair was sticking up like a baby chicken's feathers. She indulged the urge to smooth it back, drawing her fingers through the soft strands, lightly scratching his scalp. He hummed. She stroked down the nape of his neck, felt the warm muscles of his shoulders bunch and flex under her hand. He was such an odd man.

And she'd fallen in love with him.

"Morning," she said, belatedly. She couldn't tell him. She might never be able to tell him.

She swallowed down the unexpected pain that speared through her chest like a tangible thing.

She kissed him to cover up the sob that wanted to

escape. She wondered if the kiss felt different to him. Could he feel her love? Her despair?

The kiss felt different to her; sweeter, softer. She wanted to draw it out. She wanted it to last forever.

The carnival was nearly ready. They were going to do some scenes this afternoon, then break and come back for night shoots. Selena was glad for so much going on at work, because it made saying goodbye to Warner easier. He'd left for New York in the minivan around the same time she'd left for the set. He'd seemed awkward, more awkward than usual.

"There are lasagna leftovers in the fridge," he'd said as they stood in the driveway next to their respective vehicles, keys in hand, his overnight bag already loaded inside. "And a frozen chicken pot pie you could make if you want."

"I won't starve in the two days you're gone. I promise," she'd said, smiling even though she wanted to shake him. Didn't he see that everything he did showed her he cared? Didn't he see what that meant?

But she'd said nothing, though the "I love you" felt as if it was burning in her mouth, scalding her like a sip of too-hot coffee. She swallowed it down, gave him a hug and kiss goodbye. It was only two days, but the separation felt like a dress rehearsal for the permanent one they'd have once production was over.

He'd left first, the minivan rumbling down Blue Bird

Lane. She could pretend he was only going to the nursery or the Bakeshop if she wanted. She didn't need to be so melodramatic to feel as if she was never going to see him again.

She got in her own car and ordered herself to get her head in the game. Filming on location combined with elaborate sets involving carnival rides and lots of extras was the most complicated challenge they'd had so far. The director, Christine Carlson, was a veteran. The script was tight. The crew were pros. Selena shouldn't have this anxious ball in her stomach.

Her phone pinged when she was a mile out from the boardwalk. She made it a rule not to check her phone while she was driving, but it pinged again. And again. The ball of anxiety grew. Somehow, she knew those pings were bad news.

She forced herself to keep driving, found the parking spots they had cordoned off for the crew in the municipal lot by the boardwalk, and shut off the car. With shaking hands, she picked up her phone. There was no reason to believe the pings had anything to do with Warner. He was fine. He drove like a grandpa in a safe vehicle. She looked at her notifications. Becca had texted her three times, Cami twice. Nothing from or about Warner.

She blew out a hot breath, looked at the texts.

BECCA

We have a situation with John O'Toole's article.

She'd included a link. Selena clicked on it. The headline, starkly black letters on a white background, made her stomach churn almost in triumph, as if it was saying, "Told you there was something to worry about."

She skimmed the article. It was about as bad as she had expected from the title, a mass of insinuations that the show was too woke for its own good, that the casting pandered to a certain segment of the population, that Selena Echeveria's first job as showrunner was going to be a cringeworthy disaster—she'd said so herself, after all.

One article did not make or break a show, she was aware, but this was the kind of thing that would be in everyone's feeds for at least a day. It might be the only thing they heard about the show, the only impression of it they'd get before they made up their minds to watch it or not.

"Shit."

She jumped in her seat at a tap on her window. Cami was there, pale under her camera makeup. She stepped back so Selena could get out of the car.

"Did you read it?" Cami asked.

"I read it."

"We're going to have to figure out how to respond. What an asshole. What was Brad thinking sending him to set? He had to know something like this would happen."

"Maybe he thought all publicity is good publicity?" Selena didn't know what the studio suits wanted from her. She'd done everything they asked, jumped through every hoop, made herself big when she needed to be big and small when she needed to be small. She'd done the impossible and gone from an assistant with no industry connections to a showrunner in fifteen years. She'd shown up, she'd worked hard, and she was making the best goddamn TV show she knew how to make. Nonsense like this was par for the course in this crazy, mixed-up industry, but it still made her want to rail at the system for being so fucked up.

She looked at Cami, who looked scared more than angry. Impulsively, she hugged her friend. "Hey, it's going to be okay. This is one article. Hillary's spread is going to be super positive, and that doesn't come out until next month."

Cami hugged her back. "Okay. I know. It's not a big deal. It just feels shitty."

Selena released her from the hug but put her arm around Cami's shoulders so they could walk to the tent together, a united front. "It does. But he's an idiot. And our show is going to be awesome."

"Did you really call the show cringeworthy?" Cami said. "Because we could sue him for misquoting you, or something."

Selena winced. "It was out of context. I had a whole eloquent speech about the old show and the new show, and I don't even know what I said, but yeah, I think that line was in there somewhere. But not like he made it seem."

"I know exactly what you said," Becca said, walking

up to meet them, her ever-present tablet on her arm. "I recorded the whole thing, actually."

"You what?"

"I probably should have asked you first. But I didn't trust him. I didn't like the direction his questions were going, so I hit record on my tablet when you guys were talking the other day. Just in case."

"Becca, did you know you're going to be running the studio one of these days?"

"That's the plan."

"How does a recording help us with this jerk?" Cami asked.

"You have to listen to Selena, Cami," Becca said. "She was so passionate, so magnificent. I think maybe we leak the audio of her responding to his snarky comment and let the Internet do the rest. When the fans hear her defending the show so beautifully, they'll rally, I know they will."

Selena wasn't sure this plan was a smart one. She'd have her voice out there, on the record, forever. The Internet never forgot. She was much more comfortable behind the scenes.

"I don't know. That seems extreme," she said, glancing at Cami.

"The fans made this reboot happen, remember?" Cami said. "I think we should trust them to defend it against bozos like this."

Selena fumbled in her pocket for her roll of mints and popped two in her mouth. "How would we even go about it?"

"The less you know, the better," Becca said cheerfully. "I'll take care of it, okay?"

"Okay," Selena echoed, her stomach diving again. It wasn't that she didn't trust Becca; this situation just felt like it was spiraling out of her control.

"You and Cami focus on the shoot," Becca said.

Cami pulled Selena toward the tent. "You heard the woman. We have great television to make."

Chapter Twenty-Four

Erika: One thing I always wanted was an episode where
the Cove kids all go to New York.

Jules: Ooh, good call. It's only a few hours from Cloudy
Cove, right? They could take a train.

Erika: Or pile into the North family Wagoneer and road
trip it.

Jules: It would have been awesome to see our small-
town kids in a big city.

Erika: We should mention this idea to Camille Corsair
or Selena Echeveria if we ever meet them.

Jules: Totally.

From *The Sawyer's Cove Rewatch Project Podcast: Top
Ten Episodes Show*

The midweek, midday drive from Misty Harbor to
lower Manhattan went surprisingly quickly. Too

quickly. Warner was checked into his hotel by three o'clock. Dinner wasn't until seven.

He hadn't been back to New York since Angie's funeral, but the city seemed the same, loud and crowded, exciting and tension-inducing. He'd lived here for years, but it had never quite felt like home. During college, he'd felt like a duckling swimming frantically around a giant lake, trying to get his bearings, make friends, learn something from his teachers. Then he'd met Angie and she'd unlocked a different side of the city—shows and museums and out-of-the-way restaurants. He'd learned about the city through her, had never truly had to navigate it on his own. After college, they moved into the apartment that had been owned by her family since the Depression. Sure, he had his favorite bagel place and coffee shop to write in, but everything else was shared. Their regular restaurants. Their dentist. He didn't know how to be a single person in the city.

A traitorous part of his brain reminded him he wouldn't have been a single person if he'd brought Selena with him.

God, he was so sick of himself. He was sick of being the loser on the barstool, wearing wrinkled clothes and drinking away his evenings. He'd been able to escape from that version of himself while Selena was in his life, and when she left, he'd be the same old Warner, with the gloom cloud following him around.

Well, fuck that. He didn't have to be that Warner anymore. He marched down Prince Street and went into the first men's clothing store he saw. The shop employee took one look at him and immediately pulled six things off the rack, ordered him into a dressing room, and told him to take everything off and put half of what he'd given him on.

He walked out an hour later with the clothes he'd walked in with balled up in the bottom of a shopping bag under some of his purchases. The rest of the things he wore out, a pair of gray slacks and a crisp light blue Oxford underneath a new thin black cashmere sweater. It was all similar to what he normally wore, only new and sleek and about ten times more expensive. Shoes next. He went to the shop the man from the first store had recommended, came out in a pair of comfortable black lace-ups, a second pair in brown in yet another bag.

His haircut still looked all right, but he dropped his purchases at the hotel and found a barbershop that gave him a shave. When he walked up to the restaurant at 6:59, he felt polished and, if not new, then at least presentable.

Joanna was there with her husband, Bruno. She gave him a tight, longer than socially acceptable hug. His eyes were only burning a little by the end of it.

"Thanks for coming."

"Of course," he said awkwardly, as if she hadn't had to badger him into it.

He shook hands with Bruno, then Daphne and her longtime boyfriend arrived. Joanna and Daphne had been Angie's college roommates and the friends she'd kept up the most with as everyone's lives went in different directions. They went inside and were seated at a reserved rectangular table. Warner counted three empty chairs.

"Who else are we waiting for?"

"Doug and Charlie," Daphne said, ushering him to the seat at the head of the table.

"Doug Lemieux?" He hoped he was wrong.

"Yeah, didn't Joanna mention it?"

"No." He felt slightly stunned.

"I did so," Joanna countered. "I emailed you the final guest list a couple of days ago to let you know Megan and Jill couldn't make it." Megan was Angie's friend from high school. She and her wife Jill both traveled a lot for work. "And Doug and Charlie could. And there they are."

Warner turned and saw a man a couple of years older than him, smartly turned out in a black suit with a purple shirt that on Warner would have looked clownish but on Doug looked elegant. His boyfriend, Charlie, was less formal in slacks and a sweater, like Warner.

"Doug. Charlie," Warner said, trying not to freak out. He wished for the twentieth time that day that Selena was there with him. She would have smoothed over the moment. It wasn't every day he came face-to-face with his former book agent. Doug was the man who'd believed in him and *Gunsmoke* enough that he'd held out for an auction, garnering one of the largest advances for a detective thriller in years. The man who'd helped make it a bestseller. And the man who'd never once pushed him to sell the ancillary rights when Warner told him no. The man who'd cried buckets at Angie's funeral. Over the course of Warner's short career, Doug had become more than an agent; he'd become a friend. A friend Warner had disappointed by never writing the follow-up to *Gunsmoke*. A friend he'd been thinking of reaching out to, now that he had the vague idea of the story taking shape under his fingers every day at the keyboard.

Here he was, as if the universe was listening. Or maybe it was Angie, working her magic as usual, pushing people together, giving them what they didn't know they needed.

"Warner." Doug stopped in front of him, eyed him critically, then put his arms around him in a hug so emphatic, Warner literally felt the air pushed out of his lungs. "It's good to see you, my friend."

"Hi," he said when he got his breath back. "I wasn't expecting to see you two."

"We're honored to be included," Doug said, sitting down on Warner's left.

He lowered himself into his seat mechanically, out of place at the head of the table, feeling a spotlight on him, though everyone else around the table seemed at ease, talking amongst themselves, removing jackets and scarves, stowing purses, laughing and exclaiming over one thing or another. Joanna let out a peal of laughter, and Warner winced. He thought this was supposed to be a somber affair. Weren't they there to commemorate a death?

"Warner, how was your trip down from Connecticut?" Charlie asked. He was a smiley fellow, his bright teeth shining in the well-lit restaurant. Warner frowned. He didn't want to make small talk, as if this was just another night on the town with friends. He had precious few of those anyway.

Charlie's smile faltered the longer Warner glared at him, and he felt the heads of everyone around the table swiveling to look at him, to judge him, the dour widower who didn't know how to have fun.

He heard Danica's words echo in his head. They were there to celebrate a life. Angie had touched the lives of everyone at this table. If Angie could have seen him now, she would have swatted his arm and told him to lighten up. He was being a churlish brat. He forced himself to relax, starting with his clenched jaw and going down his body, muscle by muscle, until his toes wriggled in his new shoes.

"It was uneventful," he said, about a minute too late. "Thanks. How's..."

He wracked his brain to remember something about Charlie's life he could inquire about. Why was talking to people so hard? It wasn't hard when it was Selena. The conversation between them was never stilted, never ordinary. She was easy to talk to, and she sparked idea after idea in him. But she wasn't there. He remembered Charlie had a twin brother.

"...your brother?"

Charlie's smile returned. "Chris is doing really well. Thanks for asking. He's got a new job at an art therapy nonprofit and loves it."

Belatedly, he remembered Charlie's brother was intellectually disabled. "That's wonderful."

"He's living with Doug and me now, since our mom passed last year." Charlie's smile dimmed.

"Oh, I didn't know, I'm so sorry," he said.

"It had been a while coming," Charlie said. "But thanks."

Warner wished he'd known. He could have sent flowers. He supposed it wasn't too late. Maybe he could send a donation to the art therapy center Chris worked at. Money helped alleviate guilt, didn't it?

"Anyway, it was an excellent excuse to sell our tiny apartment and get someplace bigger," Charlie went on.

"You guys moved?"

"Got ourselves a fixer-upper Park Slope brownstone," Doug said. "Because we are gluttons for punishment, apparently. We've got workers traipsing in and out every single day."

"It's a lot, but it's going to be so beautiful when we're finished," Charlie said. "Chris has his own floor, with a kitchen and everything. I've got a better commute to work, and Doug's eventually going to have an office at home."

"I'm so glad for you," Warner said. Everyone's lives had changed so much, and he'd kept himself out of the loop. What had he expected—that the world would be frozen in time while he moldered away Miss Havisham-style in Misty Harbor?

The server came, and after some discussion, they ordered drinks. Once upon a time, Warner had had a favorite order here, but the menu seemed to have changed. That was the theme of the evening. Life went on, even when you didn't want it to. He ordered a glass of red. No one seemed interested in getting a bottle of anything. Of course, they all had children, responsibilities. He alone was the single one, without so much as a goldfish to depend on him.

He glanced at the empty chair. He supposed it was symbolic, a place for Angie. But he could have brought Selena. She would have been very comfortable around these people, would have thought them interesting and easy to talk to, and she would have impressed them with her cool job and confidence. He would have loved to watch her eyes light up and hands move when she was really animated about something. He would have been so proud to have her there as his...what? Girlfriend? They hadn't talked about it, mostly because he hadn't brought it up again after she'd seemed to let it go. He hadn't known what to say. He hadn't known what she wanted to hear.

But she wasn't there. And he was faced with the consequences of his own bad decision-making once again.

Conversation moved quickly, and Warner slid into something resembling comfort. He hadn't seen most of these people in years, but being around Selena had oiled his rusty hinges, made conversation come more quickly to his lips. Writing, too, had sharpened his reflexes.

The wine helped mellow his nerves. Then the food came out. He didn't even know what he'd ordered, but plate after plate was delivered from the kitchen, and everyone talked over everyone else as they passed things around family-style.

"Charlie says you're writing a book," Daphne said, and Warner nearly dropped his forkful of tempura cauliflower in surprise. How the hell did Charlie know that? Before he could answer, Doug spoke.

"I'm trying," he said. "I thought I knew how hard writing was after fifteen years in this business, but it turns out it's easier to polish something when it's not your own work. Who knew?" He smiled self-deprecatingly. "But it's not all bad. I have an editor friend who wants first look. At the rate I'm going, that'll be sometime in the next decade, but it's fine."

"What's the book about?" Daphne's husband said, taking the words out of Warner's mouth.

Doug cast a sideways glance at Warner before he said, "It's about a mystery writer who gets caught up in a real-life mystery. It's kind of meta, but it's solidly genre fiction."

"Sounds intriguing," Warner said.

Doug turned to him. "It was Angie who gave me the idea, about a million years ago. I put it off long enough, and then when I had that heart thing a couple of years ago, I decided I was done procrastinating. The first draft took me a couple of months. This second draft has taken more than a year. But it'll be done someday."

What heart thing? Jo had never mentioned it. God, he was such an asshole. He could make amends for that later. "Angie always had the best ideas. That's terrific, Doug. I'd love to read it, too."

Doug looked surprised. "Really?"

"It would be a privilege."

"I'll send you the latest draft, if you really mean it."

"Do that. I'll read it, and we can do lunch." It was past time he made some effort with people he'd like to keep in his life. "I'll come back down to the city."

Doug smiled. "I'd like that."

"And, uh." He glanced around the rest of the table, but everyone else was deep in conversation about something else. "I've been writing, too."

Doug's smile grew broader. "Seriously?"

"It's new. And rough. But it feels like it might be something."

"Another Jake Wilton novel?"

"Yeah. But a little different."

"No pressure, Warner, but that is fantastic. Let me know if I can help with anything."

"You'd do that?"

"I'm still your agent, aren't I?"

"Well—"

"Because you never officially fired me, and I never officially dropped you. So you're stuck with me."

"I really don't deserve a second chance from you," he said, still feeling the weight of his selfish indifference.

"Everyone deserves a second chance," Doug said warmly, raising his wine glass.

Warner fervently hoped so. He raised his own glass and touched Doug's lightly. "I'll drink to that."

And if it was true, perhaps Selena would grant him one as well.

Chapter Twenty-Five

JULES: This guy needs to be fired.

ERIKA: Seriously. Is this what passes for journalism these days? Out of context quotes and innuendo?

JULES: Why does this John O'Toole guy have it out for the show anyway?

ERIKA: He's just looking for clicks.

JULES: Well, he got them. About ten thousand negative comments on his stupid post by actual fans of the show.

ERIKA: I hate to reward him with negative attention, but at least we got someone from our team leaking that awesome audio of Selena Echeveria. She's the coolest.

JULES: I'm even more sure that the show is in the right hands after today.

ERIKA: We love you, Selena!

FROM THE SAWYER'S COVE REWATCH PROJECT PODCAST: SPECIAL DROP

"Let's go one last time," Christine, the director of the episode, said.

Selena shivered. It was cold by the Atlantic Ocean in the middle of the night in November. This felt like the longest day of her life. She'd started it off by saying goodbye to Warner, and she was ending it by stamping her feet to stay warm as she watched the monitor behind the camera. This would have to be the last shot of the day, before their time ran out with the union workers, and the town, too, who'd agreed to let them keep the lights on until midnight.

Stephanie and Henry were in line at the Ferris wheel. They'd already done the more complicated shots of them riding around the wheel with a smaller, more portable camera. This was a simpler shot of them getting into the Ferris wheel car.

"Roll sound," Christine called.

One of the crew answered, "Sound speeds."

"Roll camera."

"Camera speeds."

"Action."

Steph and Henry ran through their blocking, Steph carefully navigating into the car while wearing her prosthesis and staying in character as an eager and excited Grace. Henry, as Kai, was trying to seem too cool for school and failing in the face of Grace's almost innocent wonder. Grace had never been on a Ferris wheel before, and she thought Kai had, but he hadn't either, so they both nervously swung in their seats as the wheel took off.

"Cut," the director said. "We got it. And that's a wrap for the day. Let's get out of here."

Selena and the other crew members, who all looked as cold as she felt, clapped. They'd pack up their gear and go home to sleep for their twelve hours of turnaround, then they'd start again at noon tomorrow.

"That looked fantastic," she told Christina, who agreed. The carnival professionals, supervised by the stunt director, carefully disembarked the extras from the Ferris wheel, car by car.

"Selena, there you are!" Becca ran up, out of breath.

"What are you still doing here? Didn't I tell you to go home hours ago?"

"I came back. I had to show you this." She pulled out her tablet, tapped on it, then swiveled it around to show Selena.

"What am I looking at?" Selena asked, feeling old as she tried to parse the different boxes and comments and emojis on the screen.

"You're trending!" Becca said. "And it's nearly all positive stuff. The audio clip went viral, and everyone's calling you a hero. It worked!"

"Seriously?" Selena had been trying to put the bad press out of her mind all day, figuring her best revenge was making the best show possible. And today's shoot had gone really well.

She scanned the comments to get the general gist. The comments section of the original article had been overrun with *Sawyer's Cove* fans making their opinion on the casting known—they loved it, and they thought the author was trying to stir up controversy over a non-issue. Selena's heart swelled with gratitude. She'd known Cove fans were the best fans in the world, but this was the proof. She hoped Brad was seeing this.

"I sent some screenshots to Brad," Becca said, reading her mind. "Hope that's okay."

"Have I given you a raise lately?" Selena asked. "Because you're worth your weight in gold, you know that, right?"

Becca smiled. "You did give me a raise recently, as a matter of fact. How about making me an associate producer on the second season?"

"If we get one," Selena said, slightly nervously.

"We'll get one," Becca said confidently. "Which reminds me, Darren's travel plans are set. He'll be here Friday, and he doesn't have to leave until Thursday."

"Which means we have four shooting days with him, if you count Wednesday." They were trying to be done with the final episode by Wednesday at the latest, so they could celebrate with a wrap party before the set breakdown started. Selena hadn't made her flight arrangements yet, but she'd probably head home Friday at the latest. With Thanksgiving the following week, she didn't want to push her travel too far into the holiday week. Her parents were chill, but they would be pissed if she missed Thanksgiving. They missed her, and she missed them. She missed her house, too, and her favorite coffee shop around the corner from it, and her zippy little convertible, and having more than the same six dresses to wear to work.

But she would miss things about Misty Harbor, too. Zelda's coffee and cookies. The way Trevor greeted her like she was a long-lost friend every time she walked through the Bakeshop's doors. The ten-minute commute to work on traffic-less roads lined by towering trees. The way she could be at the beach in five minutes. She'd miss Warner's radiant heat tile floors and his cooking and sleepy kisses at the end of the day and stubbly kisses first thing in the morning. She'd never actually lived with a man before, and she liked it more than she thought she would.

It was as if her time in Misty Harbor had shown her another version of what her life could have been—a domestic partnership with another creative-minded person, doing the job she loved while getting the full package with a man she enjoyed.

But the last two months hadn't been real life. They were a parallel universe, an interlude. At least she'd had it that long.

She said goodnight to the crew, certain they knew their jobs and would be able to wrap up efficiently. She confirmed with the electrician that the power to the carnival would be shut off soon, that the security team they'd hired was in place to keep anyone from sneaking onto the carnival set and hurting themselves. Becca had left for the inn. All she had to do was drive home, tumble into bed. Only tonight, Warner wasn't there to catch her.

Selena unlocked her rental car, flipped on the head-lights. The streets of Misty Harbor were deserted. Hers was the only car on the road. She blasted the heat; the beach breeze had cut through her layers, and she was chilled to the bone. She turned onto the long, twisty road that led to Warner's and felt her eyelids droop. It was late and dark, and the cabin of the car was now uncomfortably hot. She wanted nothing more than to sink into Warner's bed, preferably into his arms, but he wasn't there. He was in New York, paying homage to his wife. The woman she could never compete with, because she wasn't dead.

Her vision went blurry, the light of the headlights filtering through her eyelashes. She shut her eyes, only for a second, until she realized what she was doing. She gasped as her eyes flew open. She'd nearly fallen asleep still a couple of miles from Warner's. She slammed the button to turn the air from hot to cold, punched the radio button. Synthy pop music blared out at her, making her ears ring, but she didn't care. She wasn't falling asleep at the wheel.

She drove the last two miles with her eyes Lucy Ricardo-wide, and her hands gripped so tight on the steering wheel, her fingers cramped up.

She turned into Warner's empty driveway, not caring about taking up both spots. She let herself in the back door with the key he'd given her weeks ago, set the alarm system as quickly as she could. She stumbled up the stairs, kicked off her shoes, stripped off her layers, and crawled into bed in her underwear. She could smell Warner on the sheets.

Chapter Twenty-Six

When Jake woke up, he was still wearing his shoes. That's what happened when you fell asleep after being awake for twenty-four hours.

— *Gunsmoke,* by Warner Mathis

Warner didn't sleep well in the too-soft hotel bed. His pillows were lumpy, the wine had given him a bit of a headache, and the scent of the hotel's soap was cloying. He tossed and turned until finally he gave up and turned on the television at four-thirty in the morning. The classic movie channel was showing *The Thin Man* again, and he remembered watching it on the couch with Selena, both of them laughing at the same lines.

Oh, God. *That's* why he couldn't sleep. He'd gotten used to Selena in bed with him, her warm curves only a breath away.

She was leaving him soon. He'd have to learn to live without her.

He flipped the television off angrily. What was wrong with him? The dinner had been stressful, but he'd gotten through it. He'd been glad to reconnect with everyone, and he was determined to do better about keeping up with what was going on in their lives. Joanna and her husband had already invited him to come down at New Year's for their annual shindig.

"I'll put it on the calendar," he promised. New Year's Eve seemed far away, but he knew it would rush up as they all hurtled downhill to the holidays. "And thank you for organizing this. Angie would be happy to know we did it."

"You're welcome," she said simply. "Be well, Warner."

He'd invited Doug and Charlie to come up to Misty Harbor the next time they wanted to get out of the city. Doug had promised to send him his book, and Warner said again he'd read it.

"If it's better than *Gunsmoke*, I'm going to be very annoyed," he'd said.

Doug had laughed. "Annoying you would be a dream come true, Warner."

Warner had laughed, and they'd hugged, and it all had been much less awkward than it could have— should have—been. Warner wasn't sure what happened to you after you died, but he could almost feel Angie smiling down at them, bemused at their incompetence.

Now he lay in his empty bed, the room dark but not, the way hotel rooms always were with overly bright alarm clocks and light coming from under the door. His eyes were open, sightless. He felt as far as he had come in making this trip, in getting over himself, in thinking about the future as something that could be better than the past, he'd been very stupid about something else.

Selena.

He hadn't looked for her, hadn't expected her, and then he hadn't been able to resist her.

And just as surely as all of that, he was going to lose her.

He'd known that from the beginning. He'd known it was only temporary, a relationship borne of proximity and physical attraction and a shared love of mysteries and noir and Zelda's baking.

But he wasn't losing her the way he lost Angie. It was nothing like that. He was not going to open the door to a stone-faced state trooper and have his world turned upside down. She was going to go back to where she came from—back to where they both came from, if he was being perfectly accurate. She was going back to the City of Angels, the city that had haunted him his entire adult life, an almost make-believe place he'd experienced more through the movies than real life, even though he'd grown up in its shadow. He'd set *Gunsmoke* in the streets and foothills and swimming pools and grimy back alleys, but those were all things he'd learned about from other books, from movies. His was a literary Los Angeles, and he was just a tourist.

But Selena belonged there, in the sun and light.

He was a spider who'd caught a beautiful butterfly in his web. He'd snared Selena so carefully, she'd been happy to live in the trap with him, but she'd started beating her wings hard enough to break the strands. She'd break free and fly away, and he'd remain behind, rebuilding the trap, but she'd know better than to fly close enough to be trapped ever again.

God, that was dark, even for him.

He rolled out of bed, scrubbed his face with his hand.

Selena's admonishments came back to him. He'd practically kept her a prisoner in the house, not taking her anywhere or suggesting they do anything together. Not even being her date to the library thing, like a chump. He'd done it to protect her, he'd thought, from his issues, but he had, as ever, done it to protect himself.

He was an asshole. He'd been faced with that fact enough times in the last twenty-four hours to have it stamped into his forehead.

Selena was better off without him, clearly. She had her escape plan lined up and ready to go. So what did it matter if they'd never gone to the movies or out to dinner? Never had a proper date? Never met any of each other's friends? That was never going to happen, so he couldn't miss it. He shouldn't, by rights, miss her.

He rubbed his sternum. Fuck, he must be getting old.

He felt like he had indigestion from all that rich food. His chest ached like he'd swallowed a tennis ball. Or was this hot, tight feeling because he knew was going to miss Selena? That he, in fact, missed her right this very minute?

But why?

Again, there was that suspicion he was missing something. Something obvious that, once he figured it out, would solve everything. He was Jake looking for the last piece of the puzzle that would sort out the mystery, that would clarify everything.

He stumbled to the bathroom, splashed cold water on his face, looked at himself in the mirror. He looked tired and old. He was only thirty-seven, but he felt twice that, like he had less life ahead of him than he had behind him.

What was the missing piece? The final clue that would knock the cobwebs out of his brain and mud out of his eyes? He ran his fingers through his neatly trimmed hair, looked back toward the bed.

He grabbed the remote and turned on the television again, flicking through the channels, looking for a distraction from himself. Weather. Sports. Infomercials. Teenagers in a classroom. Cartoons. Wait. He flicked back to the teenagers. He recognized one of them. Jay Orlando, a very young Jay, with a shaved head and cocky grin. This was their show. *Sawyer's Cove.* He sat back and watched for a minute, trying to figure out what was happening. Jay—Parker, his name on the show—was teasing Camille—Amy—in that way boys do when they like someone. She was pretending to be annoyed. So far, so standard. Then she looked him right in the eye, outside their classroom, the backdrop of lockers so universally high school.

"You know if you ask me to the dance, I'll say yes," Amy was saying.

"I did ask you. You told me to go to hell."

"I was mad."

"What's changed?"

Amy sighed. "Everyone deserves a second chance, Parker. Especially you."

"I want to believe you."

Warner froze. Second chance. Second chances. Selena couldn't be his second chance. He couldn't actually be *with* her.

Could he?

He scrambled back from the screen, as if it was poison. Was that what this horrible aching feeling in his chest was about? The wave of sadness every time he thought about her going back to L.A.?

The ache had moved from his chest to his stomach. He thought he might be sick.

No, this wasn't happening. He had to be wrong. There was no way he'd fallen in love with Selena. He couldn't be that stupid, that much of an asshole.

This overwhelming need to be near her, to see her and talk to her and touch her—that was all friends with benefits stuff. *Tenant* with benefits, more precisely. She was, admittedly, awesome. But love?

How massive a mistake had he made by inviting her

in for soup that night? He should have left her to her dark, cold pool house. They'd both be better off for it.

He managed to turn off the TV, then crawled back into his too-soft bed, pulled the covers over his head, and lay there motionless in the dark.

Chapter Twenty-Seven

ERIKA: I've been trying not to speculate about the show too much, because that way lies madness, but I have to say, if Parker and Amy don't at least have some scenes together, I'm not going to be happy.
JULES: Oh, they're going to have scenes together. We don't know what their relationship is like, but they'll definitely be on screen together.
ERIKA: And did you see the teaser? God, everyone looks amazing.
JULES: All I know is, they are lighting the hell out of everyone's cheekbones, and I am here for it.

FROM THE SAWYER'S COVE REWATCH PROJECT PODCAST: SPECIAL DROP

Brad called her cell first thing Thursday morning. Well, technically it was eleven, but thank God she'd already been awake for twenty minutes and was able to operate Warner's coffee maker well enough to have hot, aromatic coffee coming from it, even if she hadn't gotten any in her body yet.

"I've been following the O'Toole debacle."

"Hardly a debacle," she said mildly. Brad was given to overstatement. She refrained from reminding him it was his idea to send the guy to set.

"But so far, we seem okay. In fact, with your mysteriously leaked audio clip going viral, it's driven up awareness around the premiere twenty percent. So it's probably going to be a net win for us."

She silently felt relieved, but she sensed a "but." "But?"

"Kathleen wants to up our advertising spend, to take advantage of the buzz."

"That's good, right?" The more money spent, the more eyeballs on the show, theoretically.

"That makes *Sawyer's Cove* the most expensive show on the winter slate. Makes it that much harder of a fall, Selena." It sounded like a threat, but Brad had been the one who'd pushed for the project, and she knew he was only thinking about his own reputation if the reboot missed expectations.

"Well, we won't fall, then," she said evenly.

"That's what I want to hear," Brad said, with faux brightness. "We're all rooting for you, truly. It's going to be a huge smash, and we'll be begging you to sign up for another season."

"Why not sign the contract now, while we'll still work for cheap?" she had to ask.

His laugh sounded forced. "We'll see how it debuts, okay?"

She didn't say anything, and his voice softened. "Look, you really are doing a terrific job. Getting Darren Silverstein for the finale is a stroke of genius casting. Everyone's going to be gagging for more. Be patient."

Hollywood was a place where patience was both rewarded and punished equally.

She stifled a sigh. "Darren's here tomorrow. We have six shooting days left. Then I'll be back in L.A. for post and we're going to polish the show until it shines."

"Atta girl, Selena. It's going to be awesome."

She knew he was only telling her what she wanted to hear, but she appreciated the effort. "Talk to you later, Brad."

"Don't talk to any more journalists until the L.A. junket."

She faked a laugh. "Right."

He hung up, and she gulped her coffee, dressed in record time, and made it to set for day two of the carnival shoot. She was so busy, the midafternoon text from Warner barely registered.

> I'll be staying another night. Back tomorrow.

Okay, that was a lie. She felt it like a gut punch. An irrational referendum on their ill-conceived affair. He could be staying over for any number of reasons, none of which had to be that he was avoiding her.

But she carried on because the show was what

mattered. *Sawyer's Cove* was her legacy, and the show people were her family in a way a grumpy author she'd just happened to fall in love with would never be.

It was another late night, but they wrapped on time. She thought about sleeping in the pool house when she got back to Warner's, but he wasn't going to be there one way or the other, so she might as well be comfortable and stay in the room that felt as much hers as his these days.

Friday morning, Selena scrubbed her face with ice cold water to wake herself up. Even Zelda's coffee, less expertly prepared by herself, couldn't seem to perk her up this morning. She needed to be on it today. Her ace in the hole, Darren Silverstein, was coming in. He had the script for the finale, and she hoped he'd be able to hit the ground running. They had him shooting a couple of scenes that afternoon.

The shoot, she could admit now it was almost over, had worn her out. Ten episodes back-to-back was like ten marathons in a row. They'd left weekends sacrosanct, but she hadn't let her foot off the gas since she got there. And there was no time to recover once she got back home.

L.A. *was* home, she reminded herself fiercely.

She'd be able to rest when the show was on the air. She'd penciled in a month of doing nothing in the new year. If—when—they got picked up for a second season, she'd negotiate a longer production timeline than this whirlwind.

Selena was nearly finished getting ready when she heard a noise on the stairs and froze in the act of putting on her lipstick. She grabbed her cell from the top of the dresser, flicked it to the emergency call screen, her heart in her throat. She'd set the alarm, hadn't she? She'd stumbled in bleary-eyed the night before, but she always set the alarm after Warner had showed her how to do it.

Footsteps, then a soft knock on the half-open door of the bedroom.

Did home intruders knock?

She whirled around, and Warner was there. He looked tired, too, and as if he hadn't shaved. He was wearing an unfamiliar sweater and slacks. She peered at his feet. Were those new shoes?

The double wave of relief at it being him, then it being *him*, made her lightheaded.

"Hey," he said. His voice was the same. She'd been without him for two days, and she hadn't realized exactly how much she'd missed him until he was back.

Her knees sagged, and she went to sit on the edge of the bed before she did something ridiculous like faint or throw herself at him.

"Are you okay?" he said.

She burst into tears.

What the fuck? She tried to hide her face in her hands, but Warner was at her side in two seconds.

"Selena, what's wrong? Did something happen?" His voice was shredded with concern.

"I m-missed you," she said, feeling small and emotional and utterly unlike herself.

She felt him freeze next to her. He hadn't touched her, and he didn't now. She raised her head to look at him. He looked devastated, as if she'd told him she had an incurable disease rather than she'd missed his stupid face.

She waited. He said nothing. It was a pattern she was familiar with, and one she hated more than ever. She didn't have it in her to ask if he'd missed her, too.

She felt torn. She could dry her eyes and smile, put on the can-do Selena face that had gotten her job after job, never complaining, just showing up and doing the work until it was her show to run. They could enjoy the last few days they had together. Or she could be honest —as honest as possible, anyway—with a man who'd always seemed to be honest with her. And she'd break what they had, and she'd lose him.

But wasn't she going to lose him anyway?

"I hope you had a good trip," she said.

"It was—illuminating," Warner said haltingly.

"Do you want to talk about it?"

Warner opened his mouth, but nothing came out.

She nodded. "I didn't think so. Well, things are racing toward the finish here. I've got to run to the set now. We only have a few shooting days left."

"I know. When are you going to L.A.?"

"Don't have my plane reservation set yet."

"Ah."

Time for her to stop stalling.

"My parents are hosting Thanksgiving. I was hoping you could come out with me for a few days. A week, maybe. I'll have to work some, but you said you have family there, maybe you could see them."

The answer came almost before she'd finished speaking. "No."

Her disappointment came out in sarcasm. "Oh, gee, think you gave it enough thought, Warner?"

"Sorry. But..." He took a shaky breath. "I think we both know it's better if things end here."

The tears came again, but different. These were hot tears, anger and loss welling up uncontrollably. "It doesn't have to be like that."

"I'm sorry," he said again, a little desperately this time.

"You're afraid. You've been afraid since she died," Selena said, needing him to hurt at least a fraction as much as she did.

"I know." His eyes looked damp, too. At least she knew he had some feelings about the implosion of what they'd had. "You don't have to tell me I'm a coward. I'm aware."

"You aren't, though," she said, angry now on his behalf. "You could have given up entirely. You didn't. You kept going. You even started writing again. You made a different life for yourself. You're still here. But that's just it. You're *here*." She swallowed hard. "And so am I."

There was the unspoken third thing. That *she* wasn't here. Would never be. And perhaps Selena was a poor substitute. But she had one advantage. She was alive. And she couldn't apologize for it.

She wouldn't apologize for it.

"You can say whatever about how we came together out of convenience, but for me it's more than that. With you, I feel like I could have a home, a purpose outside of work. Delusional, I know. We never even went on a date, and here I am, thinking we could work long-term. I guess falling in love with someone makes common sense go out the window."

His expression tightened. Her stomach ached.

"I don't know what to say." His voice sounded gritty, like maybe there were tears somewhere inside he was holding back. "I never made any promises. I never lied to you about what I was capable of. About how messed up I am."

"You didn't lie to me, Warner, but I think you're lying to yourself. Because I'm leaving here with a broken heart. That's on me. I didn't mean to fall in love with you. But at least I can acknowledge that I did." She wiped her eyes. She felt like one of her heroines, a leaky faucet, trying to get through the big speech. God, if only she could have written this differently. Some pithy one-liner, walking out with her head held high. But instead, she was almost ugly-crying, tears and snot—and where was a tissue when you needed one, dammit?

On cue, Warner got up, walked over to the dresser, and turned around, holding out a box of tissues.

"Don't think being nice to me is going to make me love you any less," she said, rather nonsensically, as she took a tissue and blew her nose inelegantly. Who cared at this point?

Warner had seen her hungover, half-asleep, in work mode, in the bathtub. They'd gone from strangers to living together in the span of weeks. The intimacy was a byproduct of that, but it was real. She knew this wouldn't have happened with just anyone who was passably attractive and made her grilled cheese sandwiches. Warner was special. He was a good man, a good writer, the guy she used to be waiting for and who she'd long ago decided wasn't going to show up. She'd been okay with being a solo act. And then he'd arrived, fitting into her life like some kind of damn missing piece. As easy as it had been to slot him in, it was going to hurt like hell to tear that piece out again.

It hurt already. Her entire body felt sore, as if she'd been careless at the beach and let the ocean currents batter her against the rocks before spitting her up on the sand.

She took another tissue. She could dry her face and fix her makeup and hold her head up and go live the rest of her life. She would do that. But she'd do one last thing first.

She stood up and kissed Warner's mouth firmly. A goodbye kiss.

He didn't kiss back.

Chapter Twenty-Eight

ERIKA: In our continued coverage in the run-up to the new season, we have "Gossip Corner with Jules."
JULES: Isn't our entire podcast Gossip Corner?
ERIKA: It's mostly "Jules and Erika Gush Over the Best TV Show Ever Made Corner."
JULES: True. Well, here's some certified uncorroborated gossip for you all. Darren Silverstein has not been announced as one of the returning cast members, however he was spotted in the Providence airport last Thursday and took a couple of selfies with fans. Some might note that Providence is a mere hour's drive from Misty Harbor, aka Cloudy Cove, aka Ground Zero for the reboot. Coincidence?
ERIKA: It's either a coincidence, or we're getting Noah back.
JULES: But why haven't they announced him? He's basically the sixth Cove kid.
ERIKA: Maybe he's only doing a cameo.

JULES: Six weeks until the first episodes, and I'm already hyperventilating.

ERIKA: Breathe, sweetie, breathe.

FROM THE SAWYER'S COVE REWATCH PROJECT PODCAST: MORE REBOOT NEWS

"So are you going to start having fun at this party, or should I get someone to drive you to the inn?" Becca poked Selena's bicep with a finger. Hard.

"Ouch." She rubbed her arm and glared at her assistant and soon-to-be co-producer. "I am having fun."

"You don't even have a drink," Becca complained. "Bo! Get Selena a drink."

"Yes, ma'am." Bo saluted and went to the table where all manner of toxic substances were laid out for the consumption of the cast and crew, courtesy of The Cove's liquor stores. The wrap party was being held in the big multipurpose room at the barn-turned-sound-stage they'd used as their home base for the show twice now.

They had officially called a wrap on principal photography three hours earlier. The crew had already started breaking down the sets. There would be ADR sessions and of course editing and, later, lots of press, but for now, cast and crew could celebrate a job well done.

Bo came back with a plastic glass full of suspiciously red punch. She took a tentative sip and coughed. It tasted like cough syrup. She longed for one of the pink drinks from the library fundraiser and wondered if she could get the recipe somewhere.

"Cami, help me cheer Selena up," Becca said, dragging Cami over and away from where she'd been talking with Jay, Nash, and Mimi.

"What's wrong?" Cami said, looking worried. "Bad news?"

"Nothing's wrong. I'm not in a party mood, I guess." She'd struggled to regain her usual buoyancy since walking out of Warner's life. She'd exercised the privilege of having an assistant and sent Becca to pick up her stuff, then she'd checked into the inn for the remainder of her stay in Misty Harbor. She hadn't seen or heard from Warner since. It was as if he'd been a ghost all along, someone she'd dreamed up, an imaginary boyfriend. She'd briefly told Cami things were over, but she hadn't elaborated. And none of the others even knew she and Warner were a thing, as far as she knew.

"I know things have been rough, and you're probably exhausted, but you're going to regret it if you don't at least try to have a little fun. We might not all be in the same place again for a while," Cami said, steering her toward Jay's group.

Mimi and Nash were talking about a house they had put an offer on.

"It's got this massive soundproofed basement," Nash was saying.

"Dude, I do not need to hear about that," Jay said, making a face.

"For music recording," his sister Mimi explained

with a roll of her eyes. "And the biggest library you've ever seen in a house."

"You guys are moving in together?" Selena was behind on gossip.

They looked at each other, exchanging sickeningly adoring glances.

"Yeah," Nash said happily. "My lease with Warner is almost up, so I needed a place to live, and Mimi's apartment is barely big enough for her. We needed somewhere bigger to put all our books. And guitars."

"Hopefully, the escrow period will be short. Of course, it does need a little work. I've already talked to a couple of contractors."

"Wait, it's here in Misty Harbor?" For some reason, Selena had assumed they'd move to Los Angeles, Nash's home base between projects.

Nash put his arm around Mimi's shoulders. They looked good together, both tall with broad smiles. They were clearly in love. It was easy to see it in other people once you felt it yourself. She was happy for them, if surprised Nash would actually move to this tiny town full time. What about his career?

It was none of her business, she reminded herself. And just because it could work for Nash, didn't mean it was an option for her. What would she do in Misty Harbor year-round? Sit at Warner's kitchen table and write? She couldn't take meetings or interview potential hires from Misty Harbor. Well, not as easily. Her house was in Los Angeles. She loved her house. And her car. And her parents. Her friends.

She shook her head. Besides, there was no reason to stay if Warner didn't love her. She had too much pride to stay with him with things so emotionally out of balance.

She excused herself from the lovebirds. She was scared to finish her appalling drink, so she tossed it in the trash, wondering if it was too soon to leave, despite her assurances to Becca. She was mature enough to admit to herself she wanted to go back to her hotel room and cry.

"Hey, Selena, can I talk to you for a minute?" Darren Silverstein jogged up. He was a tall, slim man with a handsomely angular face, curly dark hair, a smattering of light brown freckles across his nose. He'd done her a favor by squeezing these last few days into his schedule, so of course she had a minute for him. That's how Hollywood worked.

"Sure. I know I told you earlier, but solid work this week. It was like no time at all had passed since you last played Noah. Well done."

He flashed a smile. "I'm glad it worked out. Hey, I wanted to throw something out there. I've been directing more than acting these days. So if you get picked up for a season two, even if Noah doesn't come back, I'd love to be considered for an episode."

Selena hadn't been expecting him to pitch himself as a director, but she had heard he'd been working here and there.

"Send me your reel," she said. "Actually, send it to Becca. And then fingers crossed for a pickup." Brad had called to congratulate her on wrapping on time and under budget but still hadn't said anything about season two.

"From the buzz I've seen online and the incredible script for the finale, there's no way it won't get picked up," Darren said confidently. "You guys are golden."

"I hope so," she said. "And we'd love to have you back. I have lots of ideas for Noah and Will."

"Awesome." He gave her a quick hug, then something that caught his gaze over her shoulder had him stepping away. "I better go. Thanks again." And he was gone into the crowd.

She turned around to see what had snagged his attention. All she saw was Crosby standing alone with a red cup in his hand. He saw her and lifted the cup in salute, his mouth a grim line. Damn. She'd thought he'd had a positive experience these past weeks, he had seemed to get along well with the other actors and the crew, but right now he seemed as moody as she was.

Maybe he was in love with someone who didn't love him back, too.

She shoved that ridiculous thought out of her mind and took out her phone, which was buzzing in her pocket.

She smiled when she saw the name on the screen, answered the call.

"Ryan, hi!"

The smooth baritone of Ryan Saylor, the creator of *Sawyer's Cove*, came over the line. "Selena, I wanted to call and congratulate you. You did it."

"We still have so much post to do." Selena groaned.

The minute she was back in L.A. she'd be back to twelve and fourteen-hour days. "But this part feels good."

"You should be proud of yourself. I'm proud of you," Ryan said. "I know it hasn't been easy."

"You saw the casting kerfuffle online?" She'd been too distracted to reach out to Ryan, knowing he'd contact her if he thought he needed to.

"Some people are assholes," he said mildly. "But I think you and your team handled it really well."

His blessing was a warm blanket of relief. "Thanks. Hey, you want me to put you on speaker? Everyone's here, and I'm sure they'd love to say hi."

"God, no," Ryan said hastily. "I mean, this is your baby now, Selena. Better if I stay out of it."

"All right. Though I'm still planning on sending you an early cut, if you're up for it."

"You can send it to me, but I'm not going to give you any notes," Ryan said stoutly. "I want you to know that you did this all on your own."

The amount of trust he had placed in her was humbling, and inspiring, and terrifying. But she'd made it this far, and she believed the show was going to be a worthy follow-up to the original. "Thanks again. For everything."

"I didn't do anything. You made this happen. Never forget that."

She bit her tongue to stop herself from thanking him again, wished him a happy early Thanksgiving, and they hung up, agreeing to touch base soon. He wasn't in charge anymore, but to her, he'd always be the final say on all things *Sawyer's Cove*.

She put her phone back in her pocket, surveyed the room. She'd gotten to know everyone here so much better over the past months. They were a team, a family, of sorts. And even though they were shortly all going their separate ways, there were some bonds that would stay for life. She'd helped make that possible.

The show was her baby, her career was her life, and she was okay with that.

If she'd hoped she could make room for something else—someone else—well, that was a dream she was mature enough to set aside. Still, she didn't feel much like making merry. She'd done her part. Let everyone else enjoy the party. She turned around and walked away.

Chapter Twenty-Nine

She was gone. The case was over. Justice had been served, if you squinted and decided that cosmic retribution was as good as the California judicial system. Jake decided he wouldn't think about it too hard. Thinking made the knot on his head hurt worse. All he needed to know was he'd be around to see the sun rise another day. That was enough.

— *Gunsmoke,* by Warner Mathis

Warner stared at the blinking cursor on his screen. Blink. Blink. Blink. The screen went blurry as his vision gave up on making sense of the words he wasn't writing.

He shoved back from his desk. This was ridiculous.

He needed out of this prison of a house. He grabbed his wallet, hand hovering over the bowl of keys. He should take the Mercedes for a drive. It had been a while. He huffed and took the big old-fashioned metal key and garage door opener.

The tang of gasoline met his nose as the garage door opened slowly. He eased the vintage car out of the driveway. It was easy without Selena's car there. She'd erased herself as easily and completely from his life as if she'd never been there at all.

He'd been sleeping like shit since she left. He'd been writing like shit, too, though he had still forced himself to write a little every day. Making matters worse, Doug had sent him his manuscript, and he'd read it in one sitting. It was good. Damn good. He could see echoes of his own work in it, but not in a bad way. In fact, Doug's book made him want to sit down and write, but he was too irritable and distracted and too fucking pathetic to do anything about it.

He drove on autopilot to the only place he knew he could turn for the kind of comfort he craved. His favorite parking spot was free. It was a sign. He parked the Mercedes, locked it up carefully. He drew his peacoat snug. A week before Thanksgiving, winter was already nipping at fall's heels.

The Cove was open, but not particularly busy.

"Warner, hey." He was being hailed by Nash Speedwell from the back corner booth. Sitting with him were Mimi Orlando, Jay Orlando, and Camille Corsair.

He recoiled at being faced with two sets of happy

couples but went over anyway, especially when he realized his usual barstool was already occupied. Besides, they might have news of Selena. She might even be with them, off powdering her nose.

"What's happening, man?" Nash said expansively. They all had beer in front of them, and the table was littered with empty glasses.

"Er." But wait, did they know about Selena and him? Even though she worked with these people, and was friends with them, too, he had no idea if she would have shared the nature of their relationship. "Not...much?"

Jay smiled at him kindly. "Want to sit down? I see your usual spot is taken." He scooted over to make room.

Warner sat down hesitantly. This is what he'd come for, wasn't it? Company?

"Great news, Warner," Nash said. "You aren't going to have to evict me. Mimi and I found a place to buy."

They told him about their real estate triumph with excited, glowing faces. He wondered how much they'd had to drink. Then he reminded himself to be less of an asshole.

"That's terrific," he said. "I'm really happy for you." They were making a go of it, right here in Misty Harbor. His stomach tightened. They were so young and full of excitement. Just like him and Angie. She used to get high from buying a new piece of real estate, too.

"Warner Mathis, I thought you were ghosting us," Danica said, sidling up to the table. "The usual?"

He smiled at his favorite bartender. "Yes, please."

She bustled away, and he turned his attention to his table mates.

"Your last name is Mathis?" Mimi said, tilting her head. "Did you know you have the same name as a writer? A mystery writer. He's only written one book, but it was an instant classic."

Cami made a squeak. He met her wide blue eyes with his gaze.

"You're a writer, too? God, no wonder Selena—"

His ears sharpened, but she stopped herself by literally putting a hand over her mouth. Her cheeks were flushed red behind her hand. Really, how drunk was everyone at this table?

"No, he has the same name as a writer," Mimi said, as if she was explaining something simple to a child.

Oh, hell. "Actually, that's me," he said heavily. "I was —I am a writer."

"You wrote *Gunsmoke*?" Mimi sat up. "I freaking loved that book. You probably have people asking you all the time when the next one's coming out."

"Well—"

"Warner didn't come in here to get grilled by a librarian," Jay said, rescuing him from his sister. "I apologize, Warner. We came here from the wrap party, and we're kind of feeling no pain."

The wrap party—that made sense. Selena had told him Wednesday was the last day of filming. So she was still in town. Where was she staying?

"Congratulations," he said belatedly. "How did it go?"

"The shoot?" Cami asked. She groaned theatrically at his nod. "It was so much work."

"It was kind of fun," Jay said.

"One of the best-run sets I've ever been on," Nash said. "But it was a lot doing everything back-to-back. I'm looking forward to a break."

Cami stuck out her tongue. It was unnaturally red, as if she'd recently eaten a popsicle. "I don't get one. I'm going to L.A. to help Selena with post."

"You have more than a week off before that. Selena won't let you come back until after Thanksgiving."

"She's the best boss," Cami said, then her eyes narrowed at Warner. "And she's been in a crappy mood the last few days. She even left the wrap party early."

The news didn't make him feel better, exactly. He sighed. Clearly, Cami knew something was going on, even if none of the others did.

"I—" He was about to defend himself when he realized he didn't want to. "Is she all right, though?"

He sensed Jay's gaze on him as Cami continued to glare.

"She won't talk about it much. She's been all business since last week. But she goes to the bathroom and comes back with red eyes, and I think you know what that means. Anyway, she's heading back to L.A., so I guess it's moot."

He'd made her cry. And she was already gone.

Danica dropped a glass of whiskey in front of him, and he mumbled his thanks but didn't pick it up. He knew from experience drinking only put off the pain.

"What's going on?" Jay asked. "You and Selena—?"

Nash hooted. "Yeah, did any of my advice work?"

"What advice? What are you talking about?" Mimi asked.

Everyone turned to look at Warner. This was kind of his worst nightmare. He opened his mouth, but Cami spoke first. "Selena seems to think you haven't done anything wrong. She told me your wife passed away, and I'm sorry about that. But you can't just use people, then throw them away."

"That's not what happened," he said, voice bleak. "I never meant to hurt her. She's incredible. And way better off without me."

"Be that as it may," Cami said primly. "I'm not a fan, Warner."

"So you and Selena are together?" Nash said.

"Not anymore," Warner said roughly. "I fucked it up." That much he could own.

Nash winced, and Mimi dropped her head to Nash's shoulder, her expression sympathetic.

"I'm going to the bathroom," Cami announced.

Warner got out of the booth, and Jay followed. She gave him one more baleful look and headed for the restrooms in the back of the building.

"I better go with her," Mimi said. "Solidarity."

Nash got out of his side of the booth and smiled after her as she walked away in a not-quite-straight line.

Warner recognized the smile of a man besotted by his woman.

"Okay, while they're gone, real talk, man," Jay said,

with determination. He seemed to be the most sober of the group. "You fucked up. But you can fix it."

Warner flinched. He might be able to fix it, but he wasn't sure he should. "I wasn't lying when I said she'd be better off without me."

"That's a cop-out. You gotta let her decide. What does she want?"

Warner hesitated. "She said she was in love with me."

Nash whistled. "This is serious, man."

"I know!" Warner spit out. "I was scared, okay? I pushed her away."

"Being in love is scary," Jay said. "Cami and me, we wasted a lot of time because we, well, mostly *I* was scared. That I wasn't enough, that I wasn't what she needed. That if I went for the brass ring and missed, it would hurt more than if I didn't go for it at all." He paused for a dramatic sip of his beer. He was an actor, after all. "But that was all bullshit. The point of love is that you're scared together."

"Until you lose her," Warner rasped. Jay meant well, but he'd never lost the love of his life, had to face waking up day after day without her. But then he remembered Jay had, in a way. He and Cami had once been very much in love, and they'd been apart for over a decade.

"I'm sorry about your wife. I didn't know. Hell, I don't know much about you besides your drink order. That's my bad. But Selena's one of a kind. And she's alive."

Warner flinched, but Jay went on, "She's alive, man.

And so are you. Don't be an asshole and miss out on the rest of your life."

Warner was mostly pissed because Jay was only saying a version of what he'd been thinking for the past week. Since before New York, if he was being totally honest.

"I don't know what to do. She left me. I let her leave because I'm the biggest fool in Misty Harbor."

"Hey, you can fight me and Nash for that title later," Jay said. "Why don't you go get her?"

"What? In L.A.?" He imagined getting on a plane, driving to Echo Park, and wandering up and down the streets, looking for the house she'd shown him on her phone all those weeks ago. Or he could beg Jay for her address. "I have to get to the airport."

Jay's smile was brilliant. "My man, now you're talking. But also, no, you don't."

"What are you talking about? I have to tell her..." He was going to tell her so many things. If she'd let him. Please, God, let her listen to him.

"Yeah, but she's not in L.A. She's still at the inn."

Chapter Thirty

Jules: Did you see the pics someone posted of the Times Square video billboard? Camille Corsair's face was as big as a building.

Erika: They're really going all out for the promo.

Jules: Considering we only found out this was happening six months ago, they probably have a lot of ground to cover.

Erika: I still wake up sometimes and have to pinch myself. All our questions answered. A second chance for Parker and Amy and Sawyer and Lily and Will. I hope the writers don't waste this opportunity.

Jules: It's going to be epic.

FROM THE SAWYER'S COVE REWATCH PROJECT PODCAST: MORE REBOOT NEWS

So it turned out the Misty Harbor Inn wasn't that bad. She should have stayed there in the first place and saved herself the bother of falling in love with the wrong right guy.

The inn had room service and a pool and a hot tub, too. Why didn't Warner's place have a hot tub? There was plenty of room in the back yard. They could have used it when the weather turned cold and he'd covered the pool for the season, if they didn't care too much about the electric bill.

Stop thinking about Warner. Life was too short to be hung up on a guy. It had been a week—shouldn't she have moved on by now? On the other hand, Cami and Jay had stayed in love with each other for years after they broke up, so maybe she was screwed.

She was excited about heading back to L.A. tomorrow, if only to get more involved in the editing booth. She missed her parents, too, and her friends, not to mention her car.

But if the show didn't get picked up for another season, she might never come back to Misty Harbor. It felt like a missed opportunity to spend her last night here holed up in her hotel room, but outside was dark and cold, and basically everything but The Cove closed after nine anyway.

She wondered if Warner was still writing. Did he know she was leaving town tomorrow? Had she made a mistake by leaving him without a final farewell? At the time, she'd needed space to focus on finishing the show. But perhaps there were still things to say.

No. He'd had a week to call if he wanted to say anything. And she'd made her position clear. Hadn't she? Their final conversation was a bit of a blur now.

God, was she pathetic for harboring some shred of hope that if she found him and gave him a proper good-bye, he'd tell her what she wanted to hear?

Yes. The answer to that was yes. She'd never been the kind of person to harbor useless hope. If she wanted something, she worked for it until she got it. But that didn't work with people. Warner didn't want to be gotten by her. He clearly wanted to be left alone.

She eyed the tub in the bathroom of her suite. Would a bath cheer her up? She could take one before she went back to the perpetual California drought. A going-away present to herself. She ran the water, remembering against her will the last time she took a bath. Warner had gotten in with her. They'd washed each other and kissed while he fingered her, then they moved to the shower and he fucked her slowly from behind while she was pressed up against the tile.

Her mouth suddenly dry, she swallowed with diffi-culty. Well, Warner wasn't going to ruin baths for her. He wasn't going to ruin anything for her. She would take the memories with her, and if she wanted someone who would make her soup and coffee and talk to her about writing and books and give her lots of orgasms—well, there were millions of people in the greater Los Angeles area. Surely one of them would be just as good in bed as Warner Mathis.

She'd stripped down to her underwear when her

phone rang. Not her cell phone, but the hotel room phone. She looked at it suspiciously for a moment, but when she went to pick it up, it stopped ringing.

Weird.

She turned the water off in time to hear a knock at the door and the muffled words "room service" from the other side.

Huh. She hadn't ordered room service. She looked out the peephole first, like any intelligent person, and indeed saw a young woman in a uniform next to a small cart with an ice bucket and champagne flutes on it.

She almost opened the door, then remembered she was in her bra and panties. She grabbed the terrycloth robe from the closet and slipped it on, then opened the door. This was why she hadn't wanted to live here for three months. Unexpected interruptions.

"Yes?"

"I have your order," the woman said. Her name tag read Carly.

"I didn't order anything," Selena said, trying not to be rude.

Carly scanned a piece of paper and looked at the room number. "I have an order for this room. Would you like me to leave it here or bring it in?"

"Bring it in, I guess. What is it?" Selena asked suspiciously. She knew she hadn't ordered anything, but it wasn't unusual for Becca to order her food preemptively if she thought she needed it.

The woman wheeled the cart inside. "Champagne, ma'am."

She spotted the bottle on the lower rack of the cart. Becca probably wouldn't have ordered her alcohol. It was probably a gift from Brad, or maybe Ryan.

"Is there a note?"

Carly looked at her paper again. "No, ma'am."

Selena bared her teeth. She really didn't need the "ma'am" stuff. It made her feel like her mother.

Carly lifted the bottle off the rack and showed it to her. "Would you like me to open it?"

"No!" The word burst out of her loudly. "That's okay," Selena said more gently.

But Carly, who'd probably seen some shit in her days of working in the hospitality industry, set the bottle in the ice bucket and nodded. "Goodnight."

"Wait—" Selena made for her purse on the desk, but Carly shook her head.

"It's taken care of, ma'am."

And she left.

Curious. Anonymous room service champagne. Two glasses. She looked at the label. Good stuff. There was no way she could drink an entire bottle of champagne tonight, but there wouldn't be any harm in having a glass with her bath. The thought of sipping bubbles while soaking in bubbles was enticing.

She was about to open the bottle herself, but she hesitated. Hadn't she read a story once about a bottle of champagne being poisoned by a long needle through the cork? Was this safe to drink? Maybe Carly didn't even work here. Maybe she was a plant.

Except who would want to kill her? That was ridiculous.

Still, she didn't open the bottle. She could call downstairs and ask about Carly and the order. Maybe they could tell her who'd ordered it at the desk.

Meanwhile, her bath was getting cold. Dammit.

She bit her lip, debating with herself for another minute before deciding against the champagne. No sense in taking chances.

Her hand was on the belt of her robe when another knock came on the door.

What the hell? She was never staying in a hotel again.

She yanked open the door. Warner stood on the other side.

He was wearing a peacoat she didn't recognize, with a thick knit sweater underneath. Jeans, but not the usual lumpy work jeans. These were dark and fit him entirely too well. He was wearing brown lace-ups instead of sneakers. Despite his attire, he looked awful—tired, unshaven. His hair was a mess.

He flicked his gaze up and down. She was still underdressed for the occasion.

"What are you doing here?" she asked finally.

"I had to see you before you left," he said, his eyes boring into her, twin spears of icy blue.

"Come in." She stood aside and let him shut the door behind him, not sure how to feel about this particular unexpected interruption.

She sat on the edge of her big, fluffy bed, holding the

robe tight across her chest. He didn't sit, just stared at her for a minute. She sighed. As much as she'd wanted to see him again before she left, she was too tired for games.

"What is it, Warner?"

He glanced at the cart with the champagne on it but didn't comment on it.

"I've been a fool," he said.

As openers went, that one was pretty solid. She nodded to show she agreed with the statement.

"I thought when you were done with the show, it would be easy to say goodbye. That's one of the things I was foolish about." He started pacing, hands in the pockets of his peacoat. "When I realized it wasn't going to be easy at all, I took the coward's way out and pushed you away sooner, as if that would save me from having my heart broken. Which of course it didn't."

Heartbroken? What was he saying?

"After Angie died, I thought I'd be better off alone. It took me too long to realize I haven't been alone at all. I have friends who've never abandoned me and a community right here in Misty Harbor. I never expected to find a home here." He stopped and gestured to the window which overlooked the town. "I've been stuck in the past for too long. I missed out on half a decade of my friends' lives. Seeing them in New York made me realize how much of a fool I am. But I can see a future now, for myself, in a way I haven't been able to in a very long time."

Selena loved this man, and she was so happy to hear

he'd realized these things, even if they had nothing to do with her. She wanted the best for him, always.

"But the thing I've been the biggest fool about is you, Selena."

How was she supposed to take that? She waited on a razor's edge between hope and rejection.

Warner took a step toward her, dropped to his knees, his expression open and earnest. She found herself stifling an involuntary cry.

"I've loved you for a while. Maybe since the day you walked into my life and knew exactly who I was. You've always seen me, Selena. You never let me hide or let me get away with giving you anything less than you deserve. Which is why you were perfectly right to leave. I wasn't holding up my end of the bargain. I wasn't being honest with you." He stopped and took a deep breath, but his voice still broke a little on his next words. "Because I love you, too."

Her sob came back, louder now. Selena covered her mouth with her hand, as if she could force the emotion to stay inside.

Warner shuffled forward, laid his head on her lap. "I never expected to fall in love, but I could never regret falling in love with someone as incredible as you. And if you still want me, I want to make this work."

He lifted his head, stared her in the eyes. "Please say we can make this work. Because I know what my life is like without you in it, and it's bleak, Selena."

She frowned. "I can't be with you only because you need me."

He smiled with his mouth turned down at the edges. "I know. Maybe you could be with me because I—I could be someone who makes your life better, Selena. I can cook for you; I can be there for you at the end of a long day. I can take care of you. It would be an honor."

"You do make my life better, Warner. You do all those things for me wonderfully well. But our relationship doesn't have to be transactional. I think we make each other better by being in each other's lives. When I know you're there for me, I'm reminded why I work so hard, why I love what I do. But—"

"But what?"

"I want to be with you, Warner." She didn't want to put any more barriers between them. "But I have to know if I'm always going to be playing runner-up to the perfect Angeline."

His face changed again, one side of his mouth went up, and he looked like he was trying not to cry. "Oh, darling. I never want you to feel like that. I know I'm a bit obsessive. I'm like Jake Wilton—we don't know when to stop sometimes. And if I ever make you feel like you're living with a ghost—please, tell me." He smiled tremulously. "Besides, Angie wasn't perfect. She had plenty of flaws. God knows, so do I. And so do you. Thank goodness. None of us are perfect, but I'm beginning to get that some of us are lucky enough to get that second chance."

"What do you mean?"

"You've shown me that second chances aren't only about getting a do-over. They're about knowing you're worth getting a second chance. Or a third. Or a fourth. They're really about not giving up. I'm not giving up on myself. Please, will you give me a second chance?"

She had no idea what would happen next, how they were going to navigate a relationship when he was here and she was there, when their lives hadn't ever intersected until three months ago. But she flung her arms around him because she loved him, and wanted him, and because she believed in second chances, too.

He hugged her back, hard, and then they were kissing. He tasted like salt; those were her own tears she was tasting.

They found themselves embracing on the bed, him overdressed and her barely dressed at all. She laughed and pushed the peacoat off his shoulders. He took it off, kicked off his shoes, too.

"When I go back to Los Angeles, you won't be letting me leave you, will you?" she asked quietly.

"I'll come with you," he said simply. "And we'll figure the rest out."

Right now, she believed they would.

"All right. Oh!" She sat up all the way. "My bath!"

"You were going to take a bath?" His eyes darkened in anticipation.

"I was going to soak away my sorrow," she said, mostly joking, but his gaze turned sad.

"I'm sorry for hurting you."

She sucked in a breath. It was such a simple sentence, and yet it meant so much. Almost as much as hearing him say he loved her. "Thank you."

"Want to take your bath anyway? I could be your bath attendant."

She laughed. "Isn't that a bit of a waste of Warner Mathis's talents?"

"Definitely not," he said severely. "But I understand if you want me to go. We can start over, do this properly."

"Properly?" What was he talking about?

"We should go on a date," he said.

"A date?" That's not what she'd been expecting him to say.

"Yes. I'll pick you up. Bring flowers. All that stuff. I'll court you properly. I should go home, and we can start fresh."

"While I would like to someday be seen with you in public," she said mildly, "if you leave right now, I will not be happy. Besides, I'm flying to Los Angeles tomorrow. We don't have time to go on a date before then."

"Tomorrow?" His face fell, then he looked determined. "What airline? What time? I'll go on the same flight."

"Oh, God." She choked on a laugh. "You're going to be the death of me. Warner, I love you. I want to be with you. But I'm still me. I'm still independent Selena, who's never lived with any man before I accidentally started living with you. We don't need to live in each other's pockets all of a sudden. You'll be here sometimes, and I'll be there sometimes, but it's going to be okay. Okay?"

He looked chagrined. "Okay. Thanks. Sorry, it's been a while since I—well, you know. I'm rusty at this relationship stuff. You're going to have to keep giving me those second chances."

"I'll give you as many second chances as you need," she promised.

His mouth curved up. "Thanks. Now, about that bath."

In the end, they both got naked and into the tub.

Naked Warner was probably her favorite Warner, although the recent upgrade in his wardrobe was appreciated. She'd have to ask him what made him buy new clothes. She was too distracted to ask when he was sitting behind her, cradling her between his legs, carefully washing her hair. It was a tighter fit than his bathtub, but they managed. She luxuriated in the care he took lavishing attention on her body.

They showed admirable restraint by not trying to fuck in the tub, which surely would have resulted in a flood that Jay's mom, one of the hotel's managers, would have disapproved of.

Instead they toweled off and took each other to bed. There was more to say, more to discuss, more to figure out. But Selena knew they had time. Right now, she only wanted to show Warner how much she loved him.

"Make love to me, Warner."

Chapter Thirty-One

The sun was rising in Echo Park. Jake watered the succulent on the sunny counter next to the toaster. He'd picked it up on an impulse in the checkout line when he'd gone to buy a toilet plunger at a big box store that had about fifty lethal weapons per aisle, ready for sale to whatever psycho walked through the automatic sliding doors. He liked having something green in his apartment.

Kerry liked it, too. She said if he managed to keep it alive, she'd buy him a cactus and he could start a collection.

"A cactus?"

"They're prickly. Like you." And then she'd kissed him.

He was doing his best to keep the succulent alive.

— Untitled work in progress, by
Warner Mathis

Make love to me, Warner.

Selena's words unlocked something in Warner's chest that had been seized with anxiety since he left The Cove knowing he was about to either win Selena for good or lose her forever. The universe—Angie—whatever, was smiling on him, because Selena had given him another chance. And now she was underneath him on the bed, naked and warm from the bath, completely open and waiting for him to show her exactly how much he loved her.

And he loved her so much. They were only at the beginning of their story, really, and as much as he loved her today, he knew he'd love her more tomorrow, and next week, and next year. He kissed her, memorizing the way kissing her today felt, cataloging it in his memory of Selena kisses for the rest of time.

Her lips were so soft and plush, and she opened up for him so easily, so trusting even after what he'd put her through. It made it all the sweeter, though, didn't it? He tightened his hold on her. He'd almost lost her, but he hadn't. She was still there. She was still *here*, in his arms.

He shivered. She looked at him with dark eyes. "All right, Warner?" Her voice was throaty. She could say anything in that voice, and he'd be a little bit turned on.

Right now he was a lot turned on, his erection rubbing against the soft curve of her belly.

"God, it's so different when you know you love someone," he said.

She didn't seem bothered by the non sequitur. "What's different?" she murmured, stroking his arms.

"Everything."

She smiled sweetly. "Yeah," she agreed, and God, he loved her so much in that moment. That moment was all they had, really, and it was more than enough.

She surged up as he crashed down, and they met in the middle, urgent and hard, the kiss fierce. They battled to show their love with that kiss, both winning.

He didn't want to leave her mouth, but the rest of her body begged for his attention. He kissed down her throat, her skin breaking out in goosebumps as he laved over it, biting her collarbone lightly. She arched into him, thrusting her large breasts into his face. He took the invitation, latching onto her nipple and sucking hard. His cock leapt as she moaned deeply. She was clutching him and spreading her legs wider, shifting her hips to get him where she wanted him to go. It was too soon, but she was too tempting, he let his cock find her soft, hot entrance and rested it there, teasing them both with the pressure but not going any further. He switched to her other nipple, lightly scraping his teeth on the sensitive bud. She bucked up.

"Warner, I swear to God. Get inside me. Please."

"Too soon," he said, with a gasp. It would all be over too soon, in a repeat of his first, humiliating time with her. He'd barely touched himself since they'd last had sex. He wasn't going to win any records for staying power.

"Don't care," she said. "I need you."

He breached her slowly, trying to make it last, her wet channel tight and perfect. He groaned. "You feel so incredibly good, Selena."

"Yeah." She bucked her hips again. "Missed you."

He captured her mouth in another kiss, starting to move now. She'd missed him. He was so damn lucky.

She urged him on, and he let himself be pushed to the edge. Time. They had time for everything. He had to believe that. He felt his orgasm build.

"I'm going to come," he warned her.

"Yes," she said, squeezing her own nipples, clenching her pussy around him tight. "Please come inside me, Warner. I love you so much."

The words were a shock to the system, an electric defibrillator to his heart, causing it to pulse and quake along with his body as he came hard and long, pumping himself into her the way she'd told him to, the way he wanted to fill her up every day for eternity. She was crying out, too, and when they finally both slowed, he registered her scarlet cheeks and glassy eyes. She looked well fucked, even if he'd wanted it to go on longer.

"Damn," he said. "That was—"

"It was good, Warner," she finished. "You're right. It was different."

"I love you," he said, because he was pretty sure he was coming too hard to say it earlier.

She smiled. "I'm glad."

It could have been facetious, but it wasn't. She was glad he loved her, and he was glad, too. He was full of gratitude for the simple miracle of loving someone who loved him back.

He kissed her sweet, saucy lips again. "Me, too."

The morning came much too quickly. Selena would get on a plane later today and fly away. But he'd follow her, soon.

They dressed quietly, the morning routine not that different than when they were sharing a bed at his house.

She bumped into the room service cart and swore lightly. "I never opened the champagne. You want it? Someone from the studio sent it, I think."

"Actually—" He stopped, not sure if what he was about to say was too embarrassing. Too late for that, he supposed.

"What?"

"I didn't know what room you were in. Did you know they don't give out room numbers at the desk?"

Selena's eyebrows slanted together in question. "So?"

"I had to find another way. I called room service and asked them to send you a bottle of champagne. I know where the kitchen is, so I kind of staked out the elevator and followed the room service person up so I could see which room they delivered it to."

She looked astonished. "Oh my God, Warner, that is a total Jake Wilton move. You sleuthed out my room number."

That she found his plan impressive rather than stalkery was probably why they were a good match. He grinned. "I'm just happy it worked."

"Me, too. You could have called me, you know."

"I wasn't sure you'd talk to me," he admitted.

"I would have. I was too proud to try to see you again after I left, but I'm not too proud to say how happy I am to be with you, Warner."

"Maybe we should drink the bubbly now."

She groaned. "I can't. If I drink now, I'll get buzzed, and we'll fuck again and won't want to get out of this bed."

"I am hearing zero problems with this plan."

"I have a plane to catch," she said regretfully. "I have meetings tomorrow. And you probably have some work to do."

He did have work to do. He had to find a management company to take over the rental properties. He could write from anywhere—even Los Angeles—but he didn't want to let his obligations in Misty Harbor go.

He wrapped his arms around her and hugged her hard. "You're so practical."

"And I'm starving. I have time for breakfast, at least."

"Then please, allow me to take you to breakfast."

"What?" She pretended to be astonished. "You mean you don't want to hide in here and order room service?"

He deserved that, and since he kind of did want to

hide in here and order room service, he bristled. "Yes, but I want to take you out more."

"Are you sure you won't turn to dust in the sunlight? Maybe you're really a vampire."

"I'm a very human man," he protested.

"Pretty sure that's what a vampire would say."

"Come on, quit stalling. Our very first date."

She grabbed her purse. He grabbed her hand. They took the elevator to the lobby and walked out the front doors of the inn together.

"Should we drive? The Mercedes is parked around back."

"Not the minivan?"

"I'm trying to change it up."

"Of all the things I've wondered about you, Warner, I'm finally going to ask the most burning question of all. Why a minivan?"

He shrugged. "It's useful. I can fit tools, plants, bags of mulch, lumber."

"That is a surprisingly prosaic answer. I thought maybe it was for transporting bodies or your secret triplets."

"Sorry it's not more interesting."

"It's okay. Let's walk."

Misty Harbor was bright and lustrous on this late November morning. Main Street beckoned, with its handsome 19th century brick buildings. The sun glinted off the windows of the gray stone library, while the Atlantic Ocean shimmered at the end of the street. Every breath made Warner feel new.

They stopped in front of the Bakeshop. Inside, he knew they'd find friends and food. Misty Harbor had made room for both of them, welcoming him as a newcomer, cradling him through his grief, the backdrop to a new love, a new life he was going to have with Selena. She'd found something there, too. Inspiration. A community. He knew no matter how much time they spent here in the future, it was always going to feel like home.

They glanced at each other.

"Shall we?" she asked.

"We shall," he said, and he opened the door.

Chapter Thirty-Two

Erika: You know we're going to have to change our podcast title for this episode.

Jules: No! It took us so long to pick out the name of this podcast.

Erika: All I'm saying is that this is not a rewatch podcast, not today. Because today we are talking about an episode of *Sawyer's Cove* we watched for the very first time two hours ago.

Jules: The very first new *Sawyer's Cove* episode in twelve and a half years!

Erika: That's right. The episode is called "The Home-coming," and it was written by Selena Echeveria, produced by Selena Echeveria and Camille Corsair, directed by David Blakely.

Jules: I'm crying. I cried through the whole episode, and I'm going to cry talking about it.

Erika: Have a tissue. Snot doesn't record well.

From The Sawyer's Cove (Re)watch Project Podcast: The Homecoming

"Is it working? Turn it up," Selena said, poking Jay in the shoulder. "Why do you have the clicker?"

"I don't know," Jay said, scowling. "Cami gave it to me."

Selena huffed and grabbed the clicker from him, turning up the volume on the television, even though no one had technically pressed start yet.

"I have to take pictures," Cami said, pointing her phone at the room. "This is for posterity."

"And for social media," Nash called.

"Look, if we're going to all be so co-dependent that we're sitting here watching this thing on Christmas Day together, the fans might as well get a kick out of it, too," Cami said.

"Okay, I'm going to start it," Selena said, voice rising over the din of side conversations in the room.

If Warner didn't know better, he'd think his girlfriend was pissed at everyone. But he heard the irritation in her voice and knew she was simply nervous.

"Shush!" Mimi hushed them like the librarian she was.

The theme song's opening notes burst out of the speakers at an impressively high volume.

"Jesus," Crosby said, covering his ears.

Warner had only met the man this morning, but he appreciated his economy of words.

"I'm turning it down," Selena said quickly, backing up her words with action. The classic theme song morphed into an updated version, as shots of the characters transitioned from teenagers to their thirty-year-old selves.

Warner had become more familiar with *Sawyer's Cove* in the last month. He'd joined Selena in Los Angeles for Thanksgiving, which they spent with her family, who were more gracious to him than he deserved. Her mom was no-nonsense, like Selena, but pride in her daughter shone out of her pores. Her dad was a trip, not shy about asking about his writing, his favorite mysteries, the way he made a living, and his intentions toward his daughter. Warner respected his straightforward manner and tried to answer, though when Mr. Echeveria asked if they were going to have kids, and, if so, they better get a move on, he did choke on his mouthful of turkey.

Selena came to his rescue by telling her dad to mind his own business, then offering to perform the Heimlich, which thankfully wasn't necessary.

Mr. Echeveria's question did get him thinking. That night when they were in bed at Selena's, which was as charming in person as in the picture she'd shown him, he asked her if she'd ever thought about children.

She hummed noncommittally and turned the question around on him.

"Angie and I kept putting it off, but it was always a vague sort of plan," he said. "It's one of the reasons we left the city. But I'm older now. I'm not sure it's something I need." He hoped the honest answer would be the right one.

"I'm good with that," she said. "My parents would love to be grandparents, but that's not enough of a reason to have kids. I like being able to pour everything into work. The shows I work on are my babies, and I'm okay with that."

"Okay," he said, relieved. He thought Selena would be a fantastic mom, and if she wanted kids, she could make it happen, but she knew herself well enough to know if it was something she really needed or not.

The next day, they drove across the city to Eagle Rock. His parents still lived in the split-level suburban ranch house he'd grown up in, and his sister and her family lived three blocks away in a similar home. It had been so long since he'd been back, at first conversation was stilted, but then it turned out his sister was a secret *Sawyer's Cove* fan, and when she found out what Selena did for a living, she was granted instant honorary sister status. Warner's mom and dad just seemed happy to have him home at all. His nephews and niece were smart, interesting kids, even if they barely remembered him. Maybe he and Selena would end up as the cool aunt and uncle.

He went with Selena to work a few times. It was fascinating to watch her in the edit bay with the editors, piecing together the story with the director's input and incorporating notes from the studio as well.

He liked being back in Los Angeles. He wrote in the morning in Selena's sunny dining room, then went for long walks around the city, getting ideas for locations and settings for the book. He had lunch with his parents and took his niece and nephews to the movies one day so his sister could do some holiday shopping.

When Selena's schedule got busy with meetings and press, she sent him back to Misty Harbor so she could concentrate.

He read Doug's book again and sent him some notes, but Doug didn't really need his input. It was ready to submit, and he was unreservedly glad for his friend. He was slower about getting pages of his own work to Doug, but that was because he was still on the first draft. There was no sense in rushing, not when he'd waited this long already. But the words kept coming, and if he kept this up, he'd have a complete draft sometime in January.

He'd been surprisingly happy to return to Misty Harbor, with the promise that Selena would join him as soon as she could. He had to check on his rentals and do Christmas shopping of his own. He also binged all three seasons of the original *Sawyer's Cove* in two weeks. It had been jarring to see people he'd come to know in real life on the screen, babies at the start of the show, grown into young men and women by the end. He could see the brilliance in the show's matter-of-fact way of dealing with teen relationships and sexuality and family dynamics, and he even spotted some touches in the dialogue he felt certain must have come from Selena's brain. She was a full staff writer by the third season, and he swelled with pride when he saw the episode with her first solo writing credit.

They had thought to go back to L.A. for the reboot's premiere but then took inventory and realized everyone was already going to be on the East Coast—Nash and Mimi and Jay and Cami already in Misty Harbor, plus Crosby and Ariel and even Darren, who was only in the final episode but had been invited to come up from New York for the event. Jay and Cami had hosted almost everyone on Christmas Eve, and now they were all piled in Warner's den to watch the first episode.

Selena made room for him on the big armchair, and they snuggled together as the episode began, her generous hips overlapping appealingly onto his thighs. She popped a mint into her mouth and grinned at him anxiously. He grabbed her hand, stroking his thumb over her knuckles until he felt her relax in his arms.

There was a lot of groaning and laughing and ribbing as the episode unfolded and everyone had to take turns watching themselves on screen. He found himself paying less attention to the show, which he knew he could watch any time, and instead on the audience, which was a once-in-a-lifetime gathering of Cove actors all in one place.

Selena kept looking over at her actors, too, as if worried they weren't going to like the finished product, but he could tell they did. They were all swept up in the story, the reintroduction of the characters, the new characters fitting in seamlessly. A moment of silence fell when the first title card showed up on screen after the final shot of the episode. Warner sensed Selena holding her breath. Then the room burst into applause.

"It was amazing," Ariel gushed.

"You did Ryan proud," Crosby said.

There were more variations on the theme, and plenty of congratulations to go around for Cami as co-producer, as well as star, and for everyone's performances.

Selena's cheeks were stained crimson by the time people started to get up from in front of the television and drift toward the spread of holiday treats Warner had assembled on a side table. She got out of the armchair, fished her phone out of her pocket and looked at the screen.

"I have to take this," she said. "Brad? Hi."

Warner wanted to roll his eyes. Of course it was the studio wanting to congratulate her. Annoying they had to do business on Christmas, but he supposed that was a downside of the industry.

"Okay. Thanks. Yes. Are you sure?" Selena paused. She looked like she was trying not to smile—or not to cry. Warner couldn't quite tell which. "Okay, I'll be in touch."

She hung up slowly. "Um, guys?" The buzz of conversation continued. "Guys?"

Warner whistled loudly, and everyone went silent.

She shot him a quick, grateful smile.

"That was the studio. They're tracking the numbers, and, apparently, we're going to be the biggest premiere of the year. We're outperforming in all demos. And they're giving us the green light for a second—and a third—season."

The silence continued for a second, as if the group was collectively making sure Selena wasn't about to say it was all a joke, then the cheers began.

Warner grabbed Selena before she could be taken up by everyone else, just for a minute. He squeezed her shoulders, looked in her beautiful eyes. "You did it," he said, full of pride.

"Yeah." She looked a little dazed. "Two more seasons. Oh, my God. There are so many stories I want to tell."

"Now you'll get your chance." He kissed her, his brilliant, beautiful second chance. "And you'll need somewhere to stay when you're back here in Misty Harbor to shoot the next season."

Selena laughed. "Is your pool house free?"

"I'm not renting it out anymore. Too much temptation. I fell in love with the last tenant, so…"

"Well, then what am I going to do?" she said, her voice low and seductive. "I can't go around seducing another landlord."

"You'll just have to move in for good," he whispered. "We'll be roommates."

She kissed him. "Roommates with benefits?"

"Roommates in love."

Epilogue

Christmas Day

The screening of the episode had finished an hour ago, but no one seemed to be in a hurry to leave Warner's warm, cozy-despite-its-size house. Crosby stifled a sigh. He didn't want to be the guy who left the party first, the way he always seemed to be, but he was also a little tired of making small talk and scrounging up interest in his co-workers' stories. He wasn't bored, but he'd been with these people for hours already, and he was reaching his limit.

He had a long drive back to the city, and a whole bunch of episodes of his favorite podcasts all lined up in his queue to keep him company on the way back. He checked his watch one more time. Ten more minutes, then he'd find Selena and Warner and thank them for their hospitality before quietly slipping away.

It didn't help that *he* was here, being gregarious and

making everyone smile and laugh the way he always did so effortlessly. Crosby never felt like he could be himself around Darren Silverstein. It was twice as hard to put up a front of being sociable when he felt self-conscious about everything he said and did, right down to his facial expressions. Not that he was looking at Crosby or anything. In fact, he wasn't certain he wasn't literally invisible to Darren for all that he'd patently ignored him today. Which was good. That was what Crosby wanted.

He checked his watch again. Eight minutes. The mulled cider he'd been nursing for the past half-hour nearly flew out of his hand as someone threw themselves onto the couch next to him.

"Hot date?" Ariel asked. She elbowed him in the side. She'd never had issues with invading his personal space, not from the very first day he met her, when she threw her arms around him and declared they were all going to be best friends.

She'd been the first to admit he was more of a challenge than she'd anticipated, but she hadn't given up on him, and he'd been grateful for her friendship over the years.

"What?" He'd heard her, but he didn't know how to respond. Of course he didn't have a hot date. But that was none of her business.

"You keep looking at your watch. Also, who wears a watch these days? You can just use your phone."

"Lots of people still wear watches." *He* was wearing one, for instance, a dark metal watch that looked good on his wrist.

"Come on, Crosby, we're not that boring, are we?" Ariel pouted. "Let's play a game," she said before he could answer. "Harrison Ford in *Raiders*."

Crosby allowed himself a single long-suffering sigh before he answered, "Alfred Molina in *Chocolat*."

"Oooh, Juliette Binoche in *The English Patient*."

They went on like that for several minutes, building a virtual chain of actors and movies until Ariel's phone beeped loudly, simultaneously with several others in the room.

"What the hell is that?" Crosby glanced at the screen of his phone, took a moment to make sense of the alert flashing on the screen. *Snowstorm. Low visibility. Shelter in place.*

Oh, no. He looked out the nearest window, realized it had gotten dark when he wasn't paying attention. The sun went down so early this time of year, and he could see big fat snowflakes hitting the darkened windowpane like fluffy white moths attracted to the light.

"I better go," he said, standing up and looking for somewhere to deposit the dregs of his cider.

"Don't be ridiculous, Crosby," Ariel said. "You're not driving anywhere in this weather."

"I'm only going to New York," he said. How could the weather have gotten so bad in a couple of hours?

"Please don't take chances on the road," Warner, his host, said seriously. "There's plenty of room here."

Crosby felt his skin prickle at the prospect of spending the night with strangers. "No, really, I'll just go to the inn." He was sure his car could make it the few miles to downtown Misty Harbor.

"Actually, my mom told me earlier today they're completely booked up for Christmas," Jay said.

"What? There's no room at the inn?" Selena said dramatically. "On Christmas?"

"Ha ha," Crosby said coldly.

"I have a double, if you don't mind sharing."

Crosby practically snapped his neck to look at the owner of the voice who'd offered to share. Darren Silverstein held his gaze, laidback as if he'd offered him the last Christmas cookie rather than half a hotel room.

He weighed his options. He could stay here, but he'd be intruding on Warner and Selena's privacy. At least at the hotel he could see if Jay was right—maybe there was a broom closet or something he could squeeze into. He knew Mimi and Nash didn't have room for anyone at the tiny apartment they were living in until they moved into the house they'd recently bought. Jay and Cami had a guest room, but Ariel had dibs.

He thought of Trevor, a Misty Harbor local and someone he'd call a friend, but the kid still lived with his parents.

He looked back to Darren and barely believed it when he said, "I don't mind sharing. That would be great. Thanks."

Darren didn't look like he believed it either, but he nodded briskly. "Let's get going, then, before the roads get any worse."

The party broke up, hugs and kisses were exchanged,

coats found. Warner warned them all to drive carefully about sixteen times apiece.

Ariel cornered him as he was wrapping his favorite hunter green cashmere scarf around his neck by the front door.

"You going to be okay?"

"Of course."

She gave him a hug as best she could through their layers of clothes. "Be nice," she murmured into his ear.

Crosby caught Darren watching them out of the corner of his eye. He swallowed. "I'll try," he whispered.

She let him go, following Jay and Cami out.

"You need a ride?" he asked Darren. See, he could be nice.

"No, I have a car. Room four forty-four. See you there?"

"See you," Crosby agreed.

His car was a rear-wheel drive two-door coupe. It was one of the worst things to drive over snowy, slick streets, but he was an experienced driver and made it to the inn in one piece, handing his keys over to the valet, along with an extra big tip, it being a snowstorm. And Christmas.

He took a minute to get his emergency kit from the trunk—a change of clothes and another pair of shoes. The inn would have spare toiletries. He even had allergy medicine tucked into his computer bag. He was fine. No one was expecting him in the city tonight, and he could rearrange tomorrow's appointments easily.

So why was his pulse thrumming as he walked into

the lobby like he was about to audition for Martin Scorsese?

He stopped by the front desk, waited behind a woman who was pleading for a room.

"I'm sorry, ma'am, we are completely booked. If you want, I can try the other area hotels for you."

"No, I called the ones by the freeway already."

"We're not supposed to allow this, but since it's Christmas, if you're really out of options, you can sit up in the lounge tonight."

Crosby didn't wait to see what her response would be. He made for the elevator, punched the up arrow with trepidation. He could do this. He could share a hotel room with a man he'd barely exchanged ten words with in the last twelve years. The man who'd been his nemesis for a good portion of the original *Sawyer's Cove* run. The man who'd stood for everything he wanted to be and couldn't.

He knocked on the door to room 444.

Darren opened it with a sardonic smile. "Crosby. Wasn't sure you'd show."

"Sleeping in the lobby wasn't an appealing option."

"But you considered it," Darren said shrewdly.

"But I considered it," Crosby agreed. He stepped into the room. It was a nice hotel room, but it was just a hotel room. He'd been a hundred like it. There were two queen-sized beds, one of which had already been turned down. Crosby set his small bag on the other one.

"You want to take a shower?" Darren asked.

Crosby's shoulders tensed. "It's a little early to get ready for bed."

"True," Darren said. "You hungry? We could order room service."

Crosby wasn't particularly hungry, but he probably would be later. "Sure."

Darren grabbed a black leather binder from the desk and tossed it to him. Crosby fumbled it a little but didn't drop it. He felt his defenses mounting. Why hadn't Darren just handed it to him? Was he trying to make him look klutzy?

Darren's eyebrows rose, and Crosby realized he was glaring at the man. He forced himself to look away, open the binder, and examine the menu. The options were standard room service fare.

"Hell of a way to spend Christmas," Darren said idly.

Crosby shrugged. "Whatever. I'm not a huge fan of Christmas."

Darren gasped theatrically. "Spencer Crosby isn't a fan of Christmas? Stop the presses." He screwed up his face. "You could play Scrooge blindfolded."

Crosby felt the zing like an actual punch to his tender middle. He turned away, pretending to look at the menu some more.

He was angry with himself. Why had he come here? He was thirty-one years old. What did he think was going to happen—he'd share a hotel room with Darren, and he'd suddenly decide Crosby wasn't a useless waste of space? That he'd throw himself on his knees and announce he'd been crushing on Crosby for fifteen years?

The way Crosby had been crushing on him.

When he had his emotions back under control, he snapped the menu shut, deliberately threw it back to Darren, who caught it smoothly. The bastard.

"Do you want anything?" he asked. His voice sounded a little funny, so he cleared his throat.

Darren looked at him thoughtfully. "Caesar salad with chicken. No parmesan."

He hadn't looked at the menu, but Crosby took him at his word and turned for the hotel phone.

"Hey," Darren said as Crosby lifted the receiver. He set the phone back down, waited. "Sorry. About the Scrooge crack."

Being on the receiving end of Darren's derision was one thing, but being on the receiving end of his pity was another. He found himself reinforcing the shell he'd put up around his heart so many years ago and ignored the apology. He'd get through this night of torture, he'd drive back to New York tomorrow, back to his real life, and forget that spending the night with Darren Silverstein ever happened.

He picked up the phone, punched a button.

"Hello? Room service?"

Thank you for reading! I hope you loved Selena and Warner's happy ending. To find out what happens when Crosby and Darren share a hotel room during the snowstorm, pick up *Take a Chance* now. And read all about Danica, Misty Harbor's favorite bartender, in Take Another Look, featured in *A Kiss at Midnight: A Kissed by Romance Collaboration*, available now.

Scan the code to subscribe to my newsletter and download the free Sawyer's Cove: The Reboot prequel. Happy reading!

xoxo,

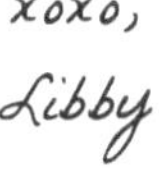

Libby

Acknowledgments

It takes an amazing team to make a book a reality. Thank you so much to my teammates at Kissed By Romance, the SALT plotters, my rockstar proofreader/blurb whisperer Sara Kettler, Jessica Snyder and the entire HEA Club crew, Amber and Karen at The Word Slayers, Dar at Wicked Smart Designs, and Jen at Jen Colburn Design.

Thanks to the Star Readers on my ARC team for your time and generosity.

Thank you to Pippa, Julie, and Dylan for your much-needed support and insight.

And thanks to my boys, for being proud of me and for always listening when I want to read them a story.

About the Author

Libby Waterford is the author of the Sawyer's Cove: The Reboot and the Never a Bride series. She's obsessed with her pollinator garden, DIY fermentation, and writing swoony first kisses and hopeful happily ever afters. Her steamy contemporary romances mix witty banter and all the feels with a solid dollop of good old-fashioned sexual tension. Libby wrangles her two ever-growing sons and a husband in Fairfield County, Connecticut.

Get a free story at libbywaterford.com and email her at libby@libbywaterford.com.

facebook.com/LibbyWaterford

instagram.com/libbywritesromance

bookbub.com/authors/libby-waterford

goodreads.com/libbywaterford

amazon.com/author/libbywaterford